By Ama

The Strange Case of Caroline Maxwell

By Amanda Harvey Purse

The Strange Case of Caroline Maxwell

Published in 2014 by FeedARead Publishing.

Copyright © Amanda Harvey Purse.

The author asserts the moral right under the Copyright, Designs and Patents Act 1988 to be identified as the author of this work.

All Rights reserved. No part of this publication may be reproduced, stored in a retrieval system, or transmitted, in any form or by any means without the prior written consent of the publisher, nor be otherwise circulated in any form of binding or cover other than that in which it is published and without a similar condition being imposed on the subsequent purchaser.

'Use of the Sherlock Holmes characters created by Sir Arthur Conan Doyle by permission of Conan Doyle Estate Ltd, www.conandoyleestate.co.uk.'

By Amanda Harvey Purse

Cover Design by

Artist, Coral De Anne

Author of Be With Me,

Requel and

Recious

The Strange Case of Caroline Maxwell

Other works by the same author

Jack the Ripper's Many Faces

A set of four linking short stories in which the reader travels through the centuries with the aim of finding out who wore Jack the Ripper's Face while meeting a few famous people such as Dr Crippen and Inspector Walter Dew.

Victorian Lives behind Victorian Crimes e-book series:

Vol:1 The women who made Jack the Ripper famous is where the victims of Jack the Ripper talk about their lives as if they were in the same room as the reader, with photographs of the murder sites as they are now.

Vol:2 The Poisoning Men has the famous Poisoners of the Victorian era such as William Palmer, H.H Holmes and Dr Cream explaining their deadly deeds with the medical and literature history of the poisons used.

Vol:3 It's a Hanging Job Now has the famous criminals such as Charles Peace, Mary Ann Cotton, James Bloomfield Rush and Amelia Dryer tell the reader their life stories to the point in which they were hanged. It also has the life stories of the hangmen, such as John Billington and William Calcraft.

By Amanda Harvey Purse

<u>Vol: 4 I am Jack, I am Jack, no I am Jack the Ripper Part One</u> has eight suspects of the famous serial killer speak to the reader with the reasons why they were suspected.

<u>Vol: 5 We are all Mad Here</u> has the famous criminals such as the artist Richard Dadd who were sent to asylums, with the history of some of the famous Victorian Asylums.

<u>Coming Soon</u>

<u>Vol: 6 The Policemen who hunted The Ripper</u> has the policemen who were involved in the Jack the Ripper Case speak to the reader

Victorian Lives behind Victorian Crimes: in Paperback.

You can even follow Victorian Lives behind Victorian Crimes on Facebook!

The Tails of Binky the Tabby Cat e-book series:

1: <u>The Detective Tails of Binklock Holmes, Purrirot and Miss Meowples</u> this is the first in the funny series where Binky the tabby cat becomes her favourite detectives and gets involved in similar but cat like versions of their favourite stories such as The Speckled Collar, Murder of the Feline Express and Pocket Full of Cat Nip.

2: <u>The Historical Tails of Binky the Tabby Cat</u> which features Leonardo Da Kitty, King Henry and his six fishes, Binkston Churchill and many more!

3: <u>The Literature Tails of Binky the Tabby Cat</u> which features The Christmas Catol, Mice in Wonderland, Cat

The Strange Case of Caroline Maxwell

Angels and Dog Demons and more! You can also join in the Christmas Spirit as Binky sings her own kitty versions of Christmas Carols!

Due to popular demand, you can now follow Binky the Tabby Cat on Facebook!

Coming Soon

Binklock Holmes Verses Jack the Slipper!

By Amanda Harvey Purse

Dead Bodies Do Tell Tales – A Jack the Ripper Novel

By Amanda Harvey Purse

'I have just finished the novel, I loved the fact it was something really different. I really like the ten year gap tool.' Ian Porter, *author of Whitechapel and Walter Sickert in Jack the Ripper: The Suspects.* On Dead Bodies Do Tell Tales – A Jack the Ripper Novel.

Whitechapel, London in 1888, Mary Kelly is the last of her group of friends left alive by Jack the Ripper...

She meets a strange woman by appearance and conversation who tells Mary her destiny is to be the last known victim of Jack the Ripper but while drinking, working the streets and remembering moments spent with

The Strange Case of Caroline Maxwell

the other Ripper victims, will Mary face her destiny? Or can Mary find out what is truly behind the strange woman's actions before it's too late for her?

Ten years after the Ripper killings we meet Thomas Dunn, an author who has an Opium addiction, which are giving him nasty nightmares about a woman who is in need of his help. Meanwhile his friend Charles, still heartbroken by an actress who disappeared ten years ago, forces Thomas to solve her murder.

After everyone Thomas questions dies in a similar fashion to the Ripper killings ten years before, his nightmares enters into his real life; he gets arrested for murder and meets a woman who knows more about him that he can remember Thomas has a meltdown. Moving to the safety of his friend's house in Kent, but has Thomas actually put himself in more danger?

Could Jack the Ripper truly be back and killing again? And what is the strange connection between Mary Kelly and Thomas Dunn?

By Amanda Harvey Purse

Praise for other books

Praise for Victorian Lives behind Victorian Crimes

Vol:1 The women who made Jack the Ripper Famous

'Amanda Harvey Purse has had the neat idea of having the Ripper's victims tell their own stories in their own words and she has executed it entertainingly.'

Described by Paul Begg (author of Jack the Ripper: The Facts and co-author of Jack the Ripper A-Z) in the Ripperologist Magazine, issue 130.

'I have just finished the novel, I loved the fact it was something really different. I really like the ten year gap tool.'

The Strange Case of Caroline Maxwell

Ian Porter, *author of Whitechapel and Walter Sickert in Jack the Ripper: The Suspects.* On Dead Bodies Do Tell Tales – A Jack the Ripper Novel.

By Amanda Harvey Purse

For my Husband, my two cats Mischief and Binky.

And, for my little daring niece, Jessica, who I don't have much to pass on to but I do have my words…

The Strange Case of Caroline Maxwell

By Amanda Harvey Purse

Friday 30th August 1901, in the City of London...

The Strange Case of Caroline Maxwell

'Miss Christie, if I have told you once I will tell you again, this just won't do! I have not got time for this, have you not heard? A Mr. Hubert Cecil Booth has invented this new thing called The Vacuum Cleaner, whatever that is but it is going to be big news and you know where The Times Newspaper wants to be when there is big news around, do you not Miss Christie?' There was a pause to which the man speaking turned from looking out of his window, seeing all the rooftops of London smoking from their chimneys in this evening's cold night air, towards me.

He looked me sternly in the eye; his grey eyes were hard and cold. I did not speak; this was not the moment to speak. I had learned that over the years, I watched as his frosty eyes turned smog like; they glazed over as if he was thinking of something else in the far off distance. He seemed to huff silently to himself and then spoke once more. 'I'm sorry but I can't allow you any more space in *The Times* newspaper!' Was, what he must have thought would be the final statement on the matter, but you see for me, it was said by the most dense and slow-witted man I

By Amanda Harvey Purse

have ever met who wasn't seeing the full picture. I gritted my teeth and counted the seconds to make me calm.

1...2...3...

'Sir,' I started 'I am deeply appreciative and indebted to you, for letting me have any space at all in the most outstanding and exceptional newspaper in Great Britain,' to that statement the editor nodded his egg shaped head so I carried on, 'But please, I know I can do so much more than a few articles here and there, let me be a part of the team you have here,' I said.

'Miss Christie... look, can I call you Amelia?' To this I could nod as I thought to myself that Victorian etiquette might be leaving us soon in this new Edwardian era and I do count myself as a very modern woman. 'I know the world is changing. These women are popping up and changing things with their slashes and chaining themselves to God knows what, but it is a slow progress and I for one can't see it happening for a long time. Don't get me wrong, you can write a good tale and your articles are worth reading but that is it; you are still a woman my dear, that fact you cannot change. So don't get ideas above your station!' My editor said as he walked to and fro in his office. If I screwed up my eyes tight enough, I swear I

The Strange Case of Caroline Maxwell

could see the invisible high horse my editor believed to be riding on at this precise moment.

1...2...3...

'Sir, May I remind you it was those little articles that brought me an interview with Sherlock Holmes! The edition sold millions because of it!'

'Yes, yes. One little interview. But to be honest with you my dear I frankly don't believe that is enough... Look, you get me a good story, I mean really good story, something to catch the heart and soul of every living person, something that no matter what class you are or,' he paused to look at me 'what sex you are, it will grab at you and make it hard for you to forget for weeks to come and I'll think about it.'

'Thank you sir,' I said as I took my turn to leave.

'You might think about speaking to that Holmes fellow again, as I recall he seemed to like you,' my editor said to me as I shut his varnished wooden door.

'That Holmes fellow,' I repeated to myself as I stood alone in the small, gloomy hallway that led to the editor's office. This corridor was like some kind of 'dead

By Amanda Harvey Purse

man walking' corridor as you await your punishment. In truth I am quite delighted to be walking in the other direction down this hall, as I feel slightly stressed and have a wanting to breathe in fresh air. As I started moving towards the way out I repeated to myself what the editor had said to me, 'That Holmes fellow'.

I am glad I am not the only one who gets shot down by that imprudent man. Sherlock Holmes has done a great deal for this country and its criminal underworld. He is willing to travel into the depths of all that is bad in this city to solve a case, putting his and more times than not Dr Watson's lives in danger. The only praise he gets is when Dr Watson is allowed to write about his adventures and even then there are many people out there that believe it is a work of fiction. Something that only happens in Dr Watson's mind, I mean how could our British Police Force be that stupid, to need help from an unprofessional member of the public? How could this lonely member of the everyday public, know so much from so few items around a murder scene, or on somebody's person? Mr. Holmes is classed in the same story bound boat as Inspector Bucket from Mr. Charles Dickens's *Bleak House,* or Inspector Cuff from Mr. Willie Collins's *The Moonstone* maybe, all

The Strange Case of Caroline Maxwell

great men with sharp and cunning intellect but surely unable to do better than the police.

How little the public truly know I thought as I shook my head with disbelief and left the offices of *The Times* newspaper and made my way home, hoping I will be able to contemplate a story worth reading before the capital's winter sets in, at the very least.

...

I had spent two days thinking of what story to write about, no scratch that and then reverse it, I had just *wasted* two days thinking of a story to write about, but my mind was an annoying and exasperating blank. I had nothing, nothing at all. I cannot believe the moment I have been waiting and working so hard for has come at long last and I could not think of anything! [punctuation?]

My mind was wondering [wandering] through the library that sat in the back of my mind and it seemed as if every book I was opening was unwritten. I moved to the window within my room, a vastly smaller sized window than the one owned by my editor I might add and it is a lot less grand. I glanced through the pane of glass towards the outside world, where my editor would have seen the grand stone

By Amanda Harvey Purse

built banks and buildings most believe are of importance to this city out of his window, I see what really is important.

Houses upon houses that accommodate large amounts of working families, these families are the breathing undertone to London, they work the clogs that grind slowly together but invisibly to make this capital live and respire. Although I live in a slightly modern area, for I have my own bathroom, I was not brought up in this area. I lived with the clogs and I suppose that is why I can't quite leave the East End, I feel as if I am always a spitting distance away and it was this East End I was watching from my window.

The smoke from their chimneys wisp through the air, rising up above my window and through the gaps in the smoke I would even spot the boats and ships lying on The Thames by the docks. This view normally helps me, it normally gives my imagination but not today and not when I need it the most.

What is wrong with me? I need something incredible, fantastic, and something sensational, to prove myself to that big simple-minded clown that I can write, that this woman can write.

The Strange Case of Caroline Maxwell

Well only when I have the right subject to write about that is. This is my chance to show the world that this tiny woman that has been looked at with disgust and antipathy for many a year can do some good, she can actually can change people's way of thinking and reasoning. I just need a subject.

Subjects seem to be drawn to only one man in London that I know of which has the gift of brilliance and intellect to play with and solve them and he undoubtedly *knows* it. Like a moth being drawn to a candle light, cases seem to almost fall from the heavenly skies through the ceiling of the now famous address, 221 B Baker Street and land right on the lap of Sherlock Holmes as he is sitting there in his dressing gown in front of his great fireplace, smoking tobacco from his Turkish slipper with his long pipe, while thinking of other things.

Stories will not be coming to me that easily and straightforwardly, no matter how hard I try not to do this, I actually agree with the repulsive and ghastly little editor. I am going to need help and assistance, I will have to be one of those many powerless and defenceless clients that always are the reason behind every 'Sherlock Holmes' story commencing, I wonder what story I will start, and

By Amanda Harvey Purse

where could it possibly lead? But more importantly to me, what would the readers learn from this new story? Would Dr Watson really write me into a contemporary and fresh novel? What would he describe me as? What would Mr. Holmes say about me when I depart from Baker Street? I questioned dreamily to myself. But of course for any of those things to happen I would have to make the first step, I would have to go and see him.

Knock, Knock.

The Strange Case of Caroline Maxwell

Chapter One

The most recognized and legendary black door opened a small amount at my presence and the most kind-hearted and compassionate elderly woman I have ever had the good fortune to meet was standing on the other side of the threshold, 'Ah Miss, there you are. I must say when Mr. Holmes got your letter; it seemed to bring him out of his black mood,' Mrs Hudson said as she opened the door wider to greet me more compassionately.

'How can what you say be possibly true?' I questioned. 'I was afraid he might think I was irritating and troublesome,' I said I walked through the doorway and felt Mrs Hudson warm and wrinkled hands on my shoulders has they had begun to take my shawl.

By Amanda Harvey Purse

'Oh no my dear, it is actually quite the opposite in fact. You have got to understand my love, now the good doctor is mostly away with his practise and wife, Mr. Holmes is more alone and well how do I put it? Loneliness doesn't become him, no matter how much he would deny it,' she replied.

'I think I understand now,' I said with a smile.

'But keep that between you and me, my dear,' Mrs Hudson whispered to me as put one of her wrinkled fingers up to her lips and waved the way to the stairs.

'It will be our little secret,' I smiled back towards her.

I walked up the flight of stairs that I had walked up only once before, counting as I go for you cannot walk up these deep red coloured famous carpeted steps without checking whether the words in the classic tale *The Study in Scarlet* are correct, were there indeed seventeen steps? How could it be otherwise? But I am afraid I have to admit I had lost count near the top as the sound I heard of some banging around in Mr. Holmes's living room, interrupted my thought progress. Sherlock Holmes was certainly up to

The Strange Case of Caroline Maxwell

something, which could only mean one thing to you and I, Sherlock Holmes had a case.

I tapped on the door, 'Mr Holmes, its Miss Christie. I have come to...' I had started.

The door unlocked and I saw in a quick glance the hand of Mr. Holmes moving past the opening of the door as he darted off back to his table, to continue working with his well used chemistry set.

There was a big bang, that jolted me and I felt goose bumps suddenly appear upon my skin. I felt as if I had witnessed a God like moment with the big bang. I knew I had seen the answer to some crime but I had yet to understand.

'Ah! Success!' Sherlock Holmes shouted through the smoke that now surrounded him.

I opened the door a little more to see that he had darted off to his writing desk and had begun writing a note. *Does this man ever move slowly? Is he always in a mad dash?* I thought to myself.

'Mrs Hudson! Mrs Hudson!' he shouted. It was only then, when I sensed Mrs Hudson behind me that I noticed I was still standing in the doorway watching this fascinating man go about his business. I moved inside the room and sat down at the dining table, covering my nose and mouth with my handkerchief to fight off the putrid, chemical smell that was filling the room and trying to admit itself into my throat.

'I'm here Mr Holmes,' she said as she moved in to the room and looked around. 'Oh Mr. Holmes! What have you done now? I can hardly see you and what's that horrid smell? I have got to open some of these windows, I don't want that fire engine to be called again, I am sure they are exhausted of coming here!'

'Send this to The Yard, it will save a man's life,' Mr. Sherlock Holmes said as he held the note he had been writing up in the air without answering or even looking at her. Mrs Hudson was still trying her best to open the living room's windows but instead of helping her, Mr. Holmes just started waving the note in the air impatiently. I was about the help her when I noticed the windows were finally opened and with a gust, the smoke drifted out of it. Mrs Hudson took a deep breath in and dusted down her apron, she glanced over to Mr. Sherlock Holmes and then to the

The Strange Case of Caroline Maxwell

note he was waving in the air. She seemed to tut quietly to herself as she moved over to him and said,

'Yes Mr Holmes,' as she snatched the important note.

'And be quick about it!'

'Yes, Mr Holmes,' she repeated as she smiled back at me, shook her head which made the white laced hat moved from side to side and she left the room.

...

'Your Mother has died, why did you not say so before, when we had spoken last,' Mr. Holmes proclaimed at me.

'I'm sorry I don't quite understand,' I said a little taken back, no one has mentioned my mother in quite some time and it was shocking to think that she is being mentioned here and by him of all people.

'Your mother has died, some time ago. I would say she died five. No I'm wrong. She died two years ago,' he said as his eyes burned into me.

By Amanda Harvey Purse

'Mr Holmes if you please! My mother passing away is not a subject to be flippant about, I am a little hurt by in the space of two minutes you have mentioned that she has died four times to me,' I said quietly but strongly back to him.

'I didn't mean for you to take offence to it, I can't help myself sometimes. I see things and know their meaning I don't tend to think of the human nature of feelings, that normally is always a red herring for me,' Mr. Holmes said, he was trying to say sorry but without actually saying the word. But what he didn't realise was that he was saying sorry with his eyes and I could detect it.

'It is fine Mr. Holmes I haven't taken an offence to it, it was just a little surprising to hear you suddenly mention my mother. How did you know?'

'I used my eyes,' was his simply reply.

'I have given myself away, you mean?' I asked as I knew what that last statement meant.

'Yes. Everybody gives theirselves away in the end.'

'How have I done such a thing?' I asked.

'The handkerchief is the answer, my dear lady.'

The Strange Case of Caroline Maxwell

'You got that my mother had died two years ago from my handkerchief?' I asked. I knew as soon as I had asked that question it was stupid of me to say such a thing. Of course Sherlock Holmes got all that from my handkerchief, this is the man that had known Dr Watson was not going to put money into shares with his club member friend from something that was as simple as the chalk between Dr Watson's first finger and thumb, so how could this be any different?

'No I had got that your mother has died from *her* handkerchief.'

Of course, how did I forget that my handkerchief, that was on show right at this very moment as it was covering my nose and throat from the smell of Mr. Holmes's Big Bang, was her handkerchief? My mother had left it to me, it was her way of reminding me that wherever I go in this *man* made world, whatever I decided to do in my chosen career, I am still a woman at heart and a woman should have a pretty handkerchief. I have carried this around with me for two years; it has almost become second nature to have it with me as much as my notepad and pen has.

By Amanda Harvey Purse

But I still haven't taken the time to unstitch the 'M' for my mother's name, Mary, and replace it with an 'A' for my name on the handkerchief. Sherlock is always right, everyone does give theirselves away in the end.

'Why do you say two years, Mr. Holmes?' I asked.

'You are not in physical mourning for your mother for you are not wearing black. You do not seem to be an upset and emotional woman, so time has passed. I had made the mistake in thinking that five years had passed, but I forgot who I was speaking too. I cannot always put you in the same case as lot of other women I meet, you are different. You are manlier which in turn makes you more strong and able to cope with,' Mr. Holmes coughed before he finished his sentence 'problems you might face. I have only met one other woman that was like you, she was very modern in her ways too. So I decided that it had been two years not five.'

I couldn't not believe what I had just heard, is it possible true? Has Mr. Sherlock Holmes really compared me to whom he has only remarked as *The Woman*? Am I really like Mrs Irene Norton aka Miss Irene Adler? I felt myself sit a little straighter in my seat as that thought came to me; I was feeling quite proud with myself.

The Strange Case of Caroline Maxwell

'Now Miss Christie, you need a story. That is correct is it not?' Mr. Holmes asked as he turned in his chair to face me once again. I waited for the last of the smoke to leave the room before I answered him.

'Ah, yes Mr. Holmes. I thought you might know of some case you don't mind me writing about,' I said as I removed my handkerchief from my face as the smell was still lingering but not as strong.

'Mmm,' he noised as he closed his eyes and put his hands in a praying position. I mistook the situation; I had thought the noise from Sherlock Holmes meant he was struggling to think of a case. I should have known I was wrong to make that presumption,

'Maybe that one you have just dealt with,' I said pointing to the door that Mrs Hudson had walked out of with the note which solved the case.

'The one I have just dealt with? Oh I see, no. That is not what I have in mind for you,' he said without opening his eyes.

'You have one in mind for me?' I asked gratefully.

By Amanda Harvey Purse

'Yes, I deduce you need a good story, a great story even. To how do I put it? To prove oneself in a world full of overgrown gorillas, that is an apt description I think.'

'Yes, I mean I am hoping to get more regular space in the paper, but of course I have to earn it and I,' I paused unable to think of a affable way of expressing what I wanted to say 'apparently haven't done so already,' I said a little disheartened.

'So that interview with me got you no special treatment then?' he asked.

'It did then, but things are always changing I guess,' I said, I knew I was sounding ungrateful but I needed to be frank, a short interview with Sherlock Holmes where you don't learn much about the great man doesn't cut the mustard anymore. There was more significant news wanted, although I hate to admit it.

'I see,' he said, still with his eyes shut. I laughed a little at the irony. I waited for him to explain and I must admit to you reader I had waited a while.

...

The Strange Case of Caroline Maxwell

'Good, you have patience then. You are going to need that quality of yours,' he finally said.

'Am I?' I asked. I knew he was building up to something incredible, something that was going to grab the attention of that impenetrable little editor of mine.

'Heard of the Ripper, by any chance?' he said.

'*Jack* the Ripper?' I asked undesirably.

'I believe he went by that name yes, but something tells me you feel a little disappointed at me for bringing him up in our little conversation.'

'There was so much wrote about him and we never got close to who he really was, I don't want to be another reporter to try to make a quick buck by using The Ripper, that's not my style. I am more than that.'

'Very admirable, but this is a little different and I would not be mentioning him if I did not believe that I had to.'

'You believe you *have* to mention Jack the Ripper?' I asked.

By Amanda Harvey Purse

'You are accurate in what you say, but then of course you have just repeated my own statement back to me, so you are always going to be correct if carry on doing that. Can you list the women killed?' he asked.

'That depends on who you start with.' I answered cleverly as I knew some people believe Jack the Ripper started his killing spree earlier than what I did, some people believe he did not actually stop. In truth until we find out who he was, we will never straightforwardly know anything about the man or dare I suggest *woman* behind the mask of the manic. But my cleverness went unrewarded I could tell, by the unembellished and unresponsive look upon Mr. Holmes's face.

'Start and finish where you want,' he said in a flippant way.

'Well the first was Mary Ann Nichols, then Annie Chapman, Elisabeth Stride, Catherine Eddowes and Mary Jane Kelly.'

'That is the normal list, yes,' was his reply.

'Of course it is the normal list, it is the only list of the main five victims.'

The Strange Case of Caroline Maxwell

'But what if one was not?' he asked chillingly.

'If one was not what Mr. Holmes? We all know they are the main victims of the Jack the Ripper.'

'Do we now? How sure can you be? Do you simply believe that because that is what the police have said? You are a journalist; a journalist that doesn't want to be a normal reporter who writes stories of make-believe so, where's your source? Where's your proof?'

'I do not understand, I know I was young in 1888 but I thought Jack the Ripper killed five women of the lower class.'

'I do not doubt that, I am not questioning how many he killed, that is provable fact that he killed five women,' he paused as I smiled to myself. He believed the same as I or in another possibly more importantly way I believed the same as Mr Sherlock Holmes! 'But of course there were others that made me in a weak moment doubt it. So I went to the unpleasant incidents of those extra killings and I can safely say that those were, at best, killed by a misguided, frenzied and unrestrained copycat that wanted his moment of fame. They were not in the same skilful and quite intelligent manner you know the killer to have. But anyway I am going off my main point I was not sceptical about how many women were killed, I am suspicious on *who* was killed.'

Mr. Sherlock Holmes had been to the other murder sites, why was this not reported? Why did he only go to those murder sites? Or did he go to them all? Did he see the faces of these poor women while their lives were at an end? Did he see the pain, the blood and the cuts? Did he see what a morbid sense of pleasure the mad man had? What did he make of it? Did he carry on as he normally would, unemotional, cold and detached only looking for the clues to lead him to the murderer, not seeing the murdered victim lying before him?

'What do you know Mr. Holmes?' I finally asked, I was starting to feel engrossed with what Sherlock Holmes was saying, which terrified me as this conversation was leading me down a dark and sickening path. I had also noticed that Mr. Holmes had not opened his eyes for a long time now, *was he picturing the scenes he saw all those years ago? Was he seeing their faces again? One will never know.*

'Interested now are we? Well what if one of the women that were killed wasn't who we all thought she

The Strange Case of Caroline Maxwell

was? What if she was someone else?' he said as if he was reading one of Edgar Allen Poe's ghost stories to a crowd of intently interested public.

'Are you saying that one of the victims wasn't Mrs. Nichols, Mrs. Chapman, Mrs. Stride, Miss Eddowes or Miss Kelly?'

'Can you imagine, what that could possibly mean?' he said as he opened his eyes for the first time since we had begun this fascinating and enthralling conversation, about the world's first famous serial killer. He had now decided to stare deeply at me, waiting impatiently for an answer but to be honest I preferred when Mr. Holmes had his eyes closed. At least then I could think whatever I wanted to think, I could even childishly stick my tongue out at him if I so wished! Now I felt tensed and that I should have the same answer that was sitting in the foremost of Mr. Sherlock Holmes's mind.

'Well that means the unthinkable,' I managed to say.

'Go on,' he said in a school master tone.

'These women have become and possibly will always be, famous in their deaths and one of them is wrong?'

'Which means,' Mr. Holmes said rolling his hands, pushing me to say more.

'That one of these famous women is still alive and living with us.'

'Precisely... my dear.'

The Strange Case of Caroline Maxwell

Chapter Two

What did I just say? One of the famous and disreputable Ripper victims is still alive? Why does every conversation about that murderer have you, ending up sounding mad and frantic yourself? Am I crazy? That thought brought me to a halt. I instantly felt sick. It is amazing is it not that one single word haunts you and brings you to your knees? I felt as if I could fall to my knees, maybe if I was not in the presence of Sherlock Holmes, maybe if I was not in his rooms in Baker Street I may well have fallen in a crying mess, how very womanly of me. But that is for another time dear reader, when you know me a little better you may think back to this moment and understand the feelings I was feeling then.

By Amanda Harvey Purse

Back to this story, if I was sitting at home I would have never said or even thought that, why now; sitting here with Mr. Sherlock Holmes would I have come out with that statement? I mean I have almost grownup with the tales about Jack the Ripper, all saying different reasons why he did what he did; there are even tales about who he really was but this? This is very diverse and contrasting, no one has ever thought about changing the victim's names. It is like saying the sky is green and the grass in blue, it just doesn't make sense. We all know who the victims were; we all cried and mourned for them and now Mr. Holmes wants me to believe that one of them is wrong.

To be honest this day is getting stranger and stranger, on one hand the information I am now holding is bizarre and almost stomach churning but on the other hand the person that has told me this information is an academic, he is smart, quick-witted and exceptional. Sherlock is the one man I feel I can trust in what he says to be true. If he has reason to disbelieve who the victims were, who am I to disagree?

'Which victim was wrong?' I finally asked.

The Strange Case of Caroline Maxwell

'This is where your patience will come to hand. You need to talk to someone, someone important but he may not want to talk about this now.'

'Who should I talk to?'

'Someone important to The Ripper case, but he despises talking about it. Even though it will always make him a celebrity for years to come, he just hasn't come to terms with it. I know how he feels some days,' Mr. Sherlock Holmes said as he at long last looked away from me.

'Who is this person? I would have thought everyone involved would like to talk about The Ripper, to have their fame in the press,' I questioned.

'Not when it all boils down to a failure and that is what Jack the Ripper was really, yes he was a serial killer, maybe the first of his kind, yes he was quite mad but all in all Jack The Ripper was an failure.'

'Because Jack the Ripper was never caught you mean, so you want me to speak to a policeman then?'

'Yes.'

'But if a policeman knows one of the victims wasn't who she was meant to be, then why didn't he say at the time?'

'He couldn't say a lot of things at that time, poor man. I felt quite sorry for him.'

'Who is he?'

'He *is* an old man.'

'He is an old man?' I repeated.

'The one and the same, he is retired now.'

'But he knew all this time?'

'Yes, but like I said, he doesn't like talking about The Ripper. He wasn't able to tell the truth, the powers of this great country stopped him,' he huffed as if he was still angry over the whole situation. 'I have even had words with my brother over this problem but one must say Mycroft is as lazy as he is loyal to the country. Oh well I guess that is another problem, my personal problem,' he said as he got up from his chair and paced to and fro in the room. He looked so different in that spilt second, was it hurt? Was it pain? Or could it possibly be confusion that I saw in his eyes?

The Strange Case of Caroline Maxwell

His brain was working overtime, that I could tell. Is this what his brother does to him because he is the only person who is able of not following Mr. Sherlock Holmes's thoughts? Mycroft Holmes is an older and more lethargic version of his younger brother after all, is he capable of making his own decisions whether or not they are different to Sherlock Holmes's? Is that why Mycroft Holmes only appears in a few of Dr Watson's amazing tales? The brothers can only get on with each other in few fleeting moments. I suppose that would be normal, almost human of Mr. Holmes to feel that way. But could Mr. Holmes really be human? There were signs of jealously in Mr. Holmes with the last case I read with them both, as Sherlock Holmes found out that Mycroft Holmes owns their father's magnifying glass. Could their also be brotherly hatred between them?

All of a sudden those feelings I saw in his eyes disappeared and he became the Sherlock Holmes we all knew. 'This policeman hated that he couldn't speak up and what with the other case,' he carried on as if there was no moment of silence between us. 'What was it called now?' he asked to himself as he stopped pacing and walked over to his files and pick up the one that said '1889'.

He scanned through the pages turning them sharply, almost with disgust that what he was looking for wasn't on that page until finally he stopped. 'That's it, the Scandal, tut, tut. That was a bad case for him as well. He had to let a noble man go. Tut, tut. Anyway I am digressing,' he said as he slammed the book shut, with a bang. 'He has grown to hate many of his cases.'

'But not *all* of his cases,' I said almost without a second thought. Mr. Holmes didn't reply to that comment; he just turned brusquely to face me and smiled. 'How do I meet him?' I asked.

'You can see him in his home in Hampshire.'

'Did you just say Hampshire?' I asked. I have never been outside London before; this really was going to be a remarkable and educational case.

'Hampshire,' was all he repeated. 'But heed my words, you will want to see him but he will not want to see you.'

...

Knock, Knock.

The Strange Case of Caroline Maxwell

The brown stained wooden living room door opened and Mrs Hudson walked in with a silver tray which had a china teapot, cups and saucers on top of it. 'I am guessing you and your guest would like some lovely sweet tea?' she said.

Sherlock Holmes huffed.

'Yes Mrs Hudson that would be very nice,' I said politely, I don't know what it is with Sherlock but you always feel you need to be even more polite than you normally are, to make up for him.

'Yes, yes very nice,' Holmes said as he waved her away. As she was leaving he said, 'Oh, Mrs Hudson?'

'Yes Mr Holmes?' She replied as she stood in the opened doorway.

'Can you do me, one... little... favour?'

'And what is that, Mr Holmes?' she said as she winked at me.

'Please could you never and I repeated this most sincerely, please could you *never ever* guess.'

By Amanda Harvey Purse

I left Baker Street with apprehensive and enthusiastic feeling, I felt like a reader at the beginning of a new Sherlock Holmes story, a story in which I have managed to place myself in the role of Dr Watson being lead by Sherlock into whatever madness he knows no bounds and I can only hope to understand at some point in this twisting tale. Where is this case going to take me? What will I discover? Will this be light hearted jolt in the county? Or will it have some sinister undertone to a disturbing mystery?

Although I don't have to be Sherlock Holmes to realise, that anything to do with Jack the Ripper leads down a dark, bloodcurdling and daunting path, a path in which I am walking clueless and naively down.

What if one of the victims was wrong? What if she is still living amongst us now? All these people in this huge city, all these people I am walking passed now; what if I am walking passed her right now? Would I know? People can hold so many secrets; would I be able to sense the most deadly secret of all, the secret life they are living? Could I see it through their eyes?

I know it sounds a little anomalous of me to talk with that tone, but I contemplate that you can tell a lot

The Strange Case of Caroline Maxwell

about a person through their eyes. The eyes can never lie while the rest of the face can.

The eyes are the gate way to a person's soul, if you study them hard enough they could tell you many things that you cannot ask. I have found this significant in the profession I have chosen for myself, but I have also established that this one fact that I know about, tends to make me look keenly and attentively into other people's eyes. This has led to some embarrassingly inept and sticky situations in the past, where people thought I was a little bizarre or outlandish or at worst, a patient that had escaped from a local asylum, but perhaps not as local as they first thought. All because they had noticed I was glaring into their faces a little too austerely and enthusiastically for their own liking.

Since then, I have developed a cunning and almost sneaky way of looking at a person without them realising I am trying to get the information out of them through their eyes rather than the answers they give to my questions. That way I get what I need from them without them thinking I am a crazy person. Eyes are important to me and help me understand a person's motives, so could I understand one of the so called victims if I looked deeply

By Amanda Harvey Purse

into her eyes? She fooled the world, she started a new life and she is the only person to have *used* Jack the Ripper and what he did to benefit herself, could I really understand all that if I saw it her eyes?

After all, she had lied to us all.

It would certainly be a different angle on the whole Jack the Ripper case, so much has been focused on the killer himself, not much has been written about one of the victims. Yes, there was uproar on the slums of Whitechapel and the destitution of the women living there, but it didn't last long. People forgot them, people just carried on with their lives, *like she must have done.*

How could she do that, just carry on with her life while the whole of London, let alone the whole world thought that she is dead and had died in a horrible way? How could someone do that? Just change their life, walk away and be someone else. That in its self is amazing and something genuinely unique, how can a woman have that much strength? I know how hard it is for a woman to work let alone live in this life time, it is still classed as scandalous and quite outrageous for a woman to have so much intensity and dilution.

The Strange Case of Caroline Maxwell

I know I have always worked hard to get a better life for myself and not have to play second fiddle to a man's world even though I haven't got much money, but could I really have the potency and dominance to leave my life and start again from scratch? I wonder would I use an 'opportunity', if I can call it that, to change my whole existence. While not knowing if it was for the better or worse.

What strength that woman must have!

I arrived back at my rooms with so many thoughts running through my head I didn't where to start. It was a curious thing, how a morning with Sherlock Holmes changes your own life. I wonder if that's what kept Dr. Watson there for so long, the not knowing what the next case would bring, where Mr. Sherlock Holmes would take him, what mood Mr. Sherlock Holmes would be in or quite simply, how Mr. Sherlock Holmes would make him feel. I feel just like that and I have only spent an hour with the man! Could I really handle a whole life time with him and his habits?

Just two days ago I was sitting at my writing desk not knowing where to start, but for an entirely different reason. I didn't have an idea for what to write about but now I have too many ideas, and still don't know where to start with any of them.

Does he always have this effect on people? I am willing to believe he does, it is just in his nature I can see it in his eyes. I sat down and wrote one word.

Why?

That has been the question to so many mysteries in life, but that word has never felt so strong and significant as it does right now. Why? Why would she do that? What made her do it? Would I have done the same? Giving the chance to become someone else, someone totally different would I take it? What effect would it have on the people, my life and me? Would I regret it? Would I regret that I can never go back to who I was? Would I want to go back?

And most crucial and somewhat imperative of all, why did Mr. Sherlock Holmes give this information to me? Why me? Sherlock Holmes never does everything on a whim, he is far too cautious and painstakingly meticulous for that, you can hardly call Mr. Sherlock Holmes slapdash. So it leads me to not understand his motives in getting me involved with such a high class mission that has a lot of

The Strange Case of Caroline Maxwell

responsibility to getting the information correct. What does he think I can do that and he can't?

How long has he known about this imperatively vital piece of information about the greatest serial murderer of this time? How did he know something wasn't quite right with the case? How did he sense that something was erroneously incorrect? While the rest of the world was satisfied and contented with knowing, what they thought was everything to do with Jack the Ripper. Mr. Holmes recognized and identified something that was flawed and inaccurate but he didn't speak up. He didn't use his detective skills in anything about the case, he left it alone.

Dr Watson has never mentioned anything about the Ripper in any of his wonderful stories, even though Sherlock Holmes and John Watson lived through it like the rest of us. The more I think about it the more it doesn't sound like a Holmes thing to do, could he really not get involved with this case? Why didn't I think of that at the time? Why didn't anyone mention or notice no participation from Mr. Sherlock Holmes? In a matter of fact, why didn't any of the newspapers pick up on the fact that Mr. Sherlock Holmes was not helping in his normal way?

By Amanda Harvey Purse

I remember reading all the reports on The Ripper, some of them scared me half to death when they were there explaining what had happen to those poor women. I read what the police were doing to help or in the case of the press, what the police wasn't doing to help. Why didn't any reporters pick up on the missing piece? The missing piece of the mystifying jigsaw had one important question of *where was Mr. Sherlock Holmes?*

How comes when a case of great consequence was on everyone's minds, the most famous killer was in our own mists, did we not hear everything from Baker Street? The most notorious murderer in London, up against the most renowned and celebrated detective in London. Why didn't that happen? Why didn't Mr. Sherlock Holmes get involved? There were too many questions and unfortunately there were no answers.

...

Start at the very beginning that is a very good place to start, I suppose. Who was this policeman? This mysterious policeman that seems to have got away with knowing what Sherlock Holmes knows and did not tell anyone, he was able to retire and move away. On a risk of repeating myself, I have got to ask *why?*

The Strange Case of Caroline Maxwell

For god's sake why do that? Why is everything to do with Jack the Ripper still unknown? It's been sixteen years! Sixteen long years and we still don't know who he was! How I am meant to understand anything to do with Jack the Ripper, when we don't know who he was or even why he starting killing? Actually while I am on this train of thought, we don't know why he stopped killing, I mean not sound unwomanly but he was getting away with it, so why stop? Is most of my report on this case going to have me writing the word 'why'?

1...2...3...

I need to calm down and think about it. Yes there is a lot of 'whys' with this subject, there was always going to be. But it might help because it would help me to focus on what I have to deal with, with every *why* there surely there must be a *'because'*.

I need to put my journalist head on, I need some facts. What do I know about this policeman? He lives in Hampshire, he has retired and he had a case in 1889. A case that Mr. Sherlock Holmes thought was noteworthy and that in its self should be noteworthy to me.

By Amanda Harvey Purse

So we need a policeman involved with the Ripper case and a famous case in 1889. Simple, well...simple if I was still in Sherlock Holmes's living room with all his notes and files to hand to help me. I suppose there really is method to the madness of his room but I don't think that will make Mrs Hudson any more ecstatic with the scene she meets when she has to do her spring cleaning! Anyway my thoughts are fleeting away from the main task of finding facts.

A policeman is what I want, so I will go to where policemen are. With the voice of Sherlock Holmes in my head I shouted to my empty room, 'Off to the yard!'

The Strange Case of Caroline Maxwell

Chapter Three

The New Scotland Yard building was very grand indeed, it was very impressive and imposing to any walker-by and it certainly inspired me. The Old Scotland Yard was a depressingly dismal and a murky place, it was so small and unimportant looking it was almost laughable to think that the great London Police Force were working inside. It was really a number of sheds pulled together behind the Royal Barracks, you wouldn't believe it was there, no one glanced a second time at it. This time it felt like the police were waving a big 'hello' to the world as the creamy white and orange brick stood out amongst the other older looking buildings along The Thames front, not including The Houses of Parliament of course. That building is definitely like chalk and cheese compared to Scotland Yard, with its golden gothic design. Money well spent uh?

The Yard almost looked like a fantasy castle, with its towers and turrets and light coloured surroundings. Could this really be the place where the little grey cells of policeman's mind can really get to work?

As I walked past the enormous, vast black gates leading to this dreamy vision of a bastion, I wondered how many other would-be detectives would pass these gates in years to come. Would there be consulting detectives from different parts of the world coming here to investigate one crime or another. Someone that was different to our Sherlock Holmes maybe?

Someone small, rounded with an air of aristocratic superior. He would of course have to be smart, clever and sharp. He would have to be quick and swift with his reasoning and deducing who the murderer was and he would have to be faster than the police. He would have a humour of his own that people would love and the murderer would feel secure by. He would act harmlessly, reliably and trustworthily but underneath there would be a man keen and determined to win the case and that's all he truly cares about. He would have to be charming, precise

The Strange Case of Caroline Maxwell

and careful; he would be clear-cut and particular with his habits and his appearance. Everything has its place; maybe he could have some facial hair.

*Who am I talking about? What am I thinking of? Have I just thought up a character for a story? Another detective that walks the streets of London, could that really happen? Could I write a detective novel like Dr Watson? The only difference would be that my detective would be purely **fictional**. No, it is a silly thought to have because the great city of London, maybe even the whole world is not ready for another detective, well not yet.*

Anyway I digress, a bad habit of mine. I walked up to the main door and a policeman walked out. 'And where do you think you're going?' He asked me in a rough and gravelled voice.

The man was tall and thin, with his pale face it seemed as if he was quite ill. His dark hair was greased and parted in the middle and with his dark moustache it gave him an almost sinister look.

'Please take a presumption,' I said, pointing to the door he had just come out off.

'I wouldn't do that if I was you,' he said as he lit the cigarette he was holding.

'Why is that?'

Between puffs of this cigarette he was smoking, the policeman managed to say,'Scotland Yard does not take kindly to reporters walking right up to their main door,' he paused to look me up and down and then he continued 'although being a woman is certainly a turn up for the books.'

'I didn't say I was a reporter,' I said abjectly.

'You didn't have to, it is written all over your face and you seem to forget who you are talking to,' he paused again, to make what he was about to say sound of great consequence to me and to take another puff. 'You are talking to a policeman of Scotland Yard no less! We all aren't as slow as that Inspector 'what's his name' now famous from the Holmes stories.'

'Well that's certainly *is* a turn up from the books,' I said with a smile.

'Well misses, what do you want?' he said not understanding my joke. Or maybe he did understand my

The Strange Case of Caroline Maxwell

joke but maybe he is not a joking man; by the look at his eyes there certainly were no life in them.

'Who am I speaking to?' I decided to ask.

'A question with question hey? Well I haven't got time for this,' he said as he threw his cigarette passed my feet and on the stair below, he turned and walked back towards the door.

'I'm here for The Ripper,' I blurted out.

He stopped and still with his back towards me he asked 'Why now?'

'What do you mean?'

'The Ripper is gone, dead. Well... most probably anyway. Leave him be.'

'We don't truly know that, you guys never caught him. *Or at least that's what you say*, why can't the files be open to the public? There may be clues left.'

'Another would be detective like the Holmes fellow, that's all we need.'

'Well if you have something to hide,' I said.

By Amanda Harvey Purse

'There is nothing hidden,' he replied as he turned to face me. I could get a better look at his eyes at this moment; they were old and exhausted with a hint of sadness. Was he sad to be here? Was he sad to work as a policeman? Why, what has happened to him? But there was no time to think about him, I needed to get inside the building so I simply said to him.

'You can prove that, I could speculate.'

The policeman dejectedly took me into the New Scotland Yard. I had never been in this new building before and I have wanted to see it for some time, but to say I was overjoyed with the new look I would be sadly overstating the mark. I was so astounded by the outside I was hoping for more than what I got inside, but there was really not much difference at all compared to the Old Yard; there were still the same old tables and chairs that were in the Old Scotland Yard with what looked liked the same piles upon piles of paperwork on them.

The room was as busy as ever, with policemen scratching their heads as they try and solve another problematical case. They were trying to put a brave face on it but I could see, even from the distance that I was away from them, that their eyes were portraying a different

The Strange Case of Caroline Maxwell

feeling. A feeling of loss and a confused state of mind was a more of accurate description of the scene that lay before me. This policeman I was walking with was right when he said that not *all* policemen were like Inspector *what's-his-name*, just I am afraid, most of them.

We walked through the room, out the other side and started to walk down a set of cast iron stairs. I couldn't believe we were going down there for the atmosphere changed instantly, the air around us had become colder and damper, which led me to ask 'The Ripper files are down here? It's so dark and dismal, so disconsolate'.

'Quite appropriate don't you think?' he answered gloomily, this really was a miserable and poignant man I thought to myself. We walked further down a hallway, it was getting darker and darker, in fact there was hardly any light at all when we reached the bottom and there was an appalling smell rinsing up and reaching my nostrils.

'What is that smell? Could it be mould? Surely not mould already,' I asked.

'Death.' he merely replied.

'Excuse me?' I said a little shocked at his reply.

'You are smelling death, that's what I think anyway. I have spent a fair few cases in a morgue to know what death smells like, this place smells the same.'

Does this guy ever cheer up? He could depress the mood at the liveliest of parties. We walked further on until we reached a door marked 'The Unsolved Crimes Office'.

'This is the morgue, number two,' he said with a huff.

'You sure are a man that loves his position aren't you?' I asked, trying to get another look at his eyes as he surely was not going to tell me anything about himself.

'This job eradicates you, slowly,' he said dodging my gaze.

'Why are you still here then?' I questioned.

'Where else would I be?' He asked shrugging his shoulders. *There was meaning behind that answer, he wouldn't be anywhere else, which means this is the only place to find him. Scotland Yard is his life. Is this why he is so sad?*

'Ah, you answer a question with a question hey?' I said jokingly. He actually smiled but he did it in such an

The Strange Case of Caroline Maxwell

awkward way, that it made it look embarrassingly unpleasant and unnerving; I don't think he had done such a thing in an exceptionally lengthy time. He placed his hand on the brass, rounded door handle and turned it slowly. With a sound of a click the door opened a little way. 'The door is not locked?' I asked.

'Doesn't have to be,' he said as he allowed his cockney accent to shine through, he released his hand from the handle. I looked at him questionably. He tried to answer my look, 'Not many people want to go in here,' he said without looking in the office or even anywhere near it. *Does he hate this place? Is it hate or is it fear? Why?*

'But why may I ask?' I asked, repeating my thoughts.

'This room is full of unsolved cases, unsolved failures. Nobody wants to be reminded of disappointment and disillusionment of frustration and regret,' he said as he began to turn away from the office.

'Don't you ever feel tempted to look in and solve the unsolvable?' I said, trying to keep his attention.

'You don't want to get caught up in the past, it's gloomy, bleak and depressingly always going to be there, you cannot change it so why try?' He asked as he again turned back to me.

'It's the not knowing, it's not final. It's like reading a book and not getting to the end,' I explained to him.

'Yes, well. I guess that's why you are here, looking up *that* case. There you go then, fill yourself with the morbid and the repugnant that fills the heads of the public and novelists alike,' he said as he pushed the door a little further open. 'Don't say I didn't warn you,' he said as he began to actually walk away, his polished shoes hitting the uncarpeted concrete flooring.

'Can I ask who the delightfully charming, jovial and cheerful policeman it is that has helped me?' I asked. He stopped for a few seconds away from me. Was he thinking of what to say to me? It was a simple question with no need to think about an answer, I was only asking his name, why the pause? When some time had gone he finally said without turning to face me,

'You're the one *playing* detective, you work it out,' he waited a few more moments to let his statement lay in the air between us. Then, when he thought that it had, he paced off in the direction of the set of stairs.

The Strange Case of Caroline Maxwell

'Oh come on! I know nothing about you!' I shouted, quite unwomanly at him.

'Isn't it the best way to start a mystery?' he said as he turned back towards me and winked. Then he walked back down the rest of hallway we had just come down, I watched him until his lean figure disappeared into the gloom. Then there I was left alone in the quiet, dark and murky stillness of the police station's basement with only the office door beckoning and taunting me to go in.

...

The room was much larger than I had thought it would have been. There were rows upon rows of shelving, reaching high enough to touch the ceiling all with files on them. There was one long lengthways window that was placed high up on the crumbing brickwork wall at the other end of where I was standing, as I tighten my eyesight to look through the window I saw a few pairs of shoes walking by, the same styled shoes as I had seen placed upon the feet of the policeman that had just left me, I wonder if they were standard issue. I really was down in the depths of a miserable place.

This is going to be a long day I could sense it.

By Amanda Harvey Purse

I sat my undersized bag down at a wooden desk in the corner of the room where there was also the only man made light in the room in a form of a candle, half burned and I noticed it hadn't been used for a while as there was a layer of dust on it and surrounding it. I lit the candle, because although it was daytime you wouldn't have known it from down here in this room. I slowly walked down the first aisle I came to trying to take a mental note of all the case names I saw.

It was quite accurate what that policeman said about the smell, it was stronger in here. I moved closer to the files folders and took a deep sniff, yes the smell was coming from these files and I suppose all these files were death. In each of these files held details about all kinds of different deaths, these files are almost keeping their deaths alive, if that makes sense.

On the middle shelf, halfway down the middle aisle I came to the word 'Ripper'. There has only been one, so far. I placed my index finger around the metal pull, it felt cold and crumbly, I glance down at my finger and it was covered in orange rusty powder. This file has not been moved for a while, no one has wanted to move or even look at. It has just been sitting here quietly knowing it is

The Strange Case of Caroline Maxwell

He was dressed in worn out garments that smelt heavily of gin. He had a billycock hat which still cast a shadow over this man's eyes; his whitening whiskers were long and grubby. Although his crooked back was obvious causing him great anguish, he must work here as he was dragging a mop and bucket behind him. Noticing that my seat was the only seat in the room, I stood up and moved aside from the desk.

'Here have my seat,' I said as I waved him to the wooden chair.

'Thank you young lady, my bones are no longer moving in a comfortable and unperturbed way,' he said as he sat down with a profoundly boisterous wheeze.

'Catch your breath,' I said, as I moved the mop and bucket out of the way. I turned to face him to see him looking intensely at the photographs I had laid out on the desk.

'Researching The Ripper are we?' He asked.

'Yes.'

'Why do you want to drag up the past?'

By Amanda Harvey Purse

'I have been told something that may change what we have come to be familiar with.'

'Will it change the past?'

'Well I don't know about that.'

'Let me put it another way, will it bring these poor women back to life?'

'Not those women, no,' I said. My statement seemed to start a silence between us, *I wonder why?*

'Then I don't see the point,' he sulked, breaking at last the stillness of the room.

'You might be able to help me,' I said, realising he must of been a mature adult at the time of The Ripper.

'I doubt that,' he said as he picked up a photograph of one of the victims and slowly started to caress it.

'I am looking for a policeman involved with the case that may be of some use to me.'

'Well I guess you are in the right place then,' he said butting in and waving one arm around while still looking at the photograph.

The Strange Case of Caroline Maxwell

'I guess so, but.'

'Did he not help you?' The old man asked.

'Who are you talking about?'

'Inspector Godley, I saw him bring you down here. He worked on the case.'

'I don't remember seeing that Inspector's name in the files.'

'He would have not been an Inspector then, only when his superior *retired*,' he paused 'Sorry miss I don't mean to be discourteous but if they catch me sitting down, they won't be best pleased. I am sorry I was no help to you,' he said as he struggled to pull himself up from the chair and gripped his mop handle and started to drag the bucket towards the direction of the door.

'No sir, you have been much help. I thank you.'

The old man, now in the shadows seemed to turn back to me and I sensed he was smiling in a way I recognise, *but from where?* Then like a notorious illusionist in a high class West End stage show, in a flash the old man was gone...

By Amanda Harvey Purse

...

I turned back to The Ripper file and reread the statements from any Inspector involved with case. There were two, one from the Metropolitan and one from the City of London Police. I had an instinct of which one it was, but I had to be sure.

I left the desk once again and headed from the shelves with the cases from 1889. As my eyes rested on the titles of the files, I tried to remember what Sherlock Holmes had called it, *The Scandal.* There was a reason for Mr. Holmes calling the case, 'The Scandal', he didn't say *a* scandal, and he said *The Scandal.* I walked up and down the aisle looking for this Scandal but there wasn't any sign of that name. Why?

I walked back over to the desk, where the file of The Ripper was spread out all over it and my notepad was lying on top with two names written in my handwriting on it.

Two names, but only one stood out to me, it almost seemed like the name was dancing on the page. I underlined it. But I had to be sure, I needed to find out about this Scandal in 1889, why isn't it here? I don't

The Strange Case of Caroline Maxwell

understand it was a police case after all, so why isn't The Scandal here?

Well, to walk out of here with two names is better than I could have hoped for, I suppose. I gathered all the files up and tried my best to place them back in the order they came out, but it had been hours ago since I took these documents out. It felt like days, someone could *genuinely* spend days in here.

As I put the paperwork back into the file box, I looked to the desk and to the photographs that lay there, *one of these women has another name.* These poor and unfortunate four women all died in vain, all died for a reason we don't truly understand.

Wait a minute, four? Wasn't there five women? I am sure I remember reading about five women were killed, why does the police only have four photographs?

I placed my notepad back in my bag, placed the file back on the shelf, walked out of the room and went to close the door. As I rubbed the door frame slowly with my right hand I took a moment to think of all the officers involved with The Ripper case. How sad they must have felt to not be able to do anything to save those women. How heartbreaking must it have been, for the officer that had to put The Ripper file in that room and shut this door, knowing this was the '*second morgue*' where all the unsolved cases go to disappear in the mists of time.

    I shook my head in remembrance, made sure the door was closed and walked down the hallway and then I remembered. What a fool I had been! I stopped and turned to face the room I had just come out of. Of Course! It all makes sense! Why didn't I think of it before? It must have been the smell or the subject, but I am working slow today. I have been researching in the wrong place!

    I wonder if this is what Mr. Holmes feels like when he comes across a clue that will lead him somewhere else. This anticipation, the eagerness to move on, the enthusiasm and excitement is all there within me. I haven't felt this way since, well since I was reading one of Mr. Sherlock Holmes's tales, now I feel I'm in one.

    I looked at the door I had just shut and my eyes moved towards the sign above it, of course! What a daft person I have been! I have not used my little grey cells! I thought to myself as I stamped my foot and slapped my forehead with my cold and rust stained hand...

The Strange Case of Caroline Maxwell

Chapter Four

The next day I went to The Times News Agency, it was as diligent as always which was beneficial and effective to me, as this meant I could go in and out without being noticed by my editor. I can't stand the mindless, senseless little man at the best of times, let alone when I'm in a middle of researching. He will want to know what I'm doing, how I am doing it, who are my sources and most importantly when will I be done. He will stare at me with those despicably unpleasant colourless eyes waiting for an answer to every question, silently judging me. I didn't need to meet him today, not with this case so heavily on my mind.

I worked my way to the other end of the main office room and pushed open the side door only enough to let myself through and I was safe. I dusted myself down, took a deep breath and carried on walking down the hallway until I reached my researching room.

I call it *my* researching room as no one else seems to be bothered about this little room, they don't seemed to realise the significance of this room. But I suppose that made it more exceptional and inspiring to me, I knew that this room would be vacant and give me the time and tranquillity I needed to make sense of this circumstance I have found myself hooked on to.

I walked in and sat at my usual desk, I looked around me and it was surprising how much this room was like the second morgue in the police station.

No one ever goes here, it is full of the past and it has a sense of tragedy and misfortune about it, no wonder I felt at home there at The Yard. I got out my notepad and folded back the pages until I reached the two names, with one underlined. I placed the notepad on the desk, I took a deep breath and turned my attention to the rows and rows of The Times newspapers from the past years, I still don't know how far back in the past these papers go but I was hoping they reached 1889 at least.

The Strange Case of Caroline Maxwell

Although yesterday was informative and seeing those poor women in their death photographs was poignant but also moving, it still hadn't left me any further on in my case. That was because I was looking in the wrong place, I had thought it would be easy finding the policeman involved with The Ripper case as well as The Scandal of 1889, and all I needed to do was go to the New Scotland Yard and pick out the files I wanted and match the names. But of course that was wrong of me because there was one major difference between the two cases.

While one was unsolved, the other was *solved*.

What did Mr. Holmes say? *That was a bad case, had to let a noble man go.* This policeman had solved The Scandal but had to let a noble man go. So of course The Scandal wasn't going to be in the Unsolved Crimes Room at Scotland Yard but it may just have made an impact to be in The Times Newspaper.

I scrutinize every newspaper article in the year of 1889, but there was nothing. Nothing called a Scandal, nothing about letting a noble man go. What is going on here? Why can't I find the information about the scandal anywhere? Maybe it is because I got the year wrong, maybe I saw 1888? 1887? 1886? Or maybe I didn't see anything. It could have been any year in the 1880's. No, I have confidence in what I see, that's what makes me a good journalist. My quick glances, the study of people's body language, knowing what sounds right and can sense what sounds wrong that is why I am good at my job, I have just got to trust myself a little more.

'Start at the beginning,' I said with a huff to myself. I went back to the newspaper articles of 1880 and 1881, as I glance at every page, nothing. As the years went on I started to recognize my own way of writing was slowly creeping in to the paper. At first it was little articles, not more than a few sentences and not even about anything important, not even at first under my own name of course but that was a whole different long winded story involving me, dressing up like a cockney sully rag boy, that story is perhaps for another time, dear reader.

Back then, I wrote about the missing blue diamond from The Langham Hotel and that's when the editor first began to notice my talent, I never thought it was the ex-con that took it so I wrote about it and was able to sign my own name to it.

I was the editor's new best thing, a writer he found and because of him The Times 'was the only newspaper

The Strange Case of Caroline Maxwell

that told the truth to their public' and didn't have to retract their story. Nothing to do with all the hard work I put into it of course, but in truth I can't complain, that article that I first signed my name to, had caught the eye of none other than *Mr. Sherlock Holmes.* That in turn lead me to have the interview all the other journalists would have loved to have got, Mr. Holmes is so quiet and unsocial it was taken as red that he would not give an interview to anyone, but of course he had to prove them wrong. He did do *one little interview,* as my editor now seemed to call it and I was the only interviewer.

That now, has led me to this case and to this room looking over all the old newspaper stories. I began again to look at the papers on the wooden rail, it was then I saw the famous article that I was just thinking about, where I met the celebrated Mr. Holmes for the first time. I knew I was busy but I couldn't help but read it over again.

'I wouldn't have thought of you as vain Miss Christie,' said a voice from behind me. I turned to see my editor standing over me as if I was a child. He had the habit of making me feel like a child and I hated him for it.

'I am researching actually,' I said.

By Amanda Harvey Purse

'Yes I can see that, researching your own past,' he said pointing to the paper that was in my hands. I pretended to have not heard that last statement and thought about how this moment could assist me as there is now nothing I can do to conceal myself from him. I looked at the ghastly little man I have to call my superior, it felt like the first time I actually took the time to glare at him.

He was a larger than average man, so such so that when he laughed at his own jokes his stomach moved up and down, it was quite possibly the only rapid exercise his body got. He lumped occasionally on his right leg; I believe it was an injury he incurred when he spent a few months in India at the height of the Boar War as a new boy reporter. I had heard from older journalists that the war had seemed to change him; I wonder what he was like before I had met him.

Now his dark hair was turning white and thinning on the top. His eyesight was failing him, something that was seriously important for him to hide as no one saw that he wore glasses but the signs of it were there as he had red marks just either side of his quite large nose and they were getting brighter and brighter each time I saw him. He now was arrogant, conceited and at the best of times pompous,

The Strange Case of Caroline Maxwell

thinking himself a better species of a human being only because he was male.

Sometimes I have managed to look at him with a grateful glance as he has allowed me to sign under my own name as a woman, one of the first newspaper editors to do that in my lifetime.

Do not get me wrong I am not saying I am the first woman journalist, god heavens no. There is another woman journalist I am very much fond of and her works, as she has wrote novels about her experiences too; her name is Ms. Nellie Bly or 'Pink' to her friends. I have often thought about writing to her, with the aim of getting some advice with my career, as she has had to dress up as someone else to get her story too. But in truth I cannot afford the postal travel fare to the United States, where she now lives and works for the' New York Post'.

She knew how it felt to be working in a man's world and getting nowhere that is why she left England for the dazzling lands across the pond where many dreams come true. I on the other hand was stuck in this depressing and dismal city I call home.

By Amanda Harvey Purse

Maybe this case will make a name for me; maybe this will be the start of something big for me. Maybe it will be my chance to be the next Ms. Nellie Bly, as I brought my attention back to where I was and what I was doing, I saw my editor's face looking jovial and self-righteous at me, although at this moment in time I hated him finding me here, he might be able to help me.

'I need to find out something, but it seems it hasn't been written about,' I managed to say.

'Then it didn't happen. The Times prides itself of being up to date and being the newspaper that the public can trust to tell them everything that is going on in the great city,' he said as he stood there like a proud little idiot that he was. I wanted to roll my eyes so I looked back at the newspaper rail for a second.

1...2...3...

'It was in 1889 and called The Scandal,' I carried on as I looked back at him.

'Ah, well, that is a different matter,' he answered losing his eye contact with me.

The Strange Case of Caroline Maxwell

'Oh, how come may I ask?' I asked, surprised to see my editor looking a little tense and uneasy. *Have I caught you off guard Mister grand editor?* As that thought crossed my mind I couldn't help but smile to myself, I don't think he noticed. *He never notices anything.*

'We have a slight condition with certain members of high society that have made this newspaper admired and stylish, that we do not publish anything that may put them in bad light.'

'Oh. Then I take it, this Scandal would have put them in bad light then.'

'Quite so, Miss Reporter.'

'Can you tell me about it?'

'I hope this researching isn't going to drag up the past and get us in to trouble *my dear,*' he said so cringingly it made me feel sick, I am not *his dear*! 'Because I can't publish anything about The Scandal, not even now,' he continued.

'I just want a few bits information to help me with what I have for a story, a big story,' I said strongly. With a

By Amanda Harvey Purse

questionable look, my editor slowly moved nearer to my desk.

'If it is for a *big* story, I suppose I better tell you. But you must promise that not only is this story is going to be big but you are the only reporter on the case.'

'I promise that no one else has even thought about this.'

'Then let me start,' he said masterly as if he was the greatest storyteller the world has ever known.

The Strange Case of Caroline Maxwell

Chapter Five

'It was in 1889 when the story broke. A young policeman was investigating a local theft at a post office, simple enough case or so he thought but what it turned out to be was something totally different. Forget the policeman's name now, Banks or Hanks something like that anyway, while the police constable was scrutinizing the working of this post office he became aware of this young telegraph boy name of Mr. Charles Winslow that worked for this particular post office. After studying him for a while the policeman decided to question the boy and found he was in possession of fourteen shillings, which of course was too much money for a simple telegraph boy to have, so with that in mind and thinking the boy had something to do with the theft, the police constable took

By Amanda Harvey Purse

the boy in for questioning at the station. After a few hours the boy finally told PC. Hanks or Banks or whatever he was called, that he had earned his fourteen shillings working as a rent boy at a brothel in Cleveland Street. Well that was the start of it.'

'Cleveland Street?' I asked.

'Of course, that's why it was called The Cleveland Street Scandal. This Mr. Charles Winslow was introduced to this brothel by an older boy who was the age of nineteen, a one Mr. Henry Newlove... curious name...anyway this brothel was run by a Mr. Charles Hammond and after a few interesting developments and a statement from Mr. Newlove, it was established that Mr. Hammond had a few note worthy clients.'

'Who were the clients?' I asked.

'Newlove just couldn't stop talking to the police; the first name was the head of the stables for the Prince of Wales, Lord Somerset.'

'Lord Somerset was in a male brothel? I think I am starting to understand. Is that why the case was hushed up?' I asked.

The Strange Case of Caroline Maxwell

'Almost, there were other members of the *highest* society involved too but that is another story.'

'A story that you can't tell, you mean.'

'Correct. Well that brought in the higher ups of the police force and the Inspector was called in.'

'The Inspector, did you say? Yes of course there had to be an Inspector, you don't happen to remember who he was?' I asked, trying to sound as if the question was unimportant to me. My editor paused for a moment and studied me before replying.

'Why do you want to know? What do you know miss? Is it anything good? Tell me now' He asked, for a foolish chap my editor can at times be quite quick witted, which is a new thing for me to hate him for.

'I'm not sure, it's probably nothing special,' I said, knowing his eyes were still studying me.

'Well I don't know what you are up to or what you have heard but you better make it special *dearie*, that is if you still want more space in the paper,' He said as he stood up, headed for the door and as he turned the handle to opened the door a small inch, I had to turn away for the

By Amanda Harvey Purse

sudden light from the hallway hitting my face. I turned back to see him still standing in the doorway facing me. 'It's Abberline, Inspector Abberline' he said as he shut the door.

As my eyes adjusted to the darkness that flooded the now empty room, I couldn't believe I had seen a new side to my editor, a side that was actually helpful. *How many more shocks lay in store for me with this case?* I put the newspapers back on the right wooden rails they belonged too, while having a lovingly look for one last time at the interview with Sherlock Holmes. That interview was the reason that all this has started and I will never forget it.

As I went back to the desk with my bag on it, I looked at the two names on my notepad and crossed out one name and left the name that was underlined. I knew I was right.

Inspector Fredrick George Abberline, I have found him Holmes! I screamed in my head.

The evening train to Hampshire was actually running on time, I quickly jumped on board and found a seat in first class, *after all the newspaper is paying for it.*

The Strange Case of Caroline Maxwell

As I relaxed back in my seat I noticed in the corner a pair of hands were holding a newspaper.

'Going all the way Miss?' said a thick Somerset accent from behind the paper.

'Sorry, what did you say?' I asked, as I wasn't expecting to speak to anyone on my way to Hampshire.

'Are you going all the way to Hampshire? My lovely,' the voice repeated.

'Oh, well yes I am.'

'Lovely part of the island, Hampshire is.'

'I wouldn't know,' I said, it was a little strange having a conversation with a newspaper and a pair of hands I had never met before.

'Ah, you're a Londoner through and through, hey? Now why would a lovely young woman want to travel such a long way? A story perhaps?' said the man's voice.

'Well as a matter of fact it is, but wait a second, how did you know I was a reporter?' I asked.

The paper moved down to his lap and the voice had a face. It was an ugly looking face, full of boils and warts, a long hooked nose, small round eyes and thin light ginger hair surrounding it. 'Why miss, I can't help but notice that you have ink on your hands and I'm afraid on the tip of your nose, where I think you must have itched yourself. No woman I have seen has had that much ink on their person, so maybe you're a writer me thinks.'

'That was very clever of you,' I said as I wiped my nose with my handkerchief.

'Ah that's very nice of you to say so miss, so what story are you on?'

'Well I'm still unsure where it will lead me at the moment.' I said.

'And you are willing to go all this way for a story you are unsure about?'

'I trust my source.'

'*That is nice to hear*, like my mother used to say, god bless her soul, what is life without trust? Where are you heading to? I may know it.'

'It's actually called Carfax St Clair it is my thinking that it is the first village you come to from the station.'

The Strange Case of Caroline Maxwell

'Oh yes, that village you say very nice, it's quiet and peaceful place I say it is. It's changed so it has.'

'Changed?' I asked.

'The village used to be full of locals. I used to be the only stranger in town when I visit my old sailing pal. Now everyone seems to retire there.'

'*Retire* there?'

'Oh yes, many. Many people like you go there, you know Londoners. Want to get away from the smoke I guess.'

'You seem to know a lot about the village.'

'I can guess you can call me a local now because of the amount of times I have been there,' he said with a chesty laugh.

'I need to get to Methuen Road,' I said as I handed him the piece of paper I had wrote Inspector Abberline's address on.

'Methuen Road, that's the road past the Silver Horse public house, turns left I would and follows the road around the cliff face, and then I would be there. Only a few cottages and an old manor house down there, it is quite out the way.'

'That would make sense,' I said as I was writing the directions down.

'You are seeing old Freddie!' the man suddenly said.

'I'm sorry?' I asked, as I looked up from my notepad.

As I looked over to him, he had turned around the piece of paper I had given him, so that the address was now facing me. I saw above '4 Methuen Road' I had written *Fred Abberline.*

'He is a new one in these parts, moved in only a few months ago. Not an easy man to talk to likes to keep himself to himself, so he does. Hardly surprising.'

'Why is it not surprising?'

'You know who he is, don't you? The Inspector that lost The Ripper, if you were the man that let a murderer of five women go, wouldn't you keep quiet? I know I would.'

The Strange Case of Caroline Maxwell

'But The Ripper isn't the only case he dealt with.'

'No?' the man asked.

'No, I have been looking into his career. He had been quite a very successful policeman.'

'But no one will remember it,' he said.

'Well maybe someone should write about them then.'

'Oh I see that's what you will be speaking to him about.'

'What else would I be doing?' I asked.

'A thought had popped into my mind, so it did, that you were speaking to Freddie about The Ripper.'

'That wouldn't be anything new.'

'Aye that'll be true so it will. He doesn't like talking about it anyways so it might have been a wasted trip,' as he said that, the train rolled into the station. I had not noticed it had got so dark outside.

'Tell me kind sir, does this Silver Horse public house have rooms to spare?'

By Amanda Harvey Purse

'I would think so at this time of year,' the man said as he opened the train door for me. I stepped on to the platform, dropped my bag on the platform to dust myself down when there was a huge amount of smoke as the train pulled away. I turned to see where the man was, but there was no one. *The man has just disappeared.*

'Best move away from the platform Miss,' said a voice in the smoke. 'Don't want to get caught under the train do you?'

As the smoke started to clear I could see an outline of a man in uniform. 'Oh I am sorry; I was just wondering where the man I had travelled with had gone,' I said.

'No one but you got off at this station Miss.'

'But he was right behind me.'

'Well he must have got back on, Miss.'

'He must of done, how very odd.'

'If you say so miss,' said the man in uniform as he began to walk away from me.

The Strange Case of Caroline Maxwell

'I'm sorry sir, but I am new here. Could you point me in the direction of The Silver Horse public house?' I asked. The man stopped and turned back around.

'Follow the road down to a large green. You'll see it.'

'Thank you, you have been very helpful.'

By Amanda Harvey Purse

Chapter Six

The Silver Horse was really a charming and enthralling little abode. Nothing like the public houses you see in London. This one had the bricks painted freshly white, the door and window frames were of darkest wood and there were pretty pink and purple flowers in the window boxes outside and in barrels by the entrance. As I walked in, the sense of being a stranger was enormous and evident as there were, what felt like thousands upon thousands of pairs of eyes looking at me. I decided to at least look bold as well as confident and went to the person that looked like a barmaid and asked if there were any free rooms for a week. She looked at me with the sense of uncertainty, her big blue eyes seemed to be asking 'who are you?' but I guess politeness got the better of her and she

The Strange Case of Caroline Maxwell

disappeared out the back. Standing at the bar friendless and alone gave me a tingling sensation which I was trying to hide as I felt every one of those pairs of eyes glaring at my back. All I kept thinking was 'please come back, quickly'. When she came back she replied 'No, sorry Miss there isn't, I just asked the landlord, the only room free has been booked.'

'Oh I see' I said a little disappointed.

'I could have another word with him, Miss. I don't see a reporter turning up anyway.'

'No that's fine. Wait a second; did you just say a reporter?' I asked.

'Yes Miss, from some newspaper in London Miss.'

'Is it The Times newspaper?'

'Why, yes it is Miss.'

'I am the reporter.'

'Oh Miss, you should have said. The room is through that door and up the stairs on your left.'

'Thank you.'

By Amanda Harvey Purse

The room was petite and trivial but it had all I needed. There was a wash basin in the corner, a table and chair in the other and a small bed, with a pillow on it. There was a window to let the light in which gave me a view of the large green that was opposite the public house. I placed my bag on the table and went to bed.

I didn't have a good night's sleep; the photographs of the four victims haunted me and invaded my dreams. I had to lie on the bed with my eyes open most of the night, when daylight shone through the window I washed, dressed and grabbed my notebook and pen.

As I walked downstairs and into the pub, a man was sitting on one of the stools alone, reading the newspaper. He noticed me and turned to face me.

'So you are the reporter? When Bessie told me it was a *woman* I thought she was joking.'

'Yes I am the reporter,' I said ignoring his last statement. 'Did the newspaper book ahead for me?'

'Didn't say he was from a newspaper, all I can say was that it was a gentleman. A posh London type, thin as a stick, was wearing one of those hats the high and mighty

The Strange Case of Caroline Maxwell

wear in the country, you know what I mean, got the flaps tied up on top with a bow.'

'You mean a deerstalker hat.'

'If that's what they are called, anyway he talked posh too. Said there would be a reporter from The Times, London calling here for a room. He paid for a week.'

'He paid?' I asked.

'Yes, he said it would be in his interest for you to have a room to stay here for a week as you have very important task in front of you.'

Holmes? Would it have been Mr. Sherlock Holmes? Why was he here?

'Oh, well thank you but I must be on my way,' I said as I wanted to get away before anyone asked what I was doing here. I needed time to think of a cover story that was believable and genuine that explained why I was here without going anywhere near the truth. *Not that I know what the truth is.*

There is something about these set of murders that happened sixteen years ago that still holds a foreboding dread and anxiety in people's hearts. Some people don't want to have anything to do with the ripper, or any story that involves him. But some people want to add their two shillings worth to the history; to able to tell future generations they had some influence on the case. Whether it is to have some emotional impact on their family, or to make them sound intelligent, exceptional or distinctive I don't know but either one I don't want to converse with.

That was the problem with the newspaper articles in 1888; they just wanted to sell their papers, to make a quick buck. Which meant the stories were never checked fully out so had no basis on the truth, sometimes the stories were made up by the revolting and horrid imaginations of journalists past and sometimes the stories have nothing to do with the murders but had cleverly used the words: *murder, Whitechapel, East End, The Ripper or Jack* to fool readers into spending money on that paper because they have faith in what they are buying would have some new information on Jack the Ripper but found out afterwards they were sadly mistaken.

I don't want to be any kind of reporter that writes a story to fool its readers, or write a story that is untrue; I want to be a reporter that writes a story that is factual, accurate and authentic. A reporter, a reader can trust with

The Strange Case of Caroline Maxwell

confidence and conviction. But the subject matter of this story did at first, make me turn away, I would have turned away if it wasn't for Mr. Holmes. To be on a Ripper quest feels me with trepidation as, can you really identify what is fact and what is fiction with this murderer? Could you even recognize it sixteen years on?

Something is telling me, I am walking on thin ice. I have never liked the winter season because of the ice and the danger it could cause, so why would I walk out on it? Why *am* I walking out on it now?

I have put trust in you Mr. Holmes, please don't let me down!

I managed to leave the pub unquestioned and headed across the large green. It was a beautiful day; the sun was shining so brightly it actually hurt my eyes to look up at it.

'I wouldn't do that too much,' said a voice ahead of me. I looked back down to eye level and was caught in a blurred vision and a sickeningly dizzy head; I couldn't focus on the person in front of me and had to sit down. I think I must have fallen down as I knew I was sitting on firm ground suddenly. 'My warning came too late I see, are you alright?' the stranger said as he or she sat down next to me. I was so dizzy and lightheaded I couldn't distinguish which gender of a person was speaking to me.

'I'm sorry I seemed to have come over all faint,' I said in a rather womanly way.

'Not used to natural sunlight without the overcast of the mucky smog are you?' said the mysterious stranger.

'Is that your way of saying I'm a Londoner? Am I really that obvious?' I asked as I focused on the grass I was sitting on. Trying to notice each little bit of growing grass rather than seeing a huge plot of green coloured flooring.

'Well you are a bit conspicuous; I am Mary by the way. Mary Yates.'

I turned to her; I could now see a young pretty lady looking with her dark, brown eyes back at me. She wasn't as fresh faced as many people I had seen here, but she looked more healthy than I did. She had freckles across the bridge of her nose which gave her a youthful appearance; as I was looking at her I noticed she was playing with the strands of her dark black hair which seemed to be in a very modern style but a little too short for the shape of her face.

The Strange Case of Caroline Maxwell

'My name is Amelia,' I said a little too late to be polite, but it had to be said at some point.

'Amelia that is a nice name, and don't worry too much. Although I noticed you were from London doesn't mean they all will. Between you and me, the people round here are nice and friendly but are a little slow on the uptake. I come from London too, so I had to be a little quicker witted to get ahead but sadly had to move.'

'Why was that?'

'My employers moved here, I've got to go where the work goes. They only moved here a few months ago but I do feel better for it, although it was very different from London life and it took a few days to get used to it.'

'In what way is it different?'

'Well the master is home more often now. In London he was away a lot working as a copper, although I don't think he walked the beat but a policeman all the same, like my brother John. Ah John, I do miss him so! Me and John went everywhere together, we were very close and now I feel so far away. Oh well, I guess I did the right thing. My mother would say so, 'go where the work is' she would say, so I did but oh how I miss John! I wonder what he is doing right now, and whether he would recognize me now I have had to cut my hair, oh I do miss my long hair!' Mary said as she looked down at her hair strands.

'Why did you cut your hair?' I asked.

'Mrs Abberline told me to, said it looked neater and as the only maid of the household now, I should look neat.'

'Mrs Abberline you say? Is your master Mr. Fredrick Abberline by any chance?' I asked.

'Why, yes Miss. You have heard of him?' she said cheerfully but in that instant her face dropped 'Oh yes, of course you would have. You are old enough to remember, Him.'

'Are you meaning Jack the Ripper?'

'Ssh, don't say the name. We are not supposed to talk about him.'

'Why can't I?' I asked. She looked very nervous and tense. She was looking around her even though there was no one else around on the green, we were sitting on. Something was scaring her, I knew the name brought fear in the most sensible of people but this was different and I couldn't quite figure out what.

'Sorry, what did you say?' she asked.

'I just asked why I can't talk about Him.' I repeated.

'Well I supposed *you* can. But I am not allowed,' she said quietly and secretly.

'Why is that?' I asked as I lowered my voice to meet hers, feeling a little stupid for having done so.

'Mr. Abberline doesn't allow it. He hates talking about it and being reminded of it. He still reads the newspapers from London; I don't know why he does it because it makes him irritated and sends him into a black mood whenever he reads a new story on Him. He stays in his library all day and no one is allowed to go near the room. He blows his top when he hears the slightest sound from anyone. He even had to get rid of our boarder because it.'

'A boarder you say?'

'Yes, he was a sort of lodger really. He was a journalist for the Daily Telegraph, it wasn't his fault really, don't tell anyone I feel this way but business was slow so he did one little story about Him to pay his bills and that was it, he was out! It was raining hard that night and he had nowhere to go and the master? Well the master didn't care; he wouldn't let a coach be sent out for him, he just stood in his study watching him leave. Master got so infuriated he couldn't even speak for about a week after that happened. You got to understand Mr. Abberline gets so furious so easily when he thinks about Him he even cries sometimes.'

'He cries! He actually cries about The Ripper, I mean Him.'

'Yes, it was last week, I came into the kitchen and there they were Mr and Mrs Abberline sitting at the table, he was crying and saying 'why don't they forget Him, why don't they forget me? I was a good policeman; I had done some good work, I helped people and solved some great cases. Why don't they ever want to talk about them? Why is it always Him?' I walked quickly out of there I can tell you. I guess that's why he moved here and left London. I feel sorry for Mr. Abberline, even after he quit the force, people still taunt him about his mistakes.'

'Was it his mistake?'

'Meaning what by that Miss?'

The Strange Case of Caroline Maxwell

'Well he wasn't the only man out there trying to catch the murderer was he? Why should he be held the fall man for that case?'

'Well I don't know anything about that Miss, and I try not to know and get myself involved with things that don't bother me but please Miss, I have said too much. Let's forget it. Are you feeling fine now?' she asked as she stood up.

'Yes, yes. I'll be fine now, I thank you Mary,' I said. With that she nodded at me and walked off towards the pub.

By Amanda Harvey Purse

Chapter Seven

I decided to sit there on the green for a while, as I was getting a little shade from the nearby trees and this was the perfect spot to watch this village life go on around me. It is always good to learn about your surroundings, it gives a base for any great story.

Even though there were many little cottages around the outskirts on the green, there seemed to be four places of importance to this modest village. One was, as I have mentioned before the Silver Horse public house. It was very busy when I came here last night, so I know if I need to find out anything that would be essential to me and this case, that place is where the gossip is to be had. A handy thing to know, as once you show that you are questioning

The Strange Case of Caroline Maxwell

the locals in formal interviews they clam up, but in a public house, things are a little less reserved and conventional.

The second place worth mentioning is the general store; where you can get most things you generally need to exist upon. I can understand how this type of store would be quite practical and reasonable, I would even say relatively feasible to have here in this sleepy village but I do hope it will not rise in popularity or become fashionable and spread to other towns. I do not want to come across as a person who does not welcome change, I do. This is somewhat different, I like going to my local butchers if I need meat for my Sunday roast or going to my local bakers for my bread or a nice sweet cake, to have it all under one roof wouldn't seem the same to me. Nevertheless as I have sat here, the door to that store seemed like it was blowing in the wind as, not for one moment was there not a person walking in or out of it. Could this be another place for where I would get my tittle-tattle?

The third place is that of Saint Peter's Church. It wasn't because it was a hive of activity like the general store or the public house, today being a Tuesday a church wouldn't be very busy at all. I counted this place of worship as fundamentally critical because of the magnitude and enormity of the building. For such a diminutively tiny cluster of locals this village holds, the vastness and dimensions of this church seemed to be inaccurate and ungrammatical. There is a porch over the considerably large entrance; above this porch was the most generously proportioned, charming and quaint stained glass window that I have ever seen. It showed a countryside scene with Saint Peter standing on a rock, looking out over the land. Still looking up, we get to the elevated spire which seemed like it was soaring into the clouds. On Sundays this structure must be very popular and an interesting place for me to visit at some point I think. The fourth place is...

'Hello Miss, you are new here aren't you? I'm sure you are, very good with faces I am. I learn everybody's face, I do. It doesn't take me long, I'm quick I am. I'm sure I haven't seen you and your face around here before, I know I'm right. I'm right aren't I?' said the most adorable and delightful little boy. He was dressed very smartly and his hair was neatly brushed.

'Well give me a second to answer you,' I said.

'Sorry, I do that I do. Always speak a lot and no one else can. People tell me to slow down I just can't. I

The Strange Case of Caroline Maxwell

guess I like talking. Yes that's it, I like talking,' he said as he sat down next to me.

'Okay, okay. Let's calm down first, yes?' I said.

'Yes let's do that.'

'Shall I start first?' I asked.

'Women always should go first,' was the reply.

'How very polite of you young man that I must say. Now what name do I call you?'

'My mother calls me Robert.'

'That's not what I asked was it?'

'No?'

'No, I asked you what you want *me* to call you.'

'Oh, well I like it when my friends call me Bobby.'

'Do you consider me a friendly person?'

'You have a kind face; I'm good at reading faces I am. Yes I think you are a friendly person,' he said as he went up on his knees to look at me closely.

'Well then, I will call you Bobby. So Bobby, are you here on your own?'

'No Miss, I'm here with my mother.'

'Oh, where is your mother?' I asked looking around.

'She is in the school.'

That was the fourth place I had considered important to this village. You may think it ridiculous, to class a school a place where you would find information, but you would be surprised what young children know. People make the mistake that children don't understand or do not know what the grownups are talking about but don't let their innocent little faces fool you. More times than not, they are fully aware of what is going on or what is being said, whether they know what they hear is right or wrong is another matter, but the basis is, children know what is going on. Let me use Bobby here, to demonstrate:

'Will she be okay with you all the way over here?'

'She never notices, she is the teacher at that school. She is always working hard, I don't blame her, there is talk of closing the school down and that means she will lose her

The Strange Case of Caroline Maxwell

job. Of course she would lose her job, I mean if she is the teacher of the school and then the school closes, there will be no school, so no need for a teacher. I mean a teacher cannot teach an empty room can she now?' he said.

See what I mean about children knowing what is going on?

'So Bobby, you like to look at faces do you?' I asked.

'Oh yes Miss, my mother thinks I'll be a policeman one day because of it.'

'So you will be a bobby, Bobby?' I asked. The child laughed, I laughed too. 'Tell me, if I was to show a face to you, a face you might have seen around here would you be able to tell me anything about that person?'

'Sure.' He replied in his cheerily childish manner.

'Okay then, what about this face?' I said as I pointed to a police group photograph of H division in London.

'What the man with the bowler hat?' asked Bobby.

'The one with a bowler hat and that beard,' I answered.

'Well, he has a kind, caring face. His eyes show a thinking man. He looks a sad man, at first I thought he looked bored but no, he is sad. Why is he sad?'

'That is what I'm here to find out.'

'Well I hope you find it out, he looks like he would be such a nice man. He shouldn't be sad.'

'Do you know this man?' I asked.

'No, should I know him?'

'He has moved here a few months ago.'

'He did? Oh I don't remember him, but I remember Mary moving here and she came with a family.'

'Mary? Do you mean Mary Yates?'

'Yes.'

'What can you tell me about Mary?'

'She is lovely and funny. She goes into the pub over there, and when she comes out she has a bright red nose and cheeks, it's so funny. She is always nice to me,

The Strange Case of Caroline Maxwell

even though sometimes I can't make out what she is saying half the time but she has a this pretty smile on her face and that is always nice to see.'

'Does she go into that pub often?'

'Quite often, I would say so. Mother tells me to not talk to her, mother saids 'she is not a good person' but I think she is wrong because I know she has a good honest face.'

'Honest you say?' I asked.

'Yes Miss and remember I can read faces, I know she is honest,' and with that he got up and ran back to the school.

The boy was only about six years old, maybe a bit older but what information I was able to get from him! He did not know Mr. Fredrick Abberline when I showed a photograph of him, *why is Mr. Abberline hiding from public view? Is he still hiding from The Ripper?* I will make a note of the description Bobby made about Mr. Abberline; it is always good to know what an outsider makes of the subject matter I am writing about.

By Amanda Harvey Purse

He knows Miss Mary Yates; she is very friendly towards him, so she likes children. She seems to also like her drink, if her nose becoming rosy is anything to go by. Someone that likes their drink normally means one or two things, the first is that they twist the truth to make their lives sounds a little less tedious and wearisome and the second is that if you were to listen to their whole story can normally pick out the bits and pieces of truth. The boy thinks she is honest, an honest drunk, she didn't seem that drunk to me when I spoke to her, even though she was headed in the direction of the Silver Horse public house.

So do I trust what she said to me about Mr. Abberline to be true? Well in truth, I have no reason to doubt her, she never said anything terrible about her master and she never said he was unscrupulous and wicked. The only thing she did do was put her master in an affectionate and compassionate light, she saw his sensitive and vulnerable side and she didn't mention that she thought of this a sign of weakness. Actually going on her tone of voice I would say it just heightens her devotion and adoration she has for her master. That fact is very singular; most servants don't openly speak of their masters in this way. But she is very fond of him and doesn't see anything wrong in saying or acting so. You may think I am drifting

The Strange Case of Caroline Maxwell

off the subject in hand but *does this tell me anything about the ex-policeman I have been sent to see?*

He hides from public because they have hurt him, but to the people who are closely around him, he is virtuous and worthy. So in turn they find him respectable and blameless. Is he truly blameless? He failed The Ripper case, yes, but is there something else he is hiding? Did he know something about the murderer? Is he hiding because of it? Why did Mr. Holmes send me to a man that doesn't like to talk about The Ripper case? How I'm I meant to make anything out of the situation Sherlock Holmes has put me in?

After a few more moments of uncertainly about the entire situation, I got up from the green, dusted down the odd crumbs of dried dirt and wisps of loosened grass that I had picked while thinking without knowing I had done so. I decided I was feeling hungry so I walked over to the local store. After purchasing an apple for my lunch I walked out of the general store and collided with a vicar.

By Amanda Harvey Purse

Chapter Eight

Isn't it strange that one quick look at a man's neck line and if you see a white dog collar, you know instantly what he does for a living? You cannot do that with any other career, and isn't it odd how you feel instantly trusting and how you have confidence in that person.

'Ah, you are a stranger from outside my flock!' He proclaimed in a genteel manner.

'Yes, I guess you could say I am,' I said.

'Well come along to the church with me Miss and let's not be strangers no more!' He said as he pushed me along the paths that led to the church.

The Strange Case of Caroline Maxwell

'Well I'm not actually what you would call a church goer,' I tried to explain.

'No need to be, my love. I get all types in my church; never turn a single one away! Not one! I was about to put the kettle on and make myself some tea, you would be doing me a great favour if you was to give an old man some company.'

'Well if you put it like that,' I said.

'I just sensed you were sympathetic to an elderly man of the church! How I was right! Can't get anything passed me! What, What! Ha!' He alleged as he opened the large, substantial door I had mention earlier.

As we walked down the aisle of the church I noticed how incredibly dark and dusty this place was. The wooden benches stood there, redundant and crying out to be sat on and the other windows were small and blocked up with some kind of material making the only light to enter this place was from the huge stained glass window at the front of the church. The only problem with that was it seemed to let one large beam of light in, which merely led to the alter and nowhere else.

By Amanda Harvey Purse

'Sorry about the disorder and clutter around here, god blesses my soul, what would the boss high upon his cloud say if he saw this? I have been away. Looking after a member of my flock and well, you can see the result!'

'I have seen worse,' I said.

'I would imagine you are right, coming from London,' He said as he pulled a heavy dark red curtain to one side for me to walk passed.

Behind the red curtain was one considerable sized room which held the vicar's kitchen, dining room, library and living quarters. I placed myself in one of the chairs belonging to the set around the dining table, which I saw was without piles of books on it. 'Am I that observable?' I asked him as he walked around me.

'What do you mean?' He asked back to me.

'Is it that apparent where I come from?'

'To the select few that have the facility to momentary look at the scene around them, yes,' *that sounds like what someone else would say, wouldn't you think so dear reader. I wonder if they could be distant cousins?*

The Strange Case of Caroline Maxwell

'I never noticed how much of a true Londoner I am, until I had left the city.'

'Most people don't if they stay in one place for all their lives, now let's get some water in the kettle and place it over the stove shall we? Mmm, that's it, now let's have a chat, while the water bubbles.'

'What would you like to know?' I asked.

'Well the obvious question is why you are here? There cannot be that many stories this sleepy village can bring?'

'Have I still got ink on my face?' I asked the friendly vicar.

'I'm sorry,' he asked a little bewilderedly. 'Do you still have ink on your face? I don't understand but in answer to your odd question, no you do not have ink on your face.'

'It is me who should be saying sorry; it is just there have been a few people guessing correctly that I am a writer.'

'Oh I see, well I can tell you, *I never guess.* The pub landlord told me that a reporter from The Times was coming here and then I saw a stranger in the local store and put those two things together.'

'Oh, I understand now, I thought for one moment I had a floating sign above my head.'

'Well that would be interesting to see and possibly for you to write about perhaps,' He laughed.

'I suppose it would.'

'The kettle is boiling its water so let me sort out the tea,' after he made us some tea, he sat back down in a chair opposite to faced me, after removing some of the book from the chair and dusting it down. 'I'm sorry for the bad tasting tea, I'm not used to making my own,' I took a sip and something indeed did not taste quite right but I smiled back him anyway, 'I don't mean to sound rude but I still don't know why you are here?' he continued.

'Oh, yes. I apologise for making you ask twice. I am here to find out about your newest locals.'

'My newest locals, you say hey? Who would that be?' he said has he tapped his long, witchy finger on his chin and then suddenly asked 'What the Abberline family?'

'Yes, that is the one.'

The Strange Case of Caroline Maxwell

'Well I say this in the most politest way I can, as you do seem a pleasant girl but how soon can you go back to London?' he whispered as he got up and went to the window, not waiting for me to reply.

'I regret I don't quite get your meaning,' I said to the back of the vicar.

'I cannot stand for it! I really can't you know! He is one of my flock now and I must protect him.'

'Protect him from *me*? I am hardly a person to be frightened of!' I declared.

'Of a person, you are quite right. But it's your words; do you not understand how important words are to people? The bible is a good example of what I am trying to say. A whole religion is based on words in a book. With you it is the same, your words control people's emotions and thoughts, you can change the world with your words. Do you not see the importance you hold?'

'I do know and understand what my words can do. I do intent to change the world with my words but for a good cause.'

'Is there such a thing in your profession?' he asked.

By Amanda Harvey Purse

'I want to change people's view of him; I disagree with the view that other journalist in the past has put on him, so I want to be able to write a wrong.'

'Change people's view on him? What do you mean?' he asked as he turned from the window to face me.

'People have this one view of him, failure. I have done some research into his career; he really did not fail at all. He was just unlucky to be put against a unique criminal, nothing like him had ever happened before; Abberline had nothing to go on. It wasn't he's fault. That's what I believe and I want to tell the world! I will be honest with you father, there was another story I was meant to write and in truth I am still following it but the more I learn about this ex-policeman the more I feel sorry for him, yes it means that I'm another journalist writing about The Ripper, and you will not know how much irritated I am to say that, but it will be from a different angle.'

The vicar moved back to the table and sat down. 'You have moved me more than you know with your words. Your conviction behind those words is strong and powerful, making me believe you. I may be the only one, I cannot see Mr. Abberline agreeing to talk about The Ripper to you, whether you are on his side or not. He is a very hurt

The Strange Case of Caroline Maxwell

man and he forgets nothing. I have often asked him to forgive those that have wronged him, but he replies that he will forgive on the day people will forget. That was not the point of what I said but he won't forgive the world and its harsh words. He is so outraged and infuriated; I fear nothing will calm him down. I fear for his soul.'

'All I can do is try, I realise it is a hard task in front of me but it is a task I have to do.'

'Well now we have that settled, do you mind me asking whether you have had some lunch?' the vicar asked as he glanced at the apple in my hand.

'This is my lunch,' I said despondently.

'It won't do, you know what happened to Adam and Eve with an apple, and it just won't do. Now pass me that sinful fodder,' he said enthusiastically. I rolled the apple across the table towards him. He took the fruit then walked over to the waste bin and while making a performance of it, discarded it from a higher than necessity height into the bin. 'Now, let's see what I can do. Do you like fish paste? Fish paste and cucumber?' he asked, I nodded. 'Well I think a sandwich will do then.'

By Amanda Harvey Purse

We sat silently as we ate our sandwiches that tasted rather odd to say in the least, which made me think of my juicy fresh apple sitting in the bin but was just slightly out of my reach but for politeness was ever further. When we finished our meal and felt as if the conversation was lacking I took my turn to leave.

The Strange Case of Caroline Maxwell

<u>Chapter Nine</u>

I left the church to find that night had fallen again, the village was empty and silent which gave the little hamlet a sinister and spine-chillingly eerie ambience. I found this fact to be a little shocking as I walked across the large green, heading in the only direction where there were lights on. I was in a sense of amazement, disbelief and quite frankly, astonishment what a change this place has at the hours of darkness. The wind was building up and going strong, if I am right, there will be a formidable and vigorous storm tonight, with that thought in mind I picked up my pace and advanced to the public house.

As I pulled at the rigid door of the entrance to the Silver Horse and the light flooded on to my face I could smell the unique and recognizable aroma that these places have, fill the night air. I walked through and found the pub to be just as full of activity as it was the night before. This is the hub of the entertainment and a pastime for many of the locals, so of course when I looked around I saw many of the people I saw today while sitting on the green. I also had noticed dissimilarity between last night and this night when I walked in, I wasn't observed tonight. I don't know how I felt about that, am I such an uninteresting, monotonous and tedious person that after just one single day the locals are bored to the death of me and why I am here? Or have the locals accepted me and I am one of them? Whatever the answer, I was proceeding to the back doors which lead to my room and more importantly to my bed for another six days.

The next morning, I awoke cheerful and optimistic that I can push on with this case. That feeling left as soon as it came the moment I walked into the bar room downstairs.

'There is a letter for you Miss,' said the landlord.

'Oh?'

'It was hand delivered,' he said as he handed me the note. I nodded at his last statement as I noticed there

The Strange Case of Caroline Maxwell

was no stamp mark on the envelope. I opened it up and my face fell. 'Bad news?' he asked.

'The worst,' I answered. The note read:

> Dear **MISS** reporter,
>
> It has been brought to my furious attention that you are in MY neighbourhood with the object of seeing and talking to me. I don't know who gave you the impression that I would willingly speak to someone like you but I am writing to inform you, that whoever it was they are miserably mistaken! I will never talk to another person of your profession again! Why can't you just leave me to the quiet life I want? Now if you would leave in the swiftest and prompt manner to wherever it was that you crawled out from under, I will not take action against you. But I promise you, if I find out you are still here in a day or two I will bring you to your knees!

By Amanda Harvey Purse

> *From the **most hounded** man the world has ever known.*

To say that I was crest fallen and a little at a loss was an understatement. I didn't know what to do or where to go. I knew that he was a hurt and upset man, but what anger! I thought that the papers had made Mr. Abberline a weak and feeble gentleman, but I was wrong. He is still outraged and infuriated with the journalists that have wronged him. He is seething and livid with the thought of a reporter in his neighbourhood, you would almost feel the heat from his pen as he wrote the note. How can I speak to him now? Do I leave as he tells me to do? Do I leave the story here and know that this very second, stopped what could have been my defining moment as a journalist? Mr. Sherlock Holmes put this story to me; he knows something, something that will give me a great story and it starts with Mr. Abberline, will it end with him too? Will the public lose out on the greatest story ever told? Do I just simply walk away?

Although I am questioning it I know in my heart of hearts I cannot walk away; I have to try to see Mr. Abberline, to at least explain why I'm here. I have to vindicate why I have travelled all this way to speak to him,

The Strange Case of Caroline Maxwell

I need to enlighten him that I'm not just another reporter looking for a quick buck, and I am here for the long haul, to go wherever this will take me. There is a magnificent story here underneath the horrendous murders of 1888, I can sense it. There is something lurking deep down that has nothing to do with Jack the Ripper and what he did or even why he did what he did. I know those two things are what most important questions people care about when they talk about him with of the mystery of who he was, but there is something additional we should be thinking about, I just don't know what that thing is yet. Yes I want to talk about The Ripper but not in the same way as most.

I started for the door of the pub. 'I wouldn't do that for a while,' said the landlord.

'Why?' I asked in a doubtful manner.

'Don't you hear it Miss?' the landlord asked. It was only at that moment I heard the outside weather howling with the expression of an ear-piercing and shattering scream. *What of earth was going on outside?*

'There is a storm?' I said rather naively and a little foolishly.

'I would say so Miss, started a few hours ago. I was worried it might keep you awake, I take pride in my paying lodgers to have a peaceful night's sleep. So you being a woman on her own, I was a bit apprehensive.'

'Put your mind at rest, I am not a sensitive and vulnerable person as you may think. I can sleep well, but I must go out.'

'I will not stand in your way but I suggest that it is not wise to go out for a few more hours.'

'Is it that dreadful outside?' I asked.

'Mr. Peterson, the driver for the Abberline's, came here this morning with that letter and he said he had to go the long way round because a whole tree trunk has been blown in the road, blocking travel to the village. Going to the long way put an extra hour on top of his travel no doubt; I would hate to think how long it would put on by foot.'

'Oh,' I said disappointedly.

'I wouldn't worry though Miss; we have storms like this at least twice a year here, and once it passes everything will get back to normal.'

The Strange Case of Caroline Maxwell

I headed back to my room disheartened, not only does the man who controls my story and quite possibly my career in his hands, doesn't want me anywhere near him but I can't write to him, I can't explain myself and I can't fight back. I'm just meant to wait, if only the landlord knew that, the few hours of waiting could mean so much or so little. I threw the letter of destiny and fate in the direction of the bed, I watched how it floated gradually and leisurely, taking care not to hurt itself has it landed softly and delicately on the bedstead. Did it somehow know how important and significant it was?

From the position I was standing in, I could see one line of the handwritten script. As to taunt and ridicule myself I read it again; *from the **most hounded** man the world as ever known.*

Is that what I am doing? Am I just like all the other journalists past, who hounded and persecuted him for a good story? Am I really doing anything different? Do I deserve the tone of letter I got?

Something is telling me not to quit, not to walk away and leave, before Mr. Abberline knows that I'm a reporter that wants to tell his side of the story, I am not here to snigger and mock him just for my own benefit. There is a more worthy and essential reason for me being here, somehow I know there is a fundamental and necessary yarn to make, I can sense it. This is more than a hearsay article about a serial murderer that held London in fear for just a few cold and wet months, I am not merely riding on the mad man's coat tails, there is something additional, something that happened sixteen years ago that is still a mystery and it's still mystifyingly unsolved.

I looked away from the letter and peered through the only miniature window of my room, out into the eye of the storm.

The sight was dark and depressing. The trees around the green, the ones in which I had sat under just the day before were bare, leafless and were being pulled up from their roots by an invisible fiend. The local store was in pitch darkness and the church had its wonderful and enchanting window demolished and destroyed. The beautiful picture was now ruined and incomplete; Saint Peter was now missing a head! Maybe they should change the name of the church to Saint John the Baptist; it would be more in keeping with the stained glass picture now. *I hope the sympathetic and benevolent vicar is safe and*

The Strange Case of Caroline Maxwell

sound. But what if he is not? He could be hurt; he might have been in the church when the window blew out. There must be glass everywhere inside, he might have cut himself. He maybe in need of some help! I ran downstairs with the attention of alarming the landlord of what I had seen but the response I got was puzzling.

'Did you hear me right Sir? I am telling you the vicar might be in trouble.'

'I heard you,' he said still chuckling to himself.

'Well what are you going to do about it?'

'Nothing.'

'I'm sorry, I don't quite understand you.'

'I will not do anything.'

'But, why? I do not understand why you will not help him.'

'Simply because my dear, he is not there.'

'Oh?'

'So I'm not going to risk my life on someone that is not in trouble.'

By Amanda Harvey Purse

'I see. Do you know where he went?'

'To finish his last rites, I suppose.'

I went back upstairs. As I stared hopelessly back into the only view I had of the outside world I speculated where the vicar could have gone in such a dash. *To finish his last rites, the landlord had said. What did the landlord mean by that? And why didn't I stop and ask him?* Perhaps he needed to take charge again of his poorly sick member of his flock. Maybe they had taken a turn for the worse and the vicar had to leave in haste. I'm glad he got away before the storm hit his beloved house of worship. He is such a kind-hearted fellow, he protects and watches over his members of his parish so vigorously and impressively that I couldn't help but be impressed. I would be proud to have a vicar like that, who I could feel, in a distant, comfortable way know that he is there to shield and safeguard me from any harm. There is only one other man in this horrid world that can make me feel like that, and he was probably sitting on his homely, comfy and cosy armchair. With his warm and pleasant fire burning, and smoking from his long, wooden pipe with a relaxing and tranquil facial expression, contemplating the world's news or some unsolvable case.

The Strange Case of Caroline Maxwell

That thought reminded me of how cold and bitter this room felt. *When will this storm end?*

I hadn't realised that day had turn to night, until there was a knock at my door. 'Hello Miss, the landlord has asked me to ask you whether you want to dine with us tonight?' said the voice of the barmaid through the door.

'Oh, yes that would be lovely, thank you,' I replied.

'Food will be ready at eight,' I heard her say; before she turned and I could hear the last of her footsteps walk slowly down the stairs.

I walked over to the wash basin and turned the tap, as I watched the flow of water run rapidly out and hammering the china bowl, I thought of the letter that had dampen my spirits. I cannot give up; this case deserves all the chances I can give it. I let the water moisten my hands and patted my face; I glanced at myself in the mirror while the drips of clear liquid ran down my cheeks and dropped of my nose.

I am a journalist, come what may, I will not give up.

By Amanda Harvey Purse

I smoothed the soft towel over my face, threw it on the bed and I travelled downstairs. As I got to the bottom of the stairs, the white painted door that has always been shut to me, opened with a creak and the landlord stood out.

'There you are, I was just going upstairs to call you.'

'I like to be prompt,' I replied.

'Right you are Miss, through this way if you please.' he said as he stood to one side of the doorway.

I walked through, to a most delightfully welcoming, unpretentious snug. A few cabinets and sideboards had been moved around, I could tell from the marks on the floor. But the room was full of homely bits and pieces; it felt very nice and lived in.

'Sorry about the mess of the place, we don't have a dining table up you see; it's just me and the misses normally. But with the storm, we couldn't let Bessie go home and with you upstairs we thought it wise to lay on some food.'

The Strange Case of Caroline Maxwell

'How very thoughtful of you and your wife,' I said as I sat down at the dining table that was set for four. 'But if you mind me asking, where are all your other lodgers?'

'Other lodgers?' he repeated as he sat to my left.

'Well when I came here, you said all your rooms were full,' I replied.

'Oh I see, well we only have two rooms to let at the moment, the other room we have needs some work and the plumbing redone again. There was a gentleman in the second room but he left last night, at rather an odd hour but he paid up front.'

'Oh, I hope he made it to where ever it was that he was going before the storm hit.'

'To be honest with you, I am a little worried. The gentleman left while the storm was picking up, he said he would be fine and he couldn't miss his train. He seemed like a man that was sensible and level-headed, so I let him go. A decision I'm starting to regret,' as he said the last sentence, a plump woman with greying long hair and the lightest colour of blue in her eyes that they were almost white, walked in the room holding two plates of steaming hot food.

'What are you regretting, my love?' she asked as she placed the food in front of me.

'Oh nothing,' he said softly.

'Come on love; don't leave me out in the dark.'

'We are Christian folk and I was just saying I am worried about the gentleman who left in the storm,' he said without looking at her. With that statement there was a mammoth bang as the dish of his food hit the table.

'Gentleman you say! Gentleman indeed! He was no gentleman!'

'Come now love, we have guests,' he said.

'Guests or not, I'm not going to lie to her or to anyone when you are talking about that crook!' she said as she walked back into what I would only presume would have been the kitchen, seeing as it was from that room I could smell food being cooked.

'I'm sorry you had to hear that,' the landlord said to me. 'You see, as I have already said we are Christians. Us Christians like nothing more than to read the bible, so as you well know we have left a book of the bible in every

The Strange Case of Caroline Maxwell

room upstairs, by the by, have you read a page or two?' he said with his piercing eyes looking intently at me.

'Oh yes, a few pages every night keeps the soul morally virtuous,' I lied as I made a mental note to look for the bible and read a few pages when I get back to my room, just in case I get asked questions about it from these 'Christian folk'.

It might sound like I am not a Christian. I guess in many ways I'm not. But I'm what you may call a believer. I am a believer of most things because I am very open-minded; you have to be if you are a woman in these times.

Anything could happen if you just believe. So I am here, believing. I am not stating this to seem weak, feeble nor even dare I say womanly, I don't believe it does. I think it makes me sound wise and shrewd; my mind is not intolerant to the spirits outside this world, or to different creatures that are living among us now that we have never met. A few years ago it was almost a fashion statement to go to a séance and speak to a loved one that has sadly passed on. People were almost using it as a get together like going to the local club or pub, not believing in the true meaning of it. It is a science form, something truly wonderful and breathtaking.

By Amanda Harvey Purse

I have never been to one but I can imagine what it would be like, to know you can see I loved one who has departed again and again whenever you wished. To know that this life isn't it, when it ends, it really doesn't. I have always wanted to go, but something seems to always hold me back from it, possibly some kind of spirit that doesn't want to be interviewed at the moment or something.

Anyway I'm going off the train of thought, I was talking about religion and it's not like I haven't been to church at all, I have when I was young and had to dress in my best gown and I do remember parts of the bible, but just not all of it.

'Well said my dear, well said. Anyway my wife, although she is a very charitable person in normal circumstances but in these circumstances she seems to have lost her charity,' the landlord said has he broke into my thoughts.

'What are these circumstances?' I asked.

'Well the gentleman seems to have stolen the bible,' the landlord said as he took a mouthful of food. *What a rather odd statement! What a rather odd thing for*

The Strange Case of Caroline Maxwell

the gentleman to do, why would he need a bible? Stealing a bible seems a little ironic to me.

'Perhaps the gentleman in question was so over come after reading the bible, he sort to become a Christian himself and every good Christian needs a good bible,' I said. I knew it sounded anomalous but I felt I needed to say something. How strange I felt that I needed to protect this man! I didn't know him; I didn't know what he even looked like. For all I know he could have been a man that had a habit to steal things and the bible was the only thing that was easy and straightforward to steal but here I was protecting his honour!

Anyway the landlord almost spat out his food when he replied 'Good show young lady! If I didn't know it I would say you have saved months of bad temper, I must remember what you said; it will surely make my wife remember happier times! Good show indeed!'

By Amanda Harvey Purse

Chapter Ten

When we had finished our meal, I expressed my gratitude and went back to the room I had already spent most of the day in. As I shut my door there was a gigantic gust of wind that pushed my petite window open, making the brawny and burly wintry weather enter my room and made what was already bitterly frozen feel more like almost arctic conditions. I rushed over to the window and with all my strength and might I forced the glass panel shut and locked it. I brushed myself down and turned back to face the room to see that the wind had blown my clothes around, the pillows were pushed to one side, my perfume bottles had fallen like dominoes and leaked a little causing three diminutive sweet smelling puddles across the wooden floor. The letter of significance was lying on the floor near

The Strange Case of Caroline Maxwell

enough to the puddles to get its top left hand corner damp and stained with my perfume.

I quickly bent down and picked up the letter, took it over to small table and patted it dry with my towel. I looked deeply at the letter; I must write back to him and post it myself.

> Dear Mr Abberline,
>
> Please let me have a chance to say why I am here. I promise I have come here on your behalf; I have done research on your career and I truly believe that you didn't deserve the bad press you have got over the years. I don't need to tell you how good of a policeman you were but I believe you were put up against an unknown killer and unknown problems. He was the first of his kind; there was no hand book to follow. I understand all of that.
>
> I am not like the other journalists you have encountered; I want to tell your side of any story you want to tell. I believe the public need to know who you truly are and what you truly did for them.

By Amanda Harvey Purse

> I can understand if you don't believe my words, I have met the local vicar of your parish and he was very protective of you and your family to someone in my profession, but he listened to me and understands that I am not here to taunt and mock you, I am here to listen to you. If you can't sense it in my words, maybe you can sense it in him.
>
> I will be here until the end of this week when my booked stay would have ended, although I am hand posting this letter to you I will not come to your home again without an invite. I am not here to hound you.
>
> For one last ditched attempt to let me have an interview with you, please allow me the possibility to prove who I am, the public have done you wrong by presuming you are someone you're not, at least see me before you decide. Thank you for your time and patience in reading this little note of mine. From, not just an ordinary journalist.

Maybe I was pushing my providence with the last sentence, but I had to show my personality and my qualities in this one letter as this might be the only chance I get to show it to him. I hope he could see what I am here to do, I hope I haven't made things worse and I really hope I

The Strange Case of Caroline Maxwell

have chosen the right thing to do. I don't want to leave the story here, I don't want to go back to London without the reason I came here in the first place. I don't want to end my story here.

...

I rose from the table, somewhat happy with what I wrote; I walked over to the locked window and took one last glance out into the terrible and battered village. Isn't it amazing what one day can do, I have optimism and faith that I will awake on a better and more improved morning hours than it was today and I pray it becomes a more productive one.

I am aware that I am obliged, even compelled to ask for some outside influence, strange as it sounds. I almost deem it an indispensable requirement to have the fundamental feeling of divine intervention. Can I put my destiny in an astonishing and enchanting presence that is entirely unknown and mysterious to me?

Now where's that bible...

I awoke with vivid and dazzling lights blinding my sight and making me slightly perplexed and unable to act. As I took a moment to get my senses into normal order I

By Amanda Harvey Purse

heard the sweet tune of the early dawn bird. It's charming and delightful song filled the fresh smelling morning air giving the awareness and belief that this day, is a new day. It's a spanking, pristine new day that could change so many things. It could be the disappointingly sour end to this story, where I will feel hard done-by and resentful as I feel it hasn't got off the ground yet, it hasn't picked up its pace, it hasn't had that one moment where all the things come together and make everything I have been through make sense. The one warming sensation of understanding why this story has happened, the astonishingly exceptional feeling of accomplishment that I feel every time I finish reading a Sherlock Holmes adventure. Or on a lighter note and in a more positive mood, today could be the very beginnings of this interesting and possibly disturbing tale that has already got its claws hooked in to me, digging deeper down into my skin, like a newly born kitten at the first time it wants to play with its owner.

It was time to start things afresh and a swift walk around this changeable village is what is called for. I washed with freezing cold water, dressed in the quickest time ever and left the public house without having breakfast, I was on a mission and I felt I needed to complete it before I did another single thing.

The Strange Case of Caroline Maxwell

I walked past the church, the stone work smelt damp and moist; it must have rained while I had been asleep, I wondered what state the inside was like because of the new hole that now ruined the picturesque window. Would the vicar now have to deal with the early stages of mould too? I carried on walking, for I had no time for wondering thoughts.

I passed the local shop, when I noticed a young adolescent who was busy decorating a table that was in front of it, with newly picked crisp green apples, I said 'good morning' and went on my way before he even looked up. For I have no time to waste on having a conversation with anyone, let alone with someone I do not need to know.

I followed the road until when I looked back the large green was nowhere in sight, all the small houses seemed to disappear and I was walking with an unbreakable view of the calming waves of the sea. I had forgotten how close to the sea this village was, you wouldn't have imagined seeing it, it was so quiet and gentle. I stopped for a moment to take in the fresh smelling sea breeze, how nice it was to see the sea in its natural form and colour, not with the man made orange substance that floated above The Thames hiding a magnitude of sins.

Even the smell was disturbingly natural and genuine; smelling what I believe the sea should smell like, not like the stench I was used to from The Thames as it passed through the centre of our great city. I will admit I had got quite used to the stink of rotting flesh from the easily imagined dead corpses and remains that have not floated for a somewhat long period of time and are hiding underneath the murky depths of the foul and contaminated water being infected with other people's stale urine and other bodily functions. *Ah home sweet home...*

What does that say about me? Why do I feel unaffected with thoughts of dead bodies? Is that what I have come accustomed to? Is that what living in London feels like? Is that why Sherlock Holmes gave me this case? After all I am a woman, and this case has something to do with a murdering mad man that has left women sliced and torn apart...

Jack the Ripper didn't just kill these women, he eradicated their souls. Some he left unrecognisable, even God himself, wouldn't know who or what they were when they met at the pearly gates. He butchered them like

The Strange Case of Caroline Maxwell

animals, I was young when it happened, I didn't truly understand. Jack the Ripper was a child's punishment, Jack the Ripper was the modern day bogie man in a sense when I was demanding my own way and not behaving in a way a good girl should 'don't be naughty sweetheart or Jack the Ripper will get you' my father used to say. We used to giggle, I used to giggle...

How could I have giggled at what Jack the Ripper was and did? Am I that immune to the bloody madness of the world? Am I that unwomanly? Is that why I'm different? I'm a woman who isn't a woman, is that why I was able to get an interview with Sherlock Holmes? Is that what he could sense in me? Am I half woman, half man? Is that what is needed for this country, the best of both sides of the sexual playing field?

They say one day The Thames will be clean and a delightful place to watch the boats and ducks pass by, but somehow I find this hard to believe, they have tried many different ways of improving the river, they have even tried straightening it and making it less wide with hopes that it will make the tide run faster, taking the dirt and other horrid things with it. But there are still areas of polluted and quite impure parts just to remind people how awful it was a few years ago, even the great houses of parliament had to drape their curtains in some kind of perfumed liquid to hide the pong of the unpleasant odour from its neighbour, not so long ago.

As my thoughts threw me back to what I was now looking at, I reflected on how different these waters were to what I am accustomed to but also how it suited the region I was now in and possibly wouldn't suit the busy and over populated London.

It gave the impression of such a tranquil and peaceful place; yesterday's storm looked as if it never happened. I didn't have to speculate why Ex-Inspector Abberline would leave London for here, it was so dissimilar. It was utterly poles apart from the smoky city; it really is like chalk and cheese. I breathed in deeply to take advantage of everything around me and took a sharp turn to the left and walked strongly to the end of the road.

There was only one house in view as I took my eyes from the sea to the land ahead of me. It was a strange manor house to be sitting there on its own; it looked like there had been other houses adjoined to it but over the years they had slowly sidestepped away and left this one

The Strange Case of Caroline Maxwell

house behind and now it stands isolated and a little forlorn about it.

The house was painted an unpolluted white which gave it an even more ethereal and ghostly sensation, there were no boundary fences or any greenery to see, a part from one single tree that was to the left of the gravelled pathway leading to the menacing black front door. There was no place for me to hide, no doubt I have already been seen, and I couldn't turn back no matter how badly I wanted to.

So without a moment to lose I walked strappingly and tenaciously up to the front door, posted the letter through the cast iron letter box pretending to myself that I hadn't just scraped my knuckles doing so and walked away again all the while, *knowing that a set of eyes were watching me.* I tried my hardest not to let the question of who was watching me enter my brain as I knew the answer would make me turn around and give the manor house one last look, and that was something I knew would be a weak mistake, a weak mistake I was not yet willing to make.

I couldn't shake off the feeling that *I was being watched,* that spine chillingly sensation like when you think you have heard a slight noise, that you know could be

By Amanda Harvey Purse

anything from a tiny mouse making his way to food or some innocent object falling off the table in the next room but there is always this something in the back of your impressible mind that tells it could be a dark and sinister man that you don't know, that has entered the place in which you live, your home.

With his piercingly colourless eyes and with the intention of slicing your throat and leaving your lifeless body to fall on the floor, as the last drop of your blood spurts out around you like a warm red blanket, he will laugh, he has a terrible harsh laugh and it's the last thing you hear. For him it's just a game, for you it is the moment you have realised you have wasted your life, thinking of what people must think of you, caring for other people's feelings before your own. Not being able to feel confident to tell the certain people how much they have hurt you, because you feel guilty of hurting them.

Not being who you truly want to be because you are afraid, letting other people wills to knock you down and letting them get away with it. All these things mean nothing because there you are lying in your own home, *dead.*

...

The Strange Case of Caroline Maxwell

That feeling was the same feeling I was getting from the sense of someone studying me from an unknown place, that feeling never left me until I had reached to protection of the village.

After feeling more myself and my walking pace was a little more my own, I decided to buy one of those sweet smelling apples from the local shop, with that in hand I sat under one of the trees on the green that was left standing after the terrible outburst of bad weather. Somehow it felt different than it did before, less strong and sturdy but I tried to make it comfortable and after a few movements I found a nice enough spot.

I had laid there with my eyes closed for what seemed like a few hours, I was trying to concentrate on the events that had past, was this all a waste of time? How could I explain this to the wretch of an editor? Would I lose all chance of writing for The Times? What would that mean for me and my attention-grabbing story?

'Glad you've got your eyes closed this time,' said a voice from above me. I lifted my hand up to my eyebrow to shade my sight from the late afternoon light of the sun as I opened my eyes.

'Hello Miss Yates, it is an improved day,' I greeted her.

'It is that Miss,' was her reply as she glanced up towards the sky. Then there was this unnerving silence, as she looked back to me. She was just standing there looking motionless at me but not saying anything.

'Is there anything I can do for you?' I asked, trying to break the uncomfortably eerie nothingness.

'I am meant to deliver this note to Silver Horse but as you are here and I know it's for you. There you go,' she said as she handed me a crisp clean white envelope.

'Oh thank you,' I said as I took the note and sat up a little straighter. To my surprise Mary sat down next to me. I put the note to one side as I sensed she wanted to say something more to me.

'You have upset the household,' she said quietly.

'I have?'

'Yes, you should have left this village when master told you too.'

'Why should I have done that?'

The Strange Case of Caroline Maxwell

'Because I thought you would have a little more respect.'

'He is not my master and I wanted to tell the reason why I am here, don't you think I had the right to tell him,' I said, a little hurt by what she had said to me.

'Everybody knows why you are here; you didn't need to tell anyone.'

'It's not about The Ripper.'

'No?' she asked. 'I find that hard to accept as true. Everything is about The Ripper with you guys.'

'Not in the way most believe.'

'I'm no writer, but how many different *ways* can you write about Him?'

'*It turns out to be quite a few.*'

'Oh?'

'You said I've upset the household, surely you meant to say I have upset your master.'

'No, I mean what I say; you have really upset the household. Mrs Abberline wrote you that note.'

'Oh?' I said as I glance back down at the note, *so the letter was from Mrs Abberline, not Fred Abberline. What could this mean?*

'You must have someone looking over you,' she said as she got up and walked slowly away.

Do I have someone looking out for me? In a bizarre way, I have always thought that to be the case ever since I left Baker Street and began my own adventure, but the question I feel I must ask myself is, is this really my adventure or am I a pawn piece sitting on a chequered board waiting for the master to move me?

When I noticed I was again on my own I turned and I opened the envelope to read the letter,

> *To an uncharacteristic journalist,*
>
> *Your letter moved me; you seem set on talking to my husband about his past career in the police force. This as you may have guessed has distressed him very much so, but I think with a little wife's persuasion his behaviour may alter, as I believe you may be able to help him improve and relieve his later life.*

> *This may sound as if I am not caring of my husband's feelings but this is not true. My husband should be resting and taking time to enjoy life, that is why we left London, but I fear this is not the case. My husband will never be at ease until he lets go of his past torments and demons this I believe, is where you hold the key for him to do that.*
>
> *I am a Christian woman at heart so:*
>
> *'Ask and it shall be given to you: seek, and ye shall find: knock and it shall be opened to you'.*
>
> *Midday, tomorrow you will come to our home. Do not be late; I cannot help you if you are late.*
>
> *From a wife that has put her trust in you.*

Someone was indeed looking out for me, I must go back to my room and practise how I am going to tackle the Abberline family, for it is *he* that holds the key to this locked mystery, now all I have to do is to find a way to unlock it...

By Amanda Harvey Purse

Chapter Eleven

The appointed time for the interview was coming too soon for my liking, I felt unprepared and ill-equipped to cope with the important task that lay ahead of me. It seemed ridiculous to say what I had just stated, how can I be so unsuspectingly unqualified for the undertaking of my duty? I had spent nearly a whole week in this sleepy village with one thing on my mind; it was becoming an obsession with me that I didn't think further than it. How dim-witted and ill-advised I am! *Sherlock Holmes would be ashamed of me.*

Now I am half an hour away from the meeting and all I have managed to do is read more of the bible I thought as I grabbed my notebook and pen and walked towards my moment of destiny, apprehensive and hesitant.

The Strange Case of Caroline Maxwell

As I walked past the village and was starting on the long stretch of empty road that sat on the cliff edge, I took a moment to breathe.

1...2...3

I carried on and instantly felt a pair of stern eyes burning into my soul; I walked through my vision of the feverish heat and up to the black door, it at once open without needing a thump from me on its lion faced knocker. A butler stood robustly in the doorway; I almost felt I needed a secret password to enter. *'Police', 'Whitechapel' or even the single word of 'Ripper' said in a whispering tone maybe.* But then the butler spoke, 'Mr and Mrs Abberline will be taking you in the drawing room,' He moved to one side and let me in.

I stood in the long and agreeable hallway with many family portraits of years gone by all looking down at me as the butler shut the door and stood beside me. 'I shall take it that as madam does not have a shawl, madam does not have a card to present in front of the master and his wife,' I could only nod, like I had been a bad school girl. 'Very well, if you could kindly follow me,' I recognized a command when I heard one, and followed in line with my head down. The butler opened a large oak door to our left and entered saying, 'The journalist is here, without a card.'

'Thank you Matters let her in please,' said a womanly voice from inside the room. The butler retreated back into the hallway and jested of me to walk in.

1...2...3

I moved slowly into the room to see Mrs Abberline sitting at the desk with Mr. Abberline standing by the window with his back to me.

The room was very grand indeed; it was lined with yellow wallpaper which gave the room a light, airy feel. It was obviously expensively done as the wallpaper paste did not have that dreadful smell to it, something I hated when I first decided to cheaply have wallpaper in my rooms, never again I can tell you, I suffered quite unfavourably with headaches for months, because of the horrifically bad smell.

There was a line of white painted wooden bookcases along the wall that were now behind me. There was no space on the bookcases for even the dust to settle, actually there was books everywhere in the room. A sign of great intelligence, if I was a questionable person I would

The Strange Case of Caroline Maxwell

wonder if those books were placed there to dispirit and suppress me. If they were, it clearly worked as I felt small and insignificant in this very significant room that I was now standing in.

As I let my eyes fall to the front of the room I noticed that on the main wall, to the side of where Mr. Abberline was standing, was row upon row of clocks but there was something wrong with the sight I was seeing, but at this moment of enormity I just couldn't put my mind in working gear and think of what that missing link was.

I glanced at the two people I have bothered and have altered their daily routines with; I noticed that Mrs Abberline was a beautiful woman, dressed in the finest silk and jewels. Her hair was neatly placed and her piercing eyes showed a woman of intelligence and skilfully talented cunning, it was her I had to thank and in that first glance at me she let me know it.

'Please shut the door; Miss,' her first words to me. 'After all this is a *private* meeting.'

'Gladly,' I replied.

'Now please could you do us an honour of sitting opposite me?'

As I sat down, in the sitting arrangement that she wanted and Mr. Abberline turned; I could see his bright red hair bouncing off the light in the room. He had a beard and moustache of the thickest kind, so much so that there was hardly any facial skin to see, but of what I could see I knew was fiercely as red as his hair. He was furious to be in the same room as me. This is going to be a problematical meeting of two sides, I could tell.

'Sign this,' he boldly said to me as he moved a document in front of me.

'Excuse me?' I asked.

'You are excused... sign this,' was his reply.

'What am I signing?' I asked.

'O generation of vipers, who hath warned you to flee from the wrath to come?' He shouted at me as he turned back to the window. I glanced at Mrs Abberline *without a clue* on what was going on.

'I am sorry for my husband's rude behaviour,' she started as he huffed. 'My husband is not able to notice he is embarrassing me,' she said looking back at him, there was silence on his part, he had been told.

The Strange Case of Caroline Maxwell

She turned back to me 'this document was the only way my husband would allow you to enter our house and see him. You have, I'm sure, a sense that my husband here has lost faith in reporters for a good reason. He does not feel the way I do about you, he does not trust you and why you are here. So this is his way of making sure that you will not betray him and what he stands for. You will write the interview you are about to have, but before you publish it you will send the only copy to my husband. Where in turn he will put it through an examination, if he is contented he will send it back to you, if he is not, he will burn it and send you a letter stating so. If he finds out that you have changed a single word after he has inspected it, he will sue you for three thousand pounds and your paper for ten thousand making sure that you never work for any paper again. If that is clear and satisfactory with you, please sign and the interview will start, if it is undesirable the meeting will stop here and you will be shown the door, never for our faces to encounter each other again. What will you do?'

This man intends to have his own way this time; I can hardly blame him after everything he has been through. Do I sign the most significant and eminent document I have ever come across in my career? This will allow him all the power of my words, he might just keep burning my verbal skill never to be happy and contented.

My story could never be told. One glance at his heated and livid face tells me, this thought of mine could be rightly so. But then on the other hand if I don't sign, it will all end here and any information Mr. Holmes thinks Mr. Abberline has will be lost. Lost forever, in the mists of time so can I really turn away now?

It's the not knowing, it's not final. It's like reading a book and not getting to the end...

'I will sign,' I replied.

The Strange Case of Caroline Maxwell

Chapter Twelve

There was a long moment of stillness after I had signed the document; it almost felt that I had suddenly materialized in an East End wax works museum.

I do remember going to one once, I still don't really understand why I went. I guess it was all the hype and the built-up excitement of seeing the 'new Jack the Ripper' waxworks, I saw the advertisement everywhere and somehow I felt I missed out on seeing the real thing, because of being so young, I thought I needed to see what all the mania was about.

I thought that! I actually thought I had missed out on seeing those horrid murder scenes! Why would I feel like that!

By Amanda Harvey Purse

All that publicity and the museum felt like a bit of a letdown because the models barely looked human, let alone looking like the victims and there wasn't any factual reality behind the sights I saw, all were models lying on the floor with a splash of red paint around their necks. I didn't feel it really showed the right atmosphere of the horror that laid in wait for the first witnesses that saw them.

As my dreamy thoughts came to an end and I was back in the grand drawing room with Mr. and Mrs Abberline I placed the pen down, beside the document and waited for the next event to happen. Mrs Abberline appeared to want to read the document, I handed it over to her as I glanced to Mr. Abberline who was motionless at the window, if I wasn't so sure it was human nature I would swear he didn't even blink. After Mrs Abberline had finished reading, she put the document in the desk drawer and locked it, putting the key in her dress pocket.

'Now that is settled, I will leave you and my husband in peace. Please take my word of warning, be patient with him, don't rush him. You will get nowhere if you rush him,' she said then she walked over to Mr. Abberline. 'I will leave you dear husband in the care of this fine lady,' He huffed again. 'I don't have to remind you of

The Strange Case of Caroline Maxwell

those many years you have wanted to tell your side of the whole HIM case, do I dear husband? This fine lady, who, I might add has signed your document, is giving you that very chance,' Mr. Abberline lowered his head.

'I thought not, now you will answer all of her questions, all of them. This is your moment to shine my husband, to show the world what you did for them. Keep this is mind when the moment comes, bless you my dear husband,' she kissed his hand and made for the door, as the door shut Mr. Abberline turned towards me. He said nothing but sat in the chair his wife was sitting in, his eyes were always on me. He was judging me; he was making his opinion of me before I had even spoken.

A part of me was longing to tell him what an ass he was making himself out to be; can't he just sense I am here to help him? How much more proving do I have to do? I was feeling insulted and disappointed when he finally spoke.

'My wife seems to think I can trust you, as I trust my wife I suppose I must trust you.'

'I am thankful to your wife, sir.'

By Amanda Harvey Purse

'So you should be, but like Saint Mark said; and if a house be divided against itself, that house cannot stand, so here we are.'

'I never meant to divide the household sir, I understand that reporters haven't shown the best work they could have done for you, but I am different.'

'Different on the outside, I can see that but what about the inside? Are you just the same on the inside?'

'Judge not, that ye be not judged.' I replied.

'Ah, you read the bible?' He asked.

'I seemed to have picked it up again, yes.'

'Needing some spiritual insight were we?'

'Wasn't I meant to be the one asking questions?'

'Ah now there *is* the journalist reply, a question with a question.'

'That's where he got that saying from,' I said quietly to myself.

'That's where *who* got that saying from?' Mr. Abberline asked me. He must have some expert hearing.

The Strange Case of Caroline Maxwell

The question caught me off guard so stupidly I asked him to repeat himself, which I was a little surprised that he did.

'That's where who got that saying from?'

'Inspector Godley, I managed to meet with him.'

'Ah he made it to Inspector, that's my boy! Good chap is old George.'

'Yes I found him very *helpful*,' I lied.

'I'm sure you did, he was always a ladies' man,' I coughed at his comment which made him smile, 'He is such an intelligent man, I was so very proud of him when he caught George Chapman. I knew he would, I managed to get back to London when they were taking the poisoner down, and it was a joyous day. I ran straight up to Godley and shouted 'You have caught him at last! You have caught...' Mr. Abberline paused in speaking, his face fell and he took a deep breath in and then said 'So go on and ask your questions.'

'Well, let's start with 1864.'

'That far back, hey?'

'You were a new constable on the force.'

'Yes, I was very young and this was my chance to start a new career.'

'A *new* career, what career did you have before?' I asked.

'You want to know that?'

'I would not have asked,' I replied. There was again silence; I was beginning to feel comfortable in these moments. Mr. Abberline seemed to be satisfied with my answer.

'Well I used to be a clockmaker, an apprentice clockmaker.'

'That explains the rows of clocks.'

'You took notice of my masterpieces then? Yes there they are sitting proud on the wall, all waiting for me to finish them.'

'You haven't finished them?'

'Can you not tell? I have not put the final mechanisms in them.'

The Strange Case of Caroline Maxwell

'Oh that's it, they are not ticking! I thought there was something wrong. Why do you not want them to work?' I asked.

'It would be all too final, it would be the end. I guess it would mean there is nothing left for me to do, when I look at them I can see that I still have, pardon the pun, *time* to finish them.'

'Sounds very shrewd of you.'

'I like to think so, but Miss Reporter we seemed to have drifted off the subject of my police career, what was we talking about?'

'We were talking of the days when you were being a young constable.'

'Ah that was it; I wanted to take on the world and all its criminals. It was the first time I hit the beat; I used to love walking around the old streets of London. My boots were polished, every night I made sure they were showing my face in them, my buttons were always shining bright. It was my third night of walking the beat when I came across them. You have got to understand that they were only children messing around; they didn't know what they were playing with. A firework went off, almost blinded one child if I hadn't grabbed him when I did. He was a sweet kid, always up to mischief, always into some minor trouble or some tribulation. The other lads back at the station thought he was a nuisance and a pest; they never really gave him the time of day, not with all the other cases they had to deal with. But somehow I knew he was worth caring about and being sympathetic to, I wasn't wrong. Old Bang became my best snitch for many years.'

'Who was Old Bang? Did you ever find out his name?'

'He was my very best snitch that is all you need to know,' Mr. Abberline said sternly. I was pushing him too much, after all no one tells on their sources; I have learned that over the years.

...

'Do you have fond memories of your time as a police constable?' I asked.

'Fond is not the word. But when my mind thinks back to those days I can't help but feel affectionate and warm-hearted. I regret not staying a constable for more years some days, life would have been a lot simpler I could tell you,' he said almost in a dreamy state. His eyes seemed

The Strange Case of Caroline Maxwell

to drift off from me and dance their way over to the corner of the room.

'You were only a constable for three years.'

'Yes, I took the promotion a little too hastily. It was quite injudicious of me, but I was young and I wanted to try to make an impression in the force, we all did. I thought I could make a change to this world the higher up I became, that thought was quite impractical of me,' he said. This was very odd of me to listen to, at moments Mr. Abberline seemed to smile and feel proud of what he did but there were other moments that came quickly and then fled.

Moments of pain, sadness and tenderness, he wasn't sure how he felt or how he was supposed to have felt about his career. He was problematically troubled. What is he hiding? I had this strange sensation that he was hiding something, something that he has been hiding for years that still caused him pain to think about it. What is it? *What has he done in the past?*

'So as a police sergeant you caught John Fleet,' I asked, there must be something in his career that has made him feel confused and baffled but where?

By Amanda Harvey Purse

'He was a horrid little man; he was ghastly to look at too. He had been a nuisance for a few months, thinking he was so cunning and ingenious; thinking he was better than us, better than the good side. But we got him in the end, on a violent attack charge. He was banged up for many years, when he came out I was there to see him, he was a broken and changed man. He never caused us any more problems. That day gave me faith in the law system; it appears to have work *sometimes*.'

'And what happened to the victim of the attack?'

'She recovered from her bruises and in a few months was back to her normal self. I kept an eye on her, just in case things went bad. But the truth is, you can't keep everyone safe but I tried, I really tried,' he said. He wasn't giving me any eye contact but his words had real meaning, he was speaking from the heart, I could sense it in his voice and it was giving me goose bumps. He was trying to tell me something, *come on brain workout what he is telling me!*

'In 1871 when they made you a detective,' I carried on.

The Strange Case of Caroline Maxwell

'Yes, I was quite sad to leave Whitechapel. It had been my home for many years; I knew the area like the back of my hand. I knew who to talk to and who not to. But I always had a feeling I would be back, can't explain it then, and can't explain it even now. I just belong there, I mean to say that I belonged there' He said as he looked sadly to one side.

'You were busy being a detective.'

'I was a little demanding yes and I suppose that was when my first marriage went down the drain. I was never at home; my mind was firmly on the job and not on my personal life, so it suffered. I wanted to be the best, be the best person I could and protect the public, I didn't realise I wasn't being the best husband,' he stopped talking and looked at me, I knew my face was betraying me as he then said 'Don't look at me like that, I'm not a pathetic man so I don't deserve a pitiable glance from you, it was nothing new. Many young detectives could tell you the same story.'

I decided this was getting me nowhere; I was dangerously close to losing him and this interview. It was best to stick with his career, so I said 'There were some quite impressive cases you had as a detective.'

'Meaning?' he asked.

'Why don't you talk about them?'

'Well there was the Gold case; two men were trying to steal as many purses as they could in a day. That was certainly different. We caught them in the end, I decided before the day was out to dress up as a lady.'

'A lady!' I proclaimed.

'I know it might sound a little laughable to some irrational people, but you can't laugh at the results can you?'

'I guess not.'

'That is what makes us dissimilar to the public,' He said pointing at me. 'We never guess,' he said as a declaration, a little like someone else I knew. I smiled when I thought of him. He was probably on a new case by now forgetting all about me and the set of circumstances he had left me in. 'What are you smiling at?' Mr Abberline asked.

'You were reminding me of someone.'

'Oh yes? Who would be?'

The Strange Case of Caroline Maxwell

Chapter Thirteen

'Mr. Sherlock Holmes,' I answered.

'Holmes!' He shouted back at me as he stood up, his face turning bright red. 'I should have presumed it, that is why you here isn't it? Holmes the meddler! Holmes the busy body! Holmes the Scotland Yard Jack in office! Don't you dare sit there in my own house and lie to me!'

'W...What have I said?'

'You have just ended this interview, goodbye Miss Reporter,' He said as he turned in his seat so his back was towards me.

'I'm sorry if I have made you angry Sir, but I have come such a long way and I truly believe the public has wronged you. Please let us finish the interview, I will obey the document you wanted me to sign, nothing will get published before you have seen it,' I said, I just couldn't understand what I had gone wrong, what had I said to make this change in his behaviour?

'You have lied to me!' he bellowed at me, without turning around.

'What have I done to anger you so?'

'You are here because that interfering and intrusive Holmes fellow sent you!'

'I was told to come to you, yes...'

'Ah! You do not deny it then! I knew it! Nothing gets past me for long.'

'No I am sure it doesn't but please Sir, I beg of you to listen to me. Sherlock Holmes sent me here to speak to you about something he believes might have happened yes I don't dispute that fact, but with every assignment I get given I do my own research. I did my research on your career and I am telling the truth when I say that people should hear what you have done for them,' I said firmly.

How could mentioning Mr. Sherlock Holmes cause this man, that seemed so calm even dreamily peaceful with his thoughts and speech to turn so frantic and hysterical?

The Strange Case of Caroline Maxwell

'Just so Miss, just so,' Said a voice from behind me, I wasn't even be aware of the door opening and of Mrs Abberline standing in the doorway until I turned to face her; I knew I was looking at her helplessly, almost like a little child.

'That Holmes fellow sent her!' screamed Mr Abberline towards his wife.

'I heard dear husband and no doubt half the neighbourhood heard it too. I have taken this opportunity to enter back into this modest interview for you my loving husband to listen to me, is it wrong of me to do so?' she asked Mr Abberline. He did not answer her and turned away; she stood there firmly and raised her eyebrows at him. 'Do I take it, that my husband will not listen to his loving and caring wife?' She asked again. Again there was silence from Mr. Abberline as his head moved so that he could glance at the floor. Mrs Abberline was not disturbed at all by the attitude her husband was giving her, she tried once again 'If that is so, what kind of marriage have I entered? I thought it was a devoted and dutiful one, where both of us are equals if this is not the case I'm afraid I have been sold a tall tale and you have been economical with the truth, is this true my dear Freddie? Have you filled our marriage with a falsehood?' This time she got an answer.

'No my love, never could that be my love. The situation I am in has upset me that is all, of course I will listen to you,' He said as he turned to face both of us. Mrs Abberline's face changed in the spilt second, she smiled back at her husband but still there was an air of sternness in her stature as she closed the door and moved towards her husband. 'I had thought that to be the case, now let's get back to the matter at hand,' she said as she glanced at me. 'I believe what this lady said is the truth.'

'How can you believe a word she said?' He asked her.

'Because she has not lied, not once dear husband,' she said as she walked over to him and grabbed at his hands and held them tightly.

'What are you talking about wife? This woman came in to this house, my house claiming she has done research in to my career!' He yelled.

'Lower you voice husband,' she said as she turned to me, 'Miss, could you kindly tell me the cases my husband was involved in when he became a detective.'

The Strange Case of Caroline Maxwell

'Well apart from the Gold case, your husband was just mentioning. There was the case about Mr Henry Muggeridge who forged cheques, a Mr Bastion who stole five shillings and The Sullivan sisters dressing like men,' I said.

'Thank you Miss, that is all we needed to hear: see husband she has done her research into your career.'

'But she was using that, to get the information Mr. Holmes told her to get!'

'But when you asked her about Mr. Sherlock Holmes and whether it was he that told her to come here, did she lie to you?'

'No she told me that it was he,' he whispered.

'Quite so, so she has come because Mr. Holmes told her to, because that man believes you could tell her something. She does research on you, SHE finds out the public has done you a great injustice, so it is HER that comes here to make up for those in her profession. Do you see now, my husband how I can believe her.'

'Yes I can,' he quietly said. 'You may leave us, wife.'

By Amanda Harvey Purse

'What about your voice?'

'Will be lowered and stay that way, dear wife.'

'Thank you, sweet husband,' she said as she dropped her husband's hands and she made her turn to leave, making sure she gave me a studied look. To which I pushed with all my might a 'thank you' through my eyes, she seemed to sense it and smiled back at me.

...

We were alone again; Mr. Abberline hadn't glanced my way for a long time. I sensed he felt a mixture of maddened frustration and the guiltiness remorse.

Suddenly his voice spoke to me, so hushed and gentle it was hard to hear, 'I had told him to leave this matter all those years ago. It's not right for him to stick his nose into other people's problems, problems that have been solved without him. Now he bothers me still, a man of old age, how disgraceful and indecent of him.'

'Mr. Sherlock Holmes is very unlike and singular to many people, he does not seem to function the way most people do. It's what makes him good and famous at what he does. He probably did not know that sending me here

The Strange Case of Caroline Maxwell

would upset you so, he just thinks of the case and that the case cannot be closed until he has all the information. He believes you are holding the missing information.'

Mr. Abberline turned to me with pleading eyes 'How right he is.'

'He is right?' I asked. I had always believed in what Mr. Sherlock Holmes had said to me but hearing it being agreed with by another was quite outstanding and shocking.

With a huff Mr. Abberline put both hands on his desk. 'When do you know him to be wrong?'

'That is true,' I said with a smile. Mr. Abberline smiled back.

'That man is so utterly annoying,' Mr. Abberline said in a stress releasing gasp 'Can you tell him that when you next see him?'

'I promise but I can't promise it will be the first time he has been called it,' I grinned at him.

'Ah I'm afraid you might be speaking the truth there, so is this where I spill my heart out to you and tell you the unknown about *that* case?'

By Amanda Harvey Purse

'I guessing it would be,' I said, but I had a feeling it wasn't going to be that easy.

...

'Well I can't, not because I'm frightened to and not even because I'm a difficult man to get along with' he smiled again at me; I couldn't help but smile back at him. It was his way of saying sorry to me without saying it, I knew so in return I smiled back to say thank you, Mr. Abberline carried on talking, 'If Mr. Holmes had asked me WHY I could not answer him, I would have told him. I would have told him all those years ago but he never did, that one time he didn't seem to ask the right question. Maybe that is why he still hounds me so. I will tell you and hope that this will take the weight of my back. It is a simple fact, maybe it's worthy of noting but simple all the same.'

'What is this simple fact?' I asked.

'Can I show you something?' He asked at me, I hoped that this wasn't going to take us off the subject.

'If it pleases you, Sir' I replied.

The Strange Case of Caroline Maxwell

'Follow me,' he said as he walked to the door. I stood up from my seat and followed this most interesting man. We walked further down the hallway in stillness; Mr. Abberline did not want to talk to me in this moving moment. I decided to look around at this wonderful modern home, the Abberline's had invested in electric lighting. Somehow it didn't seem quite right; it didn't have the warm, cosy feeling of the good old candle light. I could see the butler up head telling the maid something, then out of the corner of his eye he saw us coming nearer and quickly moved towards us.

'Mr. Abberline Sir, is there anything I can do for you?' he asked.

'If you would keep staff away from my office I would be contented with that.'

'Sir is going into his office?' The butler asked in surprise.

'Yes James, now kindly do as I say and shrug off,' Mr Abberline replied firmly.

'Shall I let Mrs Abberline know?'

'There is no need to worry Mrs Abberline, it will be fine.'

'Very well Sir,' he said as he paced off down the hallway.

'The butler seemed shocked that you were going into your office, do you not go in there often?' I asked.

'No I do not,' he said as he unlocked and opened the door that stood before him. I walked in behind him and was a little taken back.

The Strange Case of Caroline Maxwell

Chapter Fourteen

Mr. Abberline's office was a small, dark and very creepy. There were no windows or electric lighting in here and I could not see a thing because of it.

'Wait there, I will light a candle,' Mr. Abberline said to me as he moved forward and I could then hear a match being struck and then his face was in light and shadows, he reminded me of when I used to read an Elgar Allen Poe ghost story to my ma and pa at Christmas time, I used to light one candle and stick it underneath my chin to gave me a ghostly feeling.

Mr. Abberline used the light of this candle to light another one which was sitting on what I would guess should be a desk, but it was covered in so many papers I could not even see any surface wood.

With the other candle burning I could see much more of this room. There were a few bookshelves all full of files and dust on the right hand side, the desk was not only covered in what I could now see was newspapers but there was an half eaten apple which was turning brown and there were a few empty bottles of whiskey, some standing, some lying to their side, placed on the desk. I guessed that was where the stale smell, that filled this room, was coming from. The floor was covered in papers, documents and notes I could only see that there was carpeted rug underneath because of the one thin line that was free of all paper work.

'You will have to stand; there is only one chair now. The other one broke the last time I was in here,' he said as he sat down. 'It got in my way and I took a disliking to it or so I am told, to be honest I don't remember a thing.'

I knew what he meant; I was accustomed to the horrors of drinking from early childhood and living in Whitechapel.

The Strange Case of Caroline Maxwell

'Doesn't your maid come in here?' I asked.

'No, nobody comes in here. That is my orders. In fact Mrs Abberline has only been in here once... when I forgot to open the door to her.'

'Why am I in here Sir?'

'Why indeed,' he said in a huff, moments later he carried on 'You seem to want to clear my name but to do so you and I will need to talk about the elephant in the room, the elephant lives here now.'

I looked around the room, it was only then that I noticed all the newspapers were in the year of 1888 and onwards, some of the documents said the words Whitechapel, some of the notes said the words, *eye witness reports, post mortem reports, the writing on the wall reports.*

'See how he lives and breathes in here.' Mr. Abberline said sadly.

'You are still working on the case?'

'I need to know, I need to be sure we have him.'

'You believed the police have caught him?'

By Amanda Harvey Purse

'All the signs were pointing that way but there is this something, this doubting of myself that fears he is still out there.'

'But you did think they caught him?'

'Yes and then no, it was my boy Godley who did it, but I still have those dreams and now I'm not so sure.'

'Dreams, you say?' I asked.

'Nightmares, it must sound childish to you, but he is always there every time I closed my eyes, he is there... laughing at me.'

'So those dreams make you believe he is still on the loose?'

'It's got to be the only answer.'

'What if you are still dreaming of him because you never got the chance to catch him yourself, you say you believe he was this certain person that Inspector Godley caught. Have you ever doubted your instinct before? What I mean to say is, has your instincts been wrong before? If they haven't, then it could simply be about not being in the right place and in the right time period.'

'You can talk a lot you know, has anyone ever told you that?'

'Yes, it has been said, sorry.'

'You never know, I could just remember what you said and I might not need to turn to this,' he said shaking an empty bottle at me 'to help me sleep.'

'You never know Sir, I would be glad if I have been of some help to you.'

'You are right.'

'I am? What am I'm right about?'

'You are not an ordinary journalist.'

'Thank you, now do you think it would help if we said his name rather than trying to dodge it?'

'Yes it just might. But then again it might not, it is your choosing.'

'Well then, who did you think...Jack the ripper was?'

'I had thought him to be George Chapman.'

'The poisoner we were just talking about?'

By Amanda Harvey Purse

'The one and the same, there were a lot of facts pointing that way, but there was this moment.'

'What moment?'

'After the last murder, he came up to me and told me to leave the case. I thought it was because he had found out what I did but now I look back at it, he seemed to know it was going to be the end,' He said, I don't think Mr. Abberline was still talking to me.

'What did you do?' I asked.

'What?' he said with a jolt, as if I had broken the spell.

'You just said you did something that you thought you were going to be caught doing, what did you do?' I asked there was silence; Mr. Abberline was just staring at me. Then he suddenly jumped up from his desk and walked over to a long cupboard that was standing in the corner, reached inside his pocket and pulled out a gold key. He unlocked the cupboard and pulled out a walking stick.

'I wonder if it was meant to mean...' he said, then as if he suddenly remembered I was in the room, he looked at me and then back at the walking stick and then back to

The Strange Case of Caroline Maxwell

me. 'This was given to me after I finished The Ripper case.'

I walked up the line of un-papered flooring to the desk, where he had placed the walking stick on, and leaned over.

...

The walking stick was of dark brown wood; there was a golden plague on it saying 'presented to Inspector Fredrick George Abberline by seven officers engaged with him with the Whitechapel Murders of 1888'. The top of the walking stick was a man's face surrounded by a brown hood, he looked like a monk.

'What a strange thing and what a strange thing to do,' I said out loud.

'Strange you say?'

'Well, do they always give gifts to an Inspector for a case that was... uncompleted?'

'No, they don't'

'And why a hooded brother?'

'Or why a brotherhood' Mr. Abberline mumbled. I looked up at him and there was a moment I felt like he wanted to say something important to me, but then decided against it. 'It was because of the Mitre Square murder, at that place there was a temple in the 1500's where a mad monk murdered a woman.'

'They wanted to remind you of that?'

'It's a little questionable I agree.'

'You care about The Ripper case I can tell, thank you for showing me this and allowing me into this room but...'

'I have not answered why I cannot help yours and Mr. Holmes's case?'

'Yes.'

'I can't enlighten you in this case as it's not my story to tell, so I have no right to it.'

'Whose story is it?' I asked.

'Ahh now that's the correct question, and I can't believe it actually came from a woman of all people.'

The Strange Case of Caroline Maxwell

'You saddle our good name Sir, your wife seems to be a very intelligent woman so surely you can't place all women in the same basket?'

'Another quick-witted comment, well I guess you have firmly put me in my place Miss Reporter.'

'But we should all *never guess,*' I said as I smiled sweetly at him. I had done it, I had done the impossible. I had actually won over Ex-Inspector Fredrick, George Abberline. A female reporter got an interview with the most awkward and challenging man a journalist has come across, Mr Abberline. I felt proud of myself, first Sherlock Holmes now Mr. Abberline. *Who next?*

'All I have left to say on the matter is, the story you are after does not nowhere near end with me, I am afraid to tell you that you need to find someone else.'

'Who would that be?' I asked.

'You need to find Miss Caroline Maxwell.'

By Amanda Harvey Purse

Chapter Fifteen

'Miss Caroline Maxwell?' I asked. Something was telling me I had heard of that name before but this conversation had taken such a strange and perplexing turn, I was not being my normal quick and speedy self.

'If you have done your research like you have stated, that name would not be new to you, I have already said too much for me to feel comfortable with. You may not understand why saying her name, makes me undergo some nauseous and sickening sensation but you have a strength of character and determination to desire more information I can sense but I cannot talk of it anymore, please don't push me, I cannot give you any more. Please leave now'

The Strange Case of Caroline Maxwell

'Where is she?' I asked hopeful that he knew and that I wasn't pushing him.

'I do not know. I do not care to know. Please leave,' He said as he got up from the desk and walked to the door. I walked passed him as he held the door open for me. 'James will show you to the front door.'

I paused and twisted back to face him, 'Do you mind me asking why you have told me this, when you could have told Mr. Holmes so many years ago?'

'I do mind but I see that isn't important anymore. There is something different about you; my wife was able to pick up on it instantly, I, I'm afraid was a little slow. You are a woman; you probably think that's a bad thing for the time that we are living in. Things are not handed to you on a plate; you have to fight for them. So in turn, you work harder and you show emotion. You are going to need to show emotion where you're headed, something I do not believe Mr. Sherlock Holmes has,' he said as he smiled at me.

'I will never forget how gracious you have been to allow me to speak to you, how can I express my gratitude to you?'

'Believe in every choice you make, never regret the judgements you make,' he simply said as he shut the entrance into the room I was previously in and left me looking at the other side of the wooden panelled door, my nose was so close to the wooden entry I swear for a brief moment I could smell the varnish.

Mr. Abberline was on the other side in the dark and gloom surrounded by a mad man's past; I knew which side I'd preferred to be.

'This way miss,' said the butler's voice; I turned and saw him standing halfway up the hallway.

'Is Mrs Abberline still within the manor's grounds?'

'No miss, she is not.'

'Is there anywhere I could write a note for her?'

'Yes Miss, come into the library. You can write your note there.' he said. I followed him to the first door on the right. He opened the door and waited in the doorway like my very own security. I moved towards the desk in the centre of the room, I reached for a piece of clean white paper and a bottle on ink. I did not sit down; I did not want

The Strange Case of Caroline Maxwell

to make myself comfortable in a house I was lucky enough to enter and as I started to write I noticed in the corner of my eye, the butler was secretly smiling, I had chosen the right thing to do.

> Dear Mrs Abberline,
>
> I was so sorry that I missed you, but I wanted to thank you for everything you did for me. You did so much, not only allowing me into to your home but managed to stand up for me while I seemed to have upset your husband. I want you to know I never meant to distress him and was trying my best not to. I hope I have also helped with his 'dreams' but I feel I must tell you, your husband has shown me his 'office'. What that will do to his behaviour in the next few hours I am unsure.
>
> You have put your trust in me and I will not let you down, I will stick to the agreement. You have my word.
>
> Miss Amelia Christie

When I finished the letter I placed it in an envelope, after writing her name on the front I passed it to the butler. 'Can you hand this to Mrs Abberline, when she comes home?'

'Yes Miss.'

'Thank you,' I said. As the main door was being opened for me the butler said.

'I think you should have brought a shawl Miss,' I looked out of the front door and noticed it was almost dark and the wind had picked up again as the only tree on the front lawn was blowing to one side.

'I will never learn,' I said as I pulled the collar of my dress tighter to my skin and stepped outside. As I gave the butler one last smile I noticed Mr. Abberline running down the hallway towards us.

'Oh good, you haven't left yet!' said he. As he reached us he said 'James, get the coach for the lady I cannot have her walking home in that bad weather!'

'Yes Sir,' the butler said as he hurried outside and around the corner of the house.

'You do not have to do that Mr. Abberline,' I said.

'I am the gentleman of this household, so yes I do. There was something I was meant to ask you.'

'If I can help, I will. Ask away.'

The Strange Case of Caroline Maxwell

'Your letter to me....'

'Yes?'

'It was very passionate and strong.'

'Thank you.'

'It was very truthful too.'

'That was what I wanted you to feel.'

'Well I did, apart from one thing.'

'What was that?'

'The vicar of this parish...'

'What about him? I met him a few days ago and I could hardly forget him. I honestly haven't met that many men of the church but he was such a character, he cares for his flock. He felt strongly against me seeing you, he didn't want me to offend and grieve you, he wanted to protect you.'

'That is the thing I want to question.'

'Oh, what is that?' I asked. Is every conversation with this man going to be out of the ordinary?

By Amanda Harvey Purse

'Ah! There is the coach,' he said as he walked me to the coach door and opened it for me, I got in and sat down. Mr Abberline shut the door and shouted to the driver 'Take her to the public house,' I reached my head out the window and had to raise my voice above the intense wind.

'What is the problem with the vicar?'

'I have never met him!' He shouted back as the coach started to move away.

Chapter Sixteen

Back at the Silver Horse public house, I began to pack for my trip back to London. I say began, as I had difficulty in finishing the task, the last conversation I had with Mr. Abberline was bothering me too much. He had never met the vicar? That doesn't make sense, I am sure the vicar said he met him. Of course he met him, how would he know about Mr. Abberline? How would he know about Mr. Abberline now living in his parish?

But from the look in Mr. Abberline's eyes, I could see he was confused as much as I. Why would Mr. Abberline lie to me about not meeting the vicar? It was such a trivial and frivolous thing; there was no need to tell untruths.

By Amanda Harvey Purse

Another thing was bothering me, and it was the simple fact of why is this bothering me? I had just stated that this is insignificant and of no great concern and yet I am troubled and anxious about it. I cannot stop thinking about it, it feels like all my journalistic senses are boiling and going into overdrive. I can perceive a story in the making, *a story within a story*. Am I just getting ahead of myself? Do I want an article in The Times newspaper that badly, that I am thinking of all possible routes of making it so?

It is a silly thing, I am bothered about something so unimportant compared to the mission I am on now, I am being daft and foolish. It must stop. Just at that moment there was a knock at the door, 'Miss?'

'Yes,' I replied as I put the last of my things in my bag.

'The landlord would like to know if you will be dining with them on your last night here.'

'Oh I hadn't thought that far ahead, yes I guess so.' After all it would be wise to have a full meal before the long trip back to the city and it would be polite to say

The Strange Case of Caroline Maxwell

goodbye as I will be long gone before the others would be up.

'Very good Miss, I will let the landlord and his wife, know that.'

'Thank you,' I said as I heard a set of footsteps leave my door and tap their way down the stairs.

When silence returned, I sat on the end of the bed wondering about this small village and its inhabitants. Thinking back over the week, I have met some fascinating and charming people that I could hardly forget. It started with the rather strange and peculiar man I met on the train getting here; I wonder where he is now? There was the landlord and his welcoming wife, she has an excellent talent with food and I shan't forget her cooking smells or the taste!

The little school boy, Bobby. He was a cheeky chap, he reminded me of the best qualities in the Artful Dodger character in *Oliver Twist* but perhaps a more sanitary version. I wonder if he will ever make it to work in the force, should I mention dear Bobby to Mr Abberline, I wonder? Then there was Mary Yates, the housemaid to the Abberline's. She seems a loveable character, although she drinks for pleasure and exuberance I believe it has a hidden meaning for her.

She is missing her brother and she finds living so far away from him insufferable, but she feels she needs to prove herself to her family and believes to do that she must stay here in this village and although she is unhappy she knows it is a good household to work for and they will look after her.

There was of course the mysterious vicar, he seemed so energetic and animated with his love of his people, he came across so friendly and forthcoming. I simply cannot believe he would have pulled the wool over my own eyes, he surely was not pretending to be anyone he wasn't, he was a vicar and he speaks the word of god. If you cannot put your trust in a person like him, *who can you put your trust in?*

This vicar business is worrying and I don't understand why. I must forget it now it is just a part of this interesting story that will not have a solved solution, but can I live with that? Can I just leave an unanswerable tangent flapping in the wind? I guess I am going to have to, but it will be bothering me I can promise myself that!

The Strange Case of Caroline Maxwell

...

I moved away from the bed and shifted myself toward the tiny locked window of my rented room. I gazed out at the diminutive and minor village that I have grown to love. As the night draws in, it makes the scene out of my window dark and gloomily sinister, and it does not surprise me that the disturbingly creepy feeling materializes from the shadowy church with a depressingly bleak looking stained glass window. I will miss this place. It somehow has captured my inner feeling for a cosy way of living that I never knew I had. It is probably the same feeling the Abberline family had after spending most of their adult lives in the busy city.

I headed down the stairs and could instantly smell the sweet delight of the landlord's wife's cooking skills, I had the feeling I was in for an exceedingly charming treat. I tapped on the back door.

'Come in Miss, dinner is just being served,' as I opened the door and walked in the dining room there was a wave of an agreeable smelling heat that instantly watered my taste buds. 'There you go Miss,' the landlord said as he pointed to the same seat I had taken the night before. 'The wife was very pleased to hear that you wanted to eat with us again.'

'How can I not accept the chance of eating your wife's fine cooking again before I leave? It was so delicious and flavoursome last night I have not forgotten it since.'

'The wife would be ever so happy to hear that Miss.'

'My husband speaks the truth Miss,' the landlord's wife said as she walked into the room. 'I am finding it hard to keep hold of the plates that are in my hands, for I feel that I am blushing and want my hands to shield my face from you.'

'Come now, I only speak the truth. Your meals are delightful and you should be proud of them. You and your husband have made me feel so welcomed here, I thank you both heartily.'

'That is very nice of you to say so Miss,' said the landlord's wife as she placed a dish of roasted beef and vegetables in front of me.

The Strange Case of Caroline Maxwell

'If we are speaking truthfully, then I would like to speak for myself and my wife when I say that you have been the most lovely and pleasant guest we have had here,' said the landlord as he picked up his knife and fork.

'Well that's kind of you both to say so,' I said as I repeated his actions.

'Please enjoy your last meal here,' he said.

'That I can hardly deny myself,' I said as I tucked in to the appetizingly scrumptious food.

By Amanda Harvey Purse

Chapter Seventeen

Sitting on the train watching the countryside go by my mood was indifferent. Somehow I felt lost, how was I going to find this Miss Caroline Maxwell? Where have I seen the name before? Why is everything such a mystery? And what have I got myself into?

'Tickets please,' I handed the conductor my ticket. 'Ah going to the big city hey?' he asked me as he looked at my ticket.

'Actually I am going *back* to the city,' I said.

'I thought you dressed a little different from the normal country folk, so had a holiday did you?'

'A working holiday I guess you could call it.'

The Strange Case of Caroline Maxwell

'So what do you do?'

'You ask a lot of questions don't you?' was my reply.

The conductor sat down in my carriage, it was a chance for me to get a good look at him. He was quite tall, had a slick dark brown beard that followed the shape of his face. He had dark coloured eyes that seemed sharp and piercing, the brim of his conductor's hat almost covered them. 'How else am I meant meet people, I work so many hours going up and down on these rusty trains, I never get time to stop and talk to someone.'

'And you have just decided that I am the person you want to talk to?'

'Well you fascinate me.'

'Oh?'

'You're different from the ordinary; you are not the typical...'

'Woman?' I butted in and finished his sentence for him.

'Actually I was going to say... person.'

'Yes, but you were thinking, woman.'

'I cannot lie about that, you never told me what you did.'

'No I did not.'

'I see because it is touchy subject by chance?'

'No I just may not want to talk about it.'

'Can I guess?' he asked.

'Guessing is not impressive, I have recently learned that,' I said looking back to the window as we went through a tunnel, in the reflection of the glass I could swear the conductor was smiling to himself. He is not a bad guy and this trip could be a little tedious, seeing the same trees and bushes everywhere. 'But you could give it a try,' I finally said.

The conductor looked up with so much glee in his eyes and said 'Thank you, you dress like a Londoner but not a poor Londoner. No jewels, so not a rich Londoner either, so you're a working Londoner but you're different.'

'Different?'

The Strange Case of Caroline Maxwell

'I don't see you being a maid, travelling in first class anyway. You say you are on a working holiday, so you're line of work involves travelling about the place. You seem quite secretive and defensive about your work. You travel light, I see from the size of your bag, but you have not placed your bag up on the shelf above your head so whatever is in your bag means a lot to you, but what can fit in that small bag that would mean a lot? You have taken it with you on your working holiday so you need it for work. I would guess it is a notepad and pen it that bag, perhaps a little bottle of ink too. Am I wrong?'

'You should really meet a friend of mine, you two would get on like a house on fire.'

'Oh? Was I right then? You are a reporter aren't you?'

'I am trying to be.'

'Yes! I like it when I get things right!' he said like a child.

'Glad I have made you happy,' I said.

My comment broke his childish mood and with a cough he asked 'What are you working on?'

'You have got to be teasing me! You want the first hand scoop!'

'You never know, I just might be able to help.'

'I doubt that.'

'You don't know until you ask.'

'I don't have to ask.'

'Ah the secretive mood kicks back in,' he said.

'I'm sorry, I don't know where this is headed yet and I promised that only one man will get the first scoop before anyone else and that man isn't you.'

'But is it someone you have recently met?'

'Could well be.'

'Well we are coming into London now Miss, nice to meet you and all that,' the conductor said as he walked out of the carriage and with one nod of head to me he was gone...

Wait! I didn't get my tickets back...

The Strange Case of Caroline Maxwell

Chapter Eighteen

As the train rolled into the station and the bellows of stream floated passed the window of my carriage I felt mighty strange. This was my home I should feel delighted to be back but I felt a little uneasy, for the task that lay headed of me seemed worryingly foreboding as I didn't know what way to turn. I was tired and exhausted so I knew I wasn't feeling my best to make a decision right now. Homeward bound!

I treated myself to a Hansom cab which was waiting outside the station's entrance, my feet felt terrible and sore. I climbed in and almost forced myself not to say 'Home James!' As we drove along Baker Street I could not help but look up at the window of 221B, amazingly the face I was looking for was looking down at me.

By Amanda Harvey Purse

Mr. Holmes lifted his long pipe to me and nodded, I smiled back to him. As we travelled past Baker Street I couldn't help wonder why Mr. Sherlock Holmes looked so drained and fatigued, it must be another case as there no other reason for Mr. Sherlock Holmes to stop eating and looking after himself. I worry for him and I feel sorry for Mrs Hudson too, Mr. Holmes is like the complicated and demanding son she never had. She must care for him in such a passionately dedicated way, seeing him harm himself must be so very horrid for her.

When I got home, I threw my bag upon the bed and looked around, it was my room and yet it felt unfamiliar to me. I couldn't understand the feeling I was having for I was only away for a week! I didn't bother to wash myself or get dressed in my nightwear, my head hit the pillow and I was away with the *fairies*.

...

The next day I felt groggy and dazed, my head hurt badly and the light blaring in from my window hurt my eyes which made my sight a little blurry. I had to wait a few minutes for the hazy object I decided to glance at turn back into the wash basin I knew it was. I managed to gingerly walk over to the wash basin and splashed my face

The Strange Case of Caroline Maxwell

with freezing water, as I glanced at myself with a wet face I tried to speculate the time of day that it was, the light was too bright to be the morning but surely I had not slept that long!

I dressed and walked out the door, I knew where I should be heading but the truth is; I did not have the brain power to deal with the senseless and dense editor of The Times Newspaper. So I headed in the other direction and within a few minutes I walked into Regent's Park, it was a lovely day after all.

Regent's Park has always been interesting to me; it could be busy and noisy with the sound of the trumpet band playing in their stand or could be so quiet. You could feel so isolated and solitary if you keep to the lake side of the park anyway as the other side of the park has some rather odd and rare sounds you would not think you would hear from a park inside a huge city. Sounds of a hungry black American bear calling for he's lunch for instance!

Nowadays the Zoo in Regent's Park is more of a tourist place to go, rather than what it had been originally designed for, a scientific observation for the Society's Fellows. I have heard that the public have lined up for miles to see that bear, only to have their hats and bags pinched by him!

I sat down on one of the benches overlooking the lake and watched the elegant swans swim about when I heard;

'Hello Miss Amelia Christie!'

'Why it is Mrs Hudson!'

...

'Can I sit by you?' she kindly asked.

'Of course,' I said as I moved to one side.

'What have you been up to?'

'Well I'm still on that case Mr. Holmes sent me on.'

'Oh, don't talk to me about Mr. Holmes!' She said as she glanced away from me, toward the lake and the swans that I had been watching.

'What has it he done now?'

'He goes away for a few days at a time, on some kind of case I would imagine as he never tells me anything.

The Strange Case of Caroline Maxwell

I take the quiet time to clean his rooms, he then comes back in a mad rush and now it is just as big of a mess as it was before I did anything! All my hard work is down the drain!'

'Poor Mrs Hudson, you look after him so well, he would be nothing without you!'

'Nice of you to say so but some days I have so much constant worry and anxiety about that man that I am sure I am ageing before my years! I do remember not so long ago I had light auburn coloured hair, now it is white.'

'So you are avoiding him and enjoying the afternoon air then?'

'Something like that, what are you doing here?' she asked.

'I am avoiding my editor.'

'Well I couldn't pick a better spot to avoid people,' she laughed.

'That is true,' I said. As I sat there in the cosy, warm sensation of sitting next to a motherly figure I realised I knew nothing of her and her life apart from the little fragments of information in Dr Watson's stories. This fact was cataclysmic and deplorable to me; I decided to change this reality right at this moment. 'Mrs Hudson it pains me to say this, but I have just become conscious of the fact I know nothing of you.'

'Most people never ask, I am Mr. Sherlock Holmes's housekeeper and that is it.'

'I am very sorry to hear that, but I must admit I was one of those people to think that way. But if it is alright with you I would like to change that.'

'Really Miss? I am not as interesting as you may think I am, I can quite understand why a person like me gets pushed to one side when there are larger personalities around my life.'

'Come now, everyone is interesting to different people, how have you found yourself here, looking after an overgrown often self-indulgent but clever man?'

'A question I have often asked myself but I wouldn't have changed it for anything, I would never have met Mr. Holmes if I had changed it would I? I am a Scottish woman by birth, born to loving mother and a quite powerful father. I was named after my grandmother, Elaine. But she sadly died before I was born, but I was told

The Strange Case of Caroline Maxwell

I was very much like her, our family was quite influential and formidable in Scotland, the Fowler's have always owned land and animals. I wanted none of that; you see my dear, money doesn't buy you love and affection. So I decided to quite foolishly marry an Englishman who I thought was loving, Mr. Hudson had no income and would never be truly financially settled, yes he tried many different things but nothing ever arose.

We moved down to London and I brought the house in Baker Street with the money my mother gave me as a wedding gift. Things went from bad to worse, when my vigorous husband decided to fall in with the wrong crowd and became a criminal, but that was something he found he was good at. By that time I had enough of it all and asked a young man newly out of university who was making a name for himself solving little crimes in the area to stop my husband and his scandalous ways. This he did and my husband was sent to Wormwood Scrubs, it was a new prison at that time, so new in fact that I heard my husband had to build his own cell!'

'Is your husband still in prison?'

'In a way my love, he died in there.'

By Amanda Harvey Purse

'Mr. Holmes helped to put your husband in prison?'

'Yes he did Miss, he was always a good boy and he made sure I was well looked after while he did it, I never had any aggressive or vehement come back from it which now I look back at it I know I could have had. He looked after me, so in turn when he needed me I returned the favour.'

'What happened?' I asked very engrossed in the quite odd conversation I was having.

'It was raining quite heavy that night I can remember, when I opened my door to see Mr. Holmes standing there with drips running off the end of his rather large nose. I ushered him indoors and made him my famous hot lemon tea, for I was worried for his health, something that has not changed over the years! He sat there for a while silently, drinking his tea and looking at his hat, coat and gloves drying at the fireplace. I already knew to not ask Mr. Holmes any questions; he would tell me anything I needed to know in due course so I sat opposite him patiently.'

'There is no need to worry Mrs Hudson, I will be quite alright,' He suddenly said to me.

The Strange Case of Caroline Maxwell

'I'm sure you will be after you have warmed up a bit,' I replied.

'This lemon tea is quite refreshing.'

'I am glad you like it, would you like me to dish up some food? I am sure I have some curried ham leftover.'

'That would be agreeable.' He answered.

When I came back into the room with the curried ham I noticed that Mr. Holmes hadn't moved and was sitting still next to an empty cup. I placed the food in front of him and suddenly he moved to tuck into it, I took the cup away, replaced it with another tea and placed myself again opposite him. As I watched him eat like a hungry little scamp I knew then that I would be looking after him all my life, I had adopted him. I had a son.'

'That sounds like a very happy ending.'

'It is Miss, I couldn't have wanted anything more.'

'Did Mr. Sherlock Holmes ask to stay with you?'

'He didn't have to, he stayed that night and has never gone back to his lonely rooms at Montague Street, like I said before to you dear, loneliness doesn't become him.'

'I think I understand a little more now. Did you ever find out why Sherlock Holmes had appeared at your door that night?'

'I was still working as a dressmaker when Mr. Holmes entered my life, but slowly and gradually my life seemed to be overtaken by Mr. Sherlock Holmes's life and I am now his housekeeper and mother and for that reason alone I never had to ask him.'

'I can be familiar with that same feeling of Mr. Sherlock Holmes overtaking your own life; he seems to have that ability to do that.'

'It's never a bad thing,' she replied to me.

'I agree with you,' I said.

We must have sat there for another hour or so, not saying any more. It felt pleasant and calming, but all the while I was fighting the urge to think about the interview I had with Mr. Abberline, I knew I had to find Miss Caroline Maxwell to move on in this story but something was holding me back. A gut feeling that something sinister was

The Strange Case of Caroline Maxwell

just around the corner and I didn't want to face it right now but I knew I couldn't put it off forever.

After all it was a story that Mr. Sherlock Holmes had given to me, he doesn't just hand out cases to anyone he sees, it must be important, but why am I feeling so uncertain about it? Why if it is so important, hasn't Mr. Holmes got involved? Why has he left it to me? Mr. Holmes has so much faith in me and the work I do, he is confident that I am a good journalist, so confident it makes me wonder whether I am or not, I have so much to prove, there is such a lot of pressure.

'Well it is almost dinner time, I should be getting back to make Mr. Holmes his food,' Mrs Hudson said as she broke the silence.

'Do you think he will eat it?' I asked.

'I don't know, I never know. But what I *do* know is, he will miss it if it wasn't there for him to dismiss. Also I know I have done everything for him.'

'Then it is for the best.'

'I guess I will be seeing you soon at Baker Street?'

By Amanda Harvey Purse

'Yes, somehow I sense that too,' I said as I watched her walk off in the direction of 221B Baker Street. It was the truth, I had an overpowering sensation that I will be sitting in that living room of Mr. Holmes's very soon...

The Strange Case of Caroline Maxwell

Saturday 14th September 1901 in the City of London...

By Amanda Harvey Purse

The Strange Case of Caroline Maxwell

Chapter Nineteen

I managed to push myself to leave the quiet and gentle scene I was watching and took the slowest walk I had ever taken to The Times News Agency. I stopped at the bottom of the stone stairs leading up to the glassed double doors;

1...2...3...

With the last breath held for a little longer I picked up the strength the walk into the building. As the door closed behind me I took a look around, this place seemed so different to the last time I had come here. It was so peaceful and uninterrupted by other people's voices and movements, the other reporter's had gone home and what a change it made to the whole surroundings.

By Amanda Harvey Purse

I used to love this time, when I first became a reporter. I had to always report in at this time so no one saw that The Times newspaper had a woman reporter, after all I was signing myself under a fake male's name. The door to the editor's office was always opened and waiting for me, now there was a part of me that hoped it *wasn't* this time.

I walked slowly to the office and before I had chance to knock on the door, a voice boomed from within. 'Is that you Amelia?'

1...2...3

I opened the door and walked inside, 'Yes it is.'

'I thought you had changed your mind about being a journalist.'

'No I haven't.'

'Good, right tell me the story. You do have the story don't you? I haven't just spent first class train tickets for a dead end have I? You will need a great story Amelia I am afraid because while you have been running around in your little high heels in Hampshire, news has broke across the pond that the President of America, William McKinley

The Strange Case of Caroline Maxwell

has been shot by an anarchist in Buffalo. All hell is breaking loose my dear, they say that Theodore Roosevelt will be sworn in; I do not think that will happen.'

'I had heard Mr. Roosevelt will be received gratefully.'

'Never in my lifetime has a President been sworn in so young.'

'The world *is* changing.'

'Yes so you keep reminding me, you did not answer my question. Please tell me you have a story...'

'I have a story.'

'Great! Tell me.'

'I can't.'

'What!'

'I can't tell you, I signed a document saying that I would give the only copy of the story to the person, who told it, well apart of it anyway, for him to decide whether I can publish it.'

'I can't believe this! You had no right to sign such as thing! You know how I work, I need details.'

'Yes I understand that, and I know I am asking for a lot of faith and trust in me but I truly believe I am on to a great story here.'

'I have been told that before.'

'No doubt you have, but have you left a space for me in the paper?'

'Not at the moment, I was waiting to for you to prove yourself and I might add that at this precise moment you are failing.'

'So if I don't come up with the goods you can fill the space with something else then?'

'Yes I can fill the space with someone else's great work,' He said sternly, I understood his point, but I spoke up before he said anymore.

'I believe in this story so much that I signed that document to get the interview I needed,' I couldn't believe I was about to say this but, 'I believe in this story so much that I am willing to risk my career on it.'

The Strange Case of Caroline Maxwell

'What are you saying to me?'

'I will do you a deal. You trust me; you give me another two weeks at the most. I will give you a great story, a story that I can swear no other paper could have because of the document I signed. If I don't or you do not think it is great, then I will leave your office never to return again.'

'Are you saying what I think you are saying?'

'I will be a journalist no longer.'

'Wow, I am amazed. You have been the most strong-willed and determined person to become a reporter I have ever met, are you really willing to risk all that on this one story?'

'I believe in it Sir.'

'How can I say no? Yes, you have a deal,' we shook hands and I walked out the door.

...

That was that, I had made my decision. I cannot go back on my choice now; I will have to write the story no matter what happens or how I feel about it. I must be hard-hearted and callous or I will lose my career for good. Can I truly been like that I wonder? I am a woman who shows her emotion apparently after all, that's what Mr Abberline said to me anyway. It was because of that emotion I was able to get that important interview, other journalists have tried to get the interview I have but only I have it because I am different. Can I really become like every other reporter now?

Oh, I have put my total trust in you Mr. Holmes, I do hope you will not let me down.

After managing to scrap together some food for dinner and eating it, all be it so unhappily, as it was nowhere near as appetizing as the landlord's wife's food of the Silver Horse public house in Hampshire, I started to feel a little improved about my situation whether it was because my stomach was full or not I could not tell; But I would not be a proper journalist if I didn't risk it all on what I believed from time to time.

Now is the time. I must have confidence and some self-belief, I will do admirably, I will be skilful and perfectly satisfactorily with my task. I will be a journalist in my own right.

The Strange Case of Caroline Maxwell

I lit a candle as the night was drawing in fast and with the winter pushing its cold windy arms around the great city unusually early this year, I could fool myself into thinking I had some kind of warmth. This would normally have been the time I would go to bed but whether it was the long sleep I had previously or the excitement of risking everything for this story but I was unable to sleep. I needed something to read, so I started searching my bookshelves.

There was nothing that caught my eye, what can I read tonight? I was just going to give up hope with the candle light fell on the stack of The Strand Magazines I had collected over the years, with the words *The Hound of the Baskervilles* on the cover sitting on the top of the pile. This story has always interested me; it sits alone from all the other novels and short stories as Mr. Holmes, the normal main character, the main reason why the public read Dr Watson's stories, is actually hardly in it. Where was he? Why did he stay in London and why did he send the good doctor away to protect Mr. Henry Baskerville, *what was Mr. Holmes doing in London, alone?*

I sat on the edge of the bed and starting reading it all over again, after reading a note that was sent to Mr. Henry Baskerville, Mr. Holmes believed it was a friendly warning to stay off the moor but he said it would be wise for there to be someone to look out for Sir Henry.

Mr. Holmes turns down the offer to be *that person* because of a blackmail case he is working on and sends Dr Watson instead. A blackmail case? There is no mention of a blackmail case around that time in any of the other stories involving Dr Watson writing in his journal, why is that the case?

Maybe because Dr Watson was not there, he was looking after Sir Henry in Baskerville Hall. Mr. Holmes was free to pursue the blackmail case alone, why did Mr. Holmes want to be alone with this blackmail case? Something does not feel right about this and why have I just noticed this open ended part of this story now?

I looked at the date that this *Hound* of a story started, *1888! Could it be that when Jack the Ripper was having his murderous way around the East End streets of Whitechapel, Mr. Holmes sent Dr Watson away to protect him, while pretending it was because Dr Watson needed to protect Sir Henry?*

Why did Mr. Holmes believe he needed to protect Dr. John Watson against Jack the Ripper? Jack after all

The Strange Case of Caroline Maxwell

was killing women not men and anyway Mr. Holmes for some reason didn't get involved with The Ripper case. He was, as stated in The Hound of the Baskervilles story, working on a blackmail case at the same time...

At that moment Mr. Abberline's conversation ran through my head, he had got so upset and angry when I first mention Mr. Holmes's name, I had wondered why at the time, but it was just a floating thought that soon passed...

Maybe he was upset because Mr. Holmes never helped with The Ripper case perhaps? After all that would be understandable, I don't even understand why there wasn't a slightest mention of Mr. Holmes helping the police to catch a notorious serial murderer.

But wait...

'*I had told him to leave this matter all those years ago. It's not right for him to stick his nose into other people's problems, problems that have been solved without him. Now he bothers me still, a man of old age, how disgraceful and indecent of him.*'

That is what Mr. Abberline had said to me, it was him that told Mr. Holmes to not get involved with The

By Amanda Harvey Purse

Ripper case! Why did Mr Abberline not want Mr. Holmes to get involved? After all, the police needed all the help they could get, why turn down the help from the cleverest person that London has ever known? He must have had a reason, a very good reason...

...

It was not just because Mr. Abberline hated Mr. Holmes sticking his nose into other people's problems, there is something more. Jack the Ripper wasn't just a problem he was a *hindrance* to the police force.

But wait, I do not understand, did I really quote him right? I know I wrote what he said down in my notepad, it cannot be wrong. But it doesn't make sense; I knew he was trying to tell me something in that room, I could feel it, was it this? No surely not. Was he really taking about The Ripper when he said it?

'It's not right for him to stick his nose into other people's problems, problems that have been solved without him'

What had Mr. Abberline solved? Did he solve the unsolvable? But this cannot be! Mr. Abberline thought Jack the Ripper was Mr. George Chapman but now he

The Strange Case of Caroline Maxwell

doubts himself, but there is nothing else he could have solved in this case. Was it a slip of the tongue, or was he lying about Mr. George Chapman and what he thought about him, Mr. Abberline is a very secretive man after all; did he really solve The Ripper case?

And is that why Mr. Holmes thought Mr. Abberline was holding some missing information? I can't believe I am thinking what I am thinking, has Mr. Abberline knew the answer most Londoners want to know all this time?

I took another look at my notepad and read the words Mr Abberline had spoken to me just two days ago...

*'If Mr Holmes had asked me WHY I could have answered him, I would have told him. I would have told him all those years ago but he never did, that one time he didn't seem to ask the right question. Maybe that is why he still **hounds** me so'*

1...2...3...

I put the *Hound of the Baskervilles* story to one side and looked up to the heavens, for a miracle to happen. I was even listening to hear some little cherub boy singing in the far off distance and some bright light to show itself. Is

By Amanda Harvey Purse

that what I am on? I am on a Jack the Ripper quest of finding his identity?

And more importantly, what has this Miss Caroline Maxwell got to do with it?

The Strange Case of Caroline Maxwell

Chapter Twenty

The next morning I retraced my steps back to The New Scotland Yard. I needed to have another look at The Ripper files as I believe this is where I have seen the name Miss Caroline Maxwell before.

As I walked up the stairs of the orange and cream building I have visited only once before, I noticed there was now was a collection of cigarette ends sitting burnt down to the ends on one of the stairs. *I wonder if Inspector Godley is working here today.*

The scene I saw before me as I pushed hard on the door until it opened, was a little disturbing, it was a mirror image of what I saw over week ago, the same people were sitting at the same desks all still scratching their heads in the same way. Does anything change around here?

'No it doesn't,' said a voice to the side of me. I turned to see that indeed Inspector Godley was working today and sitting at a desk near where I stood. I moved to sit at the other side of the desk and asked,

'Is mind reading a skill all policemen have or are you just special?'

'I have been called special a few times in my early life, not so much now.'

'I need your help again.'

'Tell me something I don't know,' he said looking back at his paperwork.

'My middle name is Jane,' I said quietly. With that comment he looked back up at me and smiled, a little more natural than he had before. Has he been practising?

'Well do I get a first name, or do I call you Miss something Jane Reporter?'

'It's Amelia.'

The Strange Case of Caroline Maxwell

'Amelia Jane Reporter sounds sweet. Now do I take it that you are still on a case about the Ripper?' he asked as he placed his paperwork to one side of his desk as if he needed nothing to be in-between us.

'Yes,' I answered. Inspector Godley made a little frown at the answer but carried on.

'And you want my help?'

'Yes.'

'One word answers hey? Must be something important that you have found,' he said. I couldn't help myself when I replied,

'Yes,' half laughing at myself and at the situation of the one word answers.

'Can I ask what you found?'

'No.'

Now it was his turn to laugh, 'I don't know why I expected a yes to that question, but you still want me to help you even though you haven't told me why?'

'Yes.'

'Well this has been a delightful conversation, probably the best I've had in a long while,' he said as he leaned back in his chair.

'I'm sorry, I need to see The Ripper files again,' I said.

'Why?'

'Like I have said, I cannot answer that.'

'You have your sources, I know I know. But I had thought you could have trusted me.'

'Why?' I asked. 'Because you are a policeman you mean? Have you forgotten the way you treated me when we first met? You didn't even give me your name when I asked for it.'

'True, I was having a bad day. Speaking of The Ripper, well, it doesn't put me in a happier mood.'

'I see.'

'I can tell you my name now if you want Miss, but I don't want it in any of your reports.'

The Strange Case of Caroline Maxwell

'You don't have to, *Inspector Godley*. If you do help me again I promise it will not appear in the paper,' I said sweetly.

'Oh' he replied with a shocked expression on his face. 'Well I guess I better help you then, follow me again Miss,' he said as he got up from his desk and pointed in the direction of the side door and as I got up from the chair I nodded at him to suggest I was ready to make the trip down into the depths of this place once again.

We went through the door and down the stairs in silence; it wasn't until we started walking down the long, dark and smelling hallway that Inspector Godley spoke. 'Can I ask why *you* are on a story about The Ripper?'

'What do mean?'

'Well excuse me for mentioning but you are a woman.'

'Am I? What was it that gave me away? The fact that I am intellectual, strong and can hold my own, or is it because simply, I am wearing a dress.'

He started laughing to himself, 'You are all those things and I have noticed what a pretty dress you are wearing but it was more to do with the makeup on your face and the scent I can smell from you.'

'Don't you policemen put makeup on when you dress like ladies for a case?'

With that statement he suddenly turned to face me and stopped in his tracks. 'Who told you that?' he demanded in a snake like manner.

'What?'

'Who told you we have dressed like ladies for a case?' He hissed in the most evil way.

'I thought everyone knew.'

'No, they don't. Who has been talking to you? Give me a name.' He ordered, as suddenly his face changed before my eyes. You may think I am meaning 'changed' in a literary sense as I think I would if I was reading this moment but you see, it is the strangest thing, his face was *actually* beginning to change before my eyes. It was like some horrid creature had somehow got into to his skin and now under the heat of its master's anger it had started to move around his forehead. It was quite a ghastly sight I can tell you.

'What is so wrong?'

'I only know of one time we have dressed like ladies, and we were told never to mention it to anyone, let alone to a reporter.'

'I didn't realise it was a secret. But I am asking about you face.'

'My face!' he hissed again.

'Yes it is quite unpleasant; it is like there are moveable lumps under your skin,' I stated to which he looked a little shocked but soon recovered himself. Without saying anything more to me, he turned his back towards me but I could tell by the movement of his right arm that he was feeling his face. He then sharply took something out of his pocket, which I can only presume to be his hipflask as he then made a sound as if he had taken a sip of something. He then felt his face again before turning to face me once more.

He looked at me for a long while, I can sense when someone is judging me and Inspector Godley was doing so right now. 'You are speaking the truth.' He said in his normal voice as if the horrid little scene had never happened and somehow, maybe through the medium of mind control I knew I was meant to forget it too.

'Why would I lie, to a policeman of all people?'

'That's what I was thinking,' he said as he carried on walking, why do I always seem to put my foot in it with everyone I meet? We carried on walking in silence and I knew it was my turn to break it.

'Why is being a woman, a problem when on a story about The Ripper?' I asked.

'What? Oh yes, well did you see the pictures of those poor women?'

'Yes.'

'And it didn't affect you?'

'Of course it did, it was a horrid and appalling thing what Jack the Ripper did to those poor women. It makes me want to work harder and be more professional when dealing with this case,' I said as I turned to look him in the eyes. The expression I saw starring back at me was of complete confusion. 'Oh I see what you mean now, no I did not faint in a womanly way.'

The Strange Case of Caroline Maxwell

'You are certainly different.'

'And made of stronger stuff I might add.' I replied.

'That too,' he said as we got to the door of The *Second Morgue*. 'There you go again, if there is anything else I can do for you, you know where I will always be.'

'Actually now you mention it, Inspector Godley? There might be something you can do for me.'

By Amanda Harvey Purse

Chapter Twenty One

'I think it is about time you call me George,' Inspector Godley butted in.

'Thank you, George you can help me with a little question that is playing on my mind.'

'You know I can help you?' he asked in a quizzical tone and look upon his face.

'Yes.'

'Well then, I seem to be pushed in some kind of corner, ask away.'

'It's about one of your cases; I just would like some more knowledge about it,' I said, for I did need to know why Mr. Abberline thought so highly of Mr. George

The Strange Case of Caroline Maxwell

Chapman to be Jack the Ripper. It may give me some insight to the Ex- Inspector's mind.

'One of *my* cases you say, mmm very interesting. Have you been finding things out about me? What would make you do that?'

'Somebody speaks very highly of you.'

'Oh and who would that be?'

'Mr. Abberline.'

There was again this awkward silence between us and I felt suddenly colder than I did a second ago. 'You spoke to Fred?' George asked quietly.

'Yes, considering the case I am working on, you will understand that I had to.'

'You spoke to Fred about The Ripper?'

'Yes.'

'Was he well? I mean did he cope well? What I mean to say, you see the last time I saw him he was, well he was I don't know the medical term for it but I will call it unwell, he actually spoke to you about The Ripper? I can't believe it and you, being a reporter too, how did you manage to do that? You didn't blackmail him did you?'

'Hold your horses George, how am I meant to manage all those questions and what did you mean when you said blackmail? What would I have to blackmail him on?'

'*I hope nothing.*'

'I didn't blackmail him if you must know; I had to sign a document saying he was the only one to see the printed interview before I published it.'

'Now that sounds like Fred,' he laughed.

'Glad you find it funny; he was quite strong willed at times.'

'That is Fred, but he actually spoke to you about The Ripper?'

'You seemed shocked by that.'

'It is hard for me to imagine for you see, Fred doesn't talk about that subject,' George said sadly and looked down at his feet.

'You mean to say, he *didn't* talk about that subject.'

The Strange Case of Caroline Maxwell

'Yes well, what makes you so special?'

'Well it was my expert interviewing skills, a dash of caring about him and a little pinch of help from Mrs Abberline,' I said in an offhand manner.

'I see, so how was he?' He asked looking up from his hooded eyebrows.

'He is healthy; the countryside is doing him some good.'

'What about his...'

'Dreams? Yes they are still there.'

'What! Even after I had caught him?' he asked with a questionable look.

'It is him I want to talk about.'

'Oh,' he said again glancing down at his feet.

'Please tell me about him.'

'Why? Is this the new thing you have found? Something about The Ripper case by chance?'

'I need to understand why Mr Abberline once thought he was The Ripper.'

'Once thought, you say? You mean he doesn't anymore?'

'No,' I said, it was my turn to sound gloomy.

'What makes him suddenly think that?'

'There was this moment after the last murder, someone told him he can leave The Ripper case as if they knew it was going to end.'

'You scandalous woman! You can't just say something like that in such a flippant way and in here of all places!' He suddenly shouted at the top of his voice.

...

'You asked, so I answered.'

'Do you not know what you have just said to me? Do you not even understand what you have just said to me?'

'I have answered you the truth, well the truth to what Mr. Abberline believes.'

'You have got to be joking! Are you that stupid? Fred was a good man and loyal to the force and he still is. You are a woman and you got all these things running

The Strange Case of Caroline Maxwell

around your pretty little head and have made a mistake,' Inspector George said rather too loudly than what was needed and started to drag me into the Unsolved Crimes room. He threw me next to the desk which hurt my side and made me drop my bag on the floor, I started rubbing my hip as it did injure me so as I noticed he was standing with his back to me behind the door holding it open and was looking out towards the hallway.

I couldn't believe what he had just said to me, I thought he was different how wrong could I be? I wasn't going to be spoken to like that, policeman or no policeman!

'How dare you!' I shouted at the back of him.

'For pity's sake, be quiet!' he whispered strongly without looking back at me. 'I don't think anyone else was down here, good,' he said as he shut the door and then faced me.

'I don't care if anyone else is down here! I care about the way I have been spoken too!' I shouted.

'You should you know,' he said as he sat on the desk.

'Not content with insulting me you move next to telling me what I should or should not be caring about!'

'When you get angry, you really get angry don't you?' he asked in an oddly calm manner.

'Well I never!'

'That wasn't a question I wanted answering, if you let me explain...'

'Dig yourself out of a hole you mean! Well dig anyway then!' I said as I waved a hand at him.

'Do you really want the rest of the police force to hear what you said to me?' he huffed.

'What I said to *you*? What about what you said to me? Oh I forgot I am just a *woman* aren't I?'

'Please calm yourself; I am trying to explain, what did you say about Fred?'

'About Mr Abberline you mean? Well just that he thought it was a little odd for someone to tell him to finish with The Ripper case after the last murder.'

'Exactly,' he said as a matter of factly.

The Strange Case of Caroline Maxwell

'I don't quite get what you mean,' I said in a lowered voice.

'Fred doesn't lie; he has never lied about anything as long as I have known him. So I have to think to myself well maybe it is you that is lying...'

'I beg your pardon!'

'Please, I had not finished. I decided in that spilt second that you are not the type of person to lie, you have honest eyes. So it means you are telling the truth...' he said before pausing. I wondered whether he had finished now.

'So that lead you to push me hard in here, which might I add has hurt me.' I said pointing to my side.

'Sorry that I have hurt you but *yes it has*, because if anyone had heard you, you would be in a lot of danger.'

'What danger could I possibly be in? I am in a police station.'

'It is not always the safest place to be; look I feel you do not understand the full situation. The truth you have just said is that *someone* told Fred to finish the Jack the Ripper case before we all knew it was the end, the person to tell Fred to do that would have been his boss which was

Anderson...' he paused again to look at me 'Chief Inspector Anderson...' he carried on looking at me 'Another policeman, do you know what that means?'

I was looking at him questionably as I tried to figure out in my head what he was trying to say to me and then it finally hit me and must have shown on my face. 'Can you now see the importance of what you said, in this police station?' He asked me.

'Yes, I am so sorry. I never thought about it.'

'Did he say anything else important?'

'Many things, but there was this something he mumbled once to me, I knew at the time it sounded important but for the life of me I can't remember what it was...'

'Maybe it will come back to you, now you want know about The George Chapman case where do you want me to start?'

'Start wherever you think is appropriate...' I said repeating a now dear old friend of yours, dear reader.

The Strange Case of Caroline Maxwell

Chapter Twenty Two

Inspector George Godley was a handsome man for his age in his own unique way, I thought as he offered me the only seat that was in the room. I could see what the ladies must have liked about him when he was younger, there was a playful side to him which I could imagine he used to his advantage to make the ladies swoon and to be as important as a policeman as well must have helped. But now he is older there was a sad and miserable feeling to him, the years of working in the force and seeing many horrid things have taken their toll.

Maybe that is what I saw in that monstrous moment, the Inspector is ill. I am no doctor so I do not understand what is making the Inspector ill but it must be something serious for I had never seen moving lumps before. It made him seem older in that moment; it must have been my deceitful eyes for I could have sworn I saw greyer hair underneath his normal black slick hair as if he was wearing a wig.

I laughed off that silly idea as took the chair and moved it so I was facing him and sat down, 'You are settled?' he asked.

'Yes,' I replied.

'Then I will begin,' he said like an old fashioned storyteller. 'I should start by saying that Mr. George Chapman was also called Mr. Severin Antonovich Klosowski.'

'Quite a mouth full, I would say.'

'Exactly, I will call him Chapman for easy use. Now, Chapman was born in Poland 1863, worked as an apprentice surgeon.'

'So worked with knifes.'

'You can be very quick thinking, Miss Amelia Jane Reporter.'

'Thank you, carry on.'

The Strange Case of Caroline Maxwell

'Well Chapman decided to come to England in June of 1887 and started work as a hairdresser as most surgeons do when scraping around for jobs, he moved around the East End quite a lot you see making him harder to catch, of course. He moved from West Indian Dock, Cable Street, and Whitechapel High Street. He then moved to George Yard.'

'The Ripper's killing ground, some say.'

'Yes, we are on the same page, you and me. His 'wife' Miss Lucy married him in 1889 but then his real wife moved to England from Poland but disappeared quickly...'

'I could imagine she might have been in the way, so to speak.'

'Yes, quite. They both left for America but something happened and Lucy came back on her own. Loneliness wasn't for long as Chapman came back...'

'Wasn't there some murders that happened in America that was the same as Jack the Ripper's?'

'Yes there was, Chapman then decided to leave Miss Lucy with a new born baby.'

'Maybe he didn't like children.'

'Maybe or maybe Miss Lucy knew something, something about his past habits shall we say; anyway in 1893 he lived with Miss Annie Chapman.'

'Hence his new name.'

'Quite right. He again left her and started living as man and wife with Mary Spink, they lived together in a pub called the Prince of Wales and there he poisoned her. He next hired a barmaid called Miss Taylor and they 'married' and moved once again to a different pub called The Grapes and there he poisoned her a few years ago. We started taking a notice of him then, he hired Miss Maud Marsh as a barmaid she...'

'Let me guess, she married him and then died shortly after.'

'Yes, this time he claimed on her life insurance and we got involved publicly. We had to bring up the bodies of all past 'wives'.'

'My god!'

'Yes our feeling entirely, but the most horrid thing was when we saw the bodies; they looked like they had

The Strange Case of Caroline Maxwell

only just been buried even though they were actually buried years ago!'

'There was no rotting of the bodies?' I asked. There was a pause before he answered as if he was thinking that I was a woman and should not be asking those things but he quickly dismissed that idea.

...

'They looked fresh; it was because of the poison he used. There was no smell or taste to it, so he could poison them quite easily but did not realised it kept them fresh, we got him. Although I will admit, we got him a little too late to save those women.'

'Do you think he could have been Jack the Ripper?'

'That is a hard question to answer, if Fred was making the case against Chapman, I would easily agree with him. Fred is never wrong, but if he now doubts himself I don't know what to think.'

'Did you know Mr. Abberline had been told to come of the case?'

'I knew something was wrong with Fred after the 'Kelly murder' but I thought that was because of the sight he saw in Millers Court.'

'He went there?'

'Yes, he was the first one in after they broke down the door. He was sick outside and then Anderson spoke to him, I had asked what he wanted and Fred just said Chief Inspector Anderson was telling him that Sir Charles Warren had resigned his post the night before.'

'Was there anything special between Chief Inspector Anderson and Mr. Abberline? Apart from one working underneath each other I mean.'

'Not that I can think of, they did not like each other I know that, they definitely did not have the *special* relationship.'

'The special relationship?' I asked.

'Surely you have heard of it being a reporter and all, the old secret handshake stuff.'

'I may well be a reporter but I am somewhat new to the game.'

The Strange Case of Caroline Maxwell

'You learn quickly then, to manage to get Fred to talk to you.'

'Thank you but I do not know of this special relationship and secret handshake.'

'Well we have to talk quietly; you don't know who is and who isn't in it. This relationship is a sort of get together of certain important people. They dress up with hoods and have meetings; they called themselves brothers of a lodge...' he said when the door burst open and there was a tall policeman standing in the doorway.

'Inspector Godley,' the policeman said.

'Who are you? Are you new?' was George's reply.

'Yes Sir, new to the beat. I was told to fetch you; there is a bit of a riot going on upstairs sir.'

'I am talking to a lady, go fetch someone else.'

'I was told to get you, Sir. I do not want to get in trouble on my first day Sir.'

George rolled his eyes, 'Fine, fine. Can you see to it that this lady doesn't need any more help and then follow me upstairs,' he said to the policeman.

By Amanda Harvey Purse

'Righty 'o Sir.'

'I will have to go,' Inspector George Godley said to me.

'Its fine, you have been very helpful. This time round that is,' I said I smiled at him. He smiled back and left the room.

I was left in a dark office with this unknown policeman who walked slowly towards me.

'Hello there, Miss...'

The Strange Case of Caroline Maxwell

Chapter Twenty Three

'Hello,' I said plainly towards him.

'Is there anything I can help you with Miss?' he asked.

'No I am quite alright here, thank you for offering but I don't want to detain you from you duties any longer.'

'Are you sure Miss?' he asked as he stood a few feet away from me, the policeman's helmet was casting a dark shadow over his face.

'What is it with that question Sir? Have I not answered you correctly Sir?' I asked. I was beginning to think that this stranger is questioning my ambiguity.

By Amanda Harvey Purse

'Don't get me wrong Miss, if you say you are quite alright then alright you should be, but when I look down and see a lady's handbag tossed across the room in such a way such as this,' he replied pointing to the items in question, 'and in such a careless way, I do find myself a little bamboozled with your answer.'

'Oh I see,' I said bending down to pick my notepad and pen that had rolled out of my handbag and was lying by my feet. 'There is nothing to worry about, I just happened to have dropped my bag that is all,' I lied. The policeman bent down too and picked up my bag and handed it back to me. I nodded a polite thank you.

'If you say so Miss, so what case do you happen to be writing about?' he asked. It was becoming rather peculiar talking to a man with no face as it was constantly casted in shadow; it felt a rather odd thing to do.

'What I am writing about you ask? You seem to think I am a writer then.'

'Why yes Miss, why else would you have a well filled notepad and pen in such a womanly bag?'

'Well I suppose you are only doing what you have been trained to do.'

The Strange Case of Caroline Maxwell

'Trained to do Miss? I do not seem to understand,' he said rather shyly. So shyly in fact that he seemed to step back into the shadows of the doorway, as if he was hiding his bashfulness or perhaps even something else.

'You have had some training to become a policeman I presume.'

'Oh I see Miss, yes I have. We all get training here, although some I have noticed have forgotten most of it, but not me Miss, not me. I never miss anything.'

'Well I must say that you are very observant for a new copper.'

'It has been said to me a few times, now is there anything I can help you with the case Miss?'

'No, you are possibly far too young to remember The Ripper.'

'The Ripper Miss? You mean Jack the Ripper?'

'Has there been another?'

'No Miss, I mean I hope not Miss. But young as I am, I still remember The Ripper Miss, scared half the neighbourhood he did...'

By Amanda Harvey Purse

'Only half the neighbourhood you say? Then you must have been brought up in a neighbourhood of hardnosed individuals, I must say.'

'Well no Miss, it was a saying Miss, I am sorry. I should stick with the facts when speaking Miss,' He said almost as if to himself rather than addressing me. 'Jack the ripper scared everybody, well apart from me Miss, if I was older miss I would have had him, mark my words.'

'Is that why you are a copper now?'

'*At the moment* I am Miss anyway, are you trying to find him Miss? Do you really think something in here that solves the case for you?'

'You seem unsure; do you not think that somewhere, with all these documents and files, holds the answer?'

'Well Miss, don't you think it is all observably simple if it was? And as far as I know, nothing about The Ripper is that simple. Maybe you should be looking somewhere else Miss.'

'Oh,' I said a little shocked at the turn of this conversation. 'Where would you suggest?'

The Strange Case of Caroline Maxwell

'Like I say I'm new to the beat, but wouldn't it be better to be in Whitechapel? I mean after all, he did kill there and *ALL* the victims came from there.'

'I will take note in what you say but don't you think you have left Inspector Godley a little too long?'

'Oh yes Miss, righty 'o Miss,' he said as he walked backwards until he was outside the room, he then gave me a polite nod of his helmet and shut the door from the other side.

...

There I was, alone back in the Unsolved Crimes Room looking at row upon row of all different files that were attached to all different cases but I knew where mine was. I emptied out all the files again on to the desk, there seemed to be less here than before, has someone else been here? Is someone else working on the same Ripper case?

As I placed the now empty file box to one side, I suddenly had a terribly awful thought. *Was there really someone following me in Hampshire?* I was certain there was a pair of eyes burning deeply at me in definite moments within my trip. But as I always felt those sensations near the Abberline's Manor House I naturally thought the eyes were coming from the house itself, now I am not so sure. I do not understand why I am thinking this way now, but what if the pair of eyes was coming from somewhere else or someone else? Someone I did not know, but someone watching me all the same.

I am being silly I decided with a shake of my head, I mean who would be watching me? What would be the purpose? For all I am doing is following leads in an unsolved crime, an unsolved crime of a serial killer that may or may not be still alive, that is all!

I must not let thoughts of nasty goings-on alter my feelings or my journalistic competence. Putting that sinister thought to the back of my mind I scanned through the reports on the case, somewhere here is Caroline Maxwell, I am sure of it.

After what seemed like hours of reading I finally had it.

The Strange Case of Caroline Maxwell

<u>Eye Witness report of Miss Caroline Maxwell</u>

<u>Dated 10/11/88</u>

My name is Miss Caroline Maxwell; I was the daughter to Mr. Henry Maxwell landlord of the Commercial Street Chambers, commonly known Crossingham's Lodging House and I have one child.

I have known the woman in question for about four months, but have only spoken to her twice before the morning of the 9th November.

On that night I saw Marie at the corner of Dorset Street where the beginning of the passageway that leads into Miller's Court starts, time was between eight and eight thirty that morning. She was wearing a green bodice with a dark coloured skirt and her favoured red crossover shawl.

By Amanda Harvey Purse

As I got nearer to her I could see that Marie is unwell and looking quite pale. She is very young you see, and known to be very beautiful but her prettiness gets her into many troubles and I believe she has a trouble of the womanly kind.

I asked her 'Are you alright Marie?'

'No I must have the horrors of drink in me.'

'If you think so, well maybe you should have another drink at Ringers to calm your nerves.'

The Ringers being another name for a public house at the end of the street.

'I have already tried that and look where that got me,' she said pointing to some sick on the floor.

The Strange Case of Caroline Maxwell

> 'I pity your condition.' I said as I walked on by. The next time I saw Marie was in the next hour, she was talking to a rather stout looking man, I could not see his face. They were outside Ringers; the time was nine thirty on the morning of the 9th November.

The record of this eye witness account was read and wrote in front of Inspector F.G Abberline. The only witness account to do so in the entire Ripper case...

Is this why he knew about Miss Caroline Maxwell? But why remember her still? What is so important about her? What am I failing to notice? What am I missing?

Come on Amelia think, what would Mr. Holmes do? What would Mr. Holmes see?

How important is this 'Marie'?

I decided to read everything the file had on the victims, I knew it was going to take time but I needed to truly understand these women, they are more than their death photographs, they were real living, breathing women at one point. I feel I must go back to that time to accurately and sincerely be true to the quest I am on.

By Amanda Harvey Purse

I must understand them...

...

Mrs Mary Ann Nichols was a daughter to a blacksmith called Mr. Edward Walker who lived in Dean Street, Fetter Lane. There is no mention of her mother, did she die and leave Mr. Edward Walker to look after her? Mr. Edward Walker lost his daughter to Jack, did he blame himself?

Mrs Mary Nichols married a Mr. William Nichols and she gave him five children but Mr. William Nichols left with the nanny, she was alone and probably felt used so she turned to drink which lead to her to be walking the streets to earn money for drink and rent. She was feeling down and useless, no one seemed to care for her, apart from Jack that is.

Mrs Annie Chapman was born to Mr. George Smith and Mrs Ruth Chapman. She married Mr. John Chapman and the couple seemed to be financially settled and moved to Winsor. Her luck was starting to run out with her children, one daughter died and one was crippled, Mrs Annie left her family and moved back to London. What happened? Did she regret leaving them?

The Strange Case of Caroline Maxwell

She lived at the same Lodging House Mrs Caroline's father owned, did they know each other? The post mortem says that Mrs Annie was dying of a brain and lung disease, was she in pain? She had bruises from a fight a few days before she died, did it hurt to walk the streets? Did Jack seem an *easy choice to her?*

Mrs Elizabeth Stride was a foreigner, could she speak any English? Did this make her feel alone and isolated? She had married Mr. Thomas Stride and then they opened a coffee shop, sounds enchanting but where did it go wrong? She left her husband, I cannot see why but she found her way to the East End living with Mr. Michael Kidney. Did he look after her? They lived in Dorset Street together, just a few yards from where Miss Mary Kelly died, did they know each other?

It seems like her only real luck in life was that she was not mutilated, Jack only had time to slit her throat, if you can call that 'luck'.

Miss Catherine Eddowes, maybe the saddest victim of all was born to a tinplate varnisher Mr. George Eddowes. She left home to live with a pensioner called Mr. Thomas Conway but something happened. She was then on her own until she met Mr. John Kelly, by all accounts there was real love between them. He had told her to pawn his boots for the money to get a bed for her while he went to a workhouse, bare footed.

But Miss Catherine had a vice and possibly spent the money she got on drink as she was found and arrested later making an impression of a fire engine. She was let go and she walked to her death.

Jack only had minutes to take her life and could have been caught by P.C Harvey, but instead Jack the Ripper only saw Harvey's light and carried on with his ghastly work. Jack the Ripper slashed at her face.

He attacked her face? Why her face? I just wonder if Jack the Ripper knew her...

Then there was Miss Mary Jane Kelly, nothing much is known about her, her life was an undocumented blur. The only 'facts' the police seem to know about her is from a Mr. Joseph Barrett, her boyfriend and he is only repeating what Miss Mary had said to him. How very sad is all that?

She was born in Limerick and moved to Wales at an early age, she married a man called Mr. Davis but he died leaving her alone. Somehow she got to London and

The Strange Case of Caroline Maxwell

rapidly went downhill; she lived on the notorious Ratcliff Highway which was the worse place to be in the East End. She had a few lovers but then met Mr. Joseph Barrett and settled down soon after at 13 Millers Court, she came off the streets and Joseph paid for both of them but then he lost his job. She went back to the streets, Mr. Joseph Barrett left and she met Jack.

How utterly sad these lives were, there was really no hope for any of them. The saddest thing of all was that these women would have carried on living their lives in this horrid disarray and chaos right under all our noses if it wasn't for their deaths.

If it wasn't for Jack the Ripper.

I read Miss Caroline Maxwell's statement over and over again. Although it felt somewhat satisfying to know I was right that I had seen her name in the Ripper file, a major thing was still puzzling me. Although Miss Caroline only mentions 'Marie', the fact that she muses over the date of the 9th of November means that she is meaning Miss Mary Jane Kelly, but if that is true there is a very important factual problem.

By Amanda Harvey Purse

When Miss Caroline Maxwell was talking to her 'Marie', Miss Mary Jane Kelly had been dead for at least two hours...

The Strange Case of Caroline Maxwell

Chapter Twenty Four

What a fatal flaw in the most significant case there has ever been. I am surely not the first person to observe this fault. How totally bizarre it all is, there is something here and there is something worth noting I can sense it.

Miss Caroline was called to court to repeat her story, she stood by it even though it was plainly pointed out to her that she could not have possibly seen, let alone talk to Miss Mary Kelly at the time and on the day in which she had stated.

But Miss Maxwell was adamant she had seen her and had spoken to her.

Why would Miss Caroline do this? She could have quite easily said she had got the day wrong or even the time, but she didn't. She stuck to her story, every last word of it.

Surely she knew she would be laughed out of court...

She was evidently dismissed speedily and swiftly, also I could imagine the laughs in court from the public and police as she walked away, but her statement still lies in the Ripper file as if it *was* important.

It is a document worth noting to be in here but why? Why did Mr. Abberline allow her to make this statement unquestionably knowing she would be called to court to be sniggered at and no doubt have the whole court in hysterics as they doubled up and fell about laughing at her? Why would he do that to a seriously quaint and strange lady? It doesn't seem to fit with the character of Mr. Abberline, he always helped and he went out of his way to be of some assistance. What was he doing to this woman? How was he helping the situation?

Mr. Abberline was correct in his statement, I must find this woman...

The Strange Case of Caroline Maxwell

As I wrote that sentence in my notepad the door of the office opened and Inspector George Godley stood there like some kind of conqueror in the doorway.

'I thought it would not be possible, but there you still are.'

'I seem to have got caught in 1888.'

'It's a bad illness Miss and I think it's catching.'

'Oh?'

'I have been thinking about Fred, do you think he did something that the higher ups didn't like?'

'What makes you think that?'

'There is something with this hooded brother's lark, I can feel it.'

Or brotherhood...

'That was it!'

'What was what?' Inspector George asked as he moved into the room and shut the door.

'I have remembered what Mr. Abberline mumbled, 'brotherhood' is what he said, he wanted to tell me more Inspector George but he changed his mind!'

'He actually said the word brotherhood? I knew there was something; I should have done something to help, but Fred didn't let me in.'

'Oh George! Does this really mean?' I asked as I glanced back at my notepad.

'Don't say it! Don't even think it! How can I carry on knowing what they might have done?'

'Killed those poor women, you mean,' I said still looking through my notes in my notepad; I was even looking at all the ink splashes and smudges so not to look up at the Inspector.

'And Fred knew, didn't he? He knew all this time! I looked up to him.' Inspector George's voice broke off which made me look across at him. He was leaning on a book case looking at the floor, he was depleted and dwindling. I stood up and walked over to him.

'No, don't do that George. Don't lose faith in Mr. Abberline, I trust my instincts with people, Mr. Abberline

The Strange Case of Caroline Maxwell

is a friendly and loyal man. He spent his whole career helping the public; you worked with him in 1888 didn't you?'

'You know I did.'

'Did you ever see him not doing his best to catch Jack the Ripper?'

'No.'

'Did you ever feel that he couldn't be bothered with the case?'

'No.'

'So do you not believe he did everything in his power to save those women?'

'Yes, I believe he did all he could think of and more. He got into a right state over this case, he started drinking because of it and he would have died for those women,' he said as he paused for a moment to think.

'I guess in a small way he did, always fighting the demon that still haunts his soul.' I said as Inspector George looked up at me, his eyes were watering. 'He did what he had to do, let's leave it there.'

By Amanda Harvey Purse

'Thank you,' was George's only reply. I nodded at him and walked back to the desk, putting all the documents back in the box. As I was putting the box back on the shelf, George asked 'Who is *'the woman'*?'

'I'm sorry what was that you said?' I asked back as I walked back towards him to notice he was looking at my notepad.

'Oh, someone called Miss Caroline Maxwell,' I said as I took my notepad out of sight and back in my bag, 'Oh my God!' I screamed...

The Strange Case of Caroline Maxwell

Chapter Twenty Five

'What is wrong?' asked George.

'*The* handkerchief!' I shrieked at him.

'The handkerchief?' he mused.

'Oh, I mean *my* handkerchief. It is missing, it was my mother's and I always carry it around with me. It was in my bag.'

'It couldn't have gone far; this is a police station after all.'

'I don't know where it could have gone!'

By Amanda Harvey Purse

'Miss Amelia Jane Reporter, listen to me,' he said as he leaned on my shoulders, 'You look tired, you are been in here for almost eight hours.'

'Eight hours?'

'Yes eight hours, you need to go home and rest. I will look for your handkerchief.'

'Thank you,' I said as Inspector George released his grasp of me and I got my bag and started for the door.

'Dew,' George said. I stopped and turned sharply around

'What did you say?'

'Dew, you need to speak to Inspector Walter Dew, he was with Fred when they went to see Miss Caroline Maxwell to get her statement.'

'Why didn't *you* go with Mr. Abberline?'

'Your guess is as good as mine; I didn't know where they were going. Fred didn't want me with him, but they came back with her statement, mad old cow.'

'You think she was mad?'

The Strange Case of Caroline Maxwell

'Makes sense don't you think, she comes out of nowhere, makes a statement that can't possibly be true and disappears again. Probably locked up in some asylum by now, I would say.'

'There is no information on where she is?'

'None at all, a little odd isn't it?'

'Very.'

'What is even stranger is where did Fred and Walter Dew go to get her statement? There was no information on her whereabouts then or now.'

'How do I meet this Inspector Walter Dew?'

'I'll arrange it; I will tell him to meet you in The Whitechapel Library in the High Street, at seven, Thursday night.'

'At night, you say?' I asked.

'Well he is a busy man during the day.'

'Of course, thank you George,' I smiled back at him.

'Anything for someone like you,' he said back as I shut the door and left him in the dark office.

...

I walked home quickly as it was getting quite dark, for the first time I was actually nervous to be a woman in London at night. Although I could feel my anxiousness I also felt ridiculous and a little foolish for feeling that way. After all what was I scared about? This was my home town; I had spent many a night in this city, trying my best to get research on one of my stories. Why would I be fearful of it now?

It is not like Jack the Ripper is still around to jump out at me, waving his knife.

No matter how hard I tried to make myself feel better and pretended to walk as natural as I would normally have, I did jump a mile high when a ginger cat bounded out at me from an alleyway.

1...2...3

When my breathing had gone back to its normal rate, I looked down at the cat, who was now rubbing itself around my ankles, 'Hey I know you don't I? You are little

The Strange Case of Caroline Maxwell

Mischief maker aren't you?' I asked it. She meowed back at me as if that was a form of reply. 'You have been missing for over a week, my neighbour has been worried sick. She does love you so and then you go missing on her, bad kitty, tut, tut.' I was only a block away from home and decided to pick Mischief up and carry her back. As she sat comfortably on my shoulder, purring, my thoughts started to wonder if I was in some kind of story, maybe this should be a story in the future for I feel as if this story will need to be told at some point. I was in an adventure novel with that thought in mind I suddenly remembered the works of Mr. Robert Lewis Stevenson although I hope I do not have to travel on the seven seas to find the where 'x' marks the spot in the final answer to this quest of mine.

    I carried on stoking Mischief until we had reached home, I lied to myself saying that I was comforting her but the truth was that I was comforting myself as I couldn't shake off the feeling that I was being followed again and I was so scared to look back.

    I tapped on the door of Miss Violet Smith, my next door neighbour and got no answer so I dropped the cat to the floor and as she sat in the same spot licking her paw while I left my neighbour a quick note,

By Amanda Harvey Purse

> Miss Violet Smith,
>
> I wanted to let you know I have found your pussycat unharmed and brought her home with me, you were not in when I knocked so I will keep her next door with me until you pick her up.
>
> Miss Amelia Christie

As I finished writing the note there was a loud noise coming from the other end of the street, I turned to look but I could not see further than my nose in this dark, but I was sure it sounded as if someone had fallen against a fence. I quickly slid the note under the door, grasped Mischief and ran inside my home next door.

...

As I leaned my back against my front door after shutting it, Mischeif worked her way out of my arms and jumped on my bed and started again to clean herself.

'Well I guess you've made yourself at home then,' I said to her. She made a slight noise with agreement and carried on licking. 'Well I suppose I better lay on some

The Strange Case of Caroline Maxwell

milk for my new lodger,' I tipped some milk on to a small plate and left it by the side of my bed, on the floor. Mischief instantly jumped off the bed and starting drinking, I guess the milk was to her liking, I gave her a quick stoke and laid down on my bed.

It was rather out of the ordinary for Miss Violet not to have answered her door at this time of night. She is one of these routine people, got up at seven walked to work by eight and was back home by six, that kind of thing. She was a little older than me so she was able to help me through the bad days when my mother passed on, leaving me alone in this world.

'You should get a pet Miss Amelia,' she once said to me as she was sitting on my bed drinking her tea.

'A pet you say? I am hardly in need to have a pet.'

'A cat looks after itself as long as you feed it and give it a good fussing once a day.'

'A cat as a pet?' I had questioned. 'I have never thought of having a cat as a pet, are they not a working animal, to keep the river rats at bay?'

By Amanda Harvey Purse

'You will be surprised how much a cat loves and it helps the loneliness.'

'I will look in to it,' I said, I never did of course. My work got in the way and made me focus on other things. As I thought about what life would be like to have a cat, to have something you would have to look after and would want you to look after it, Mischief chose that moment to jump on my chest and look down at me. I started stoking her and her eyes gave me a glance of contentment. I fell asleep quite easily to the sound of a ginger cat's gratification of its voice box.

...

In the middle of the night I woke to the sound of a sharp scream and then there was silence, Mischief was still sleeping at the bottom of my bed. Did I imagine a scream? It sounded like it came from next door, I better check it. I got up and went to Miss Violet's door and tapped on it but again there was no answer.

I wonder where Violet is at this time of night.

Well I cannot spend all my time wondering on this little matter I do need more sleep, working in Scotland Yard's Unsolved Crimes office has given me things to

The Strange Case of Caroline Maxwell

think on and also given me a headache so I decided to go back to bed.

The next time I woke it was because of a knock at my door, I washed quickly, dressed in new clothes and answered the door to a rather short and emaciated man wearing a grey suit which matched his dull grey eyes and he was the one to speak first. 'Sorry to bother you Miss, are you Miss Amelia Christie?'

'Why! I am Miss Amelia Christie, yes.'

'Oh good Miss, may I come in?'

'I'm sorry but I do not know who you are.'

'Ah yes, please excuse my haste, my name is Lestrade, I am an Inspector of Scotland Yard.'

Chapter Twenty Six

'Oh Inspector, please come in' I said as I stood to one side.

What could this Inspector want with me?

He walked in and took off his hat. 'Please sit wherever you can, sorry for the mess I don't always tend to be at home for long,' I replied.

'I can see that Miss,' he said as he sat on the bed.

'If this is because of me visiting The Yard,' I started.

'You have visited The Yard? Why would a young sensible lady like you have done that?'

The Strange Case of Caroline Maxwell

'Well I needed some information.'

'Information you say,' he said as his grey eyes seemed to turn a shade darker and gave the impression of questioning me further.

'Yes, well as that is clearly not why you are in my rooms, can I ask why you are?' I said. I did not feel it was right to open my mouth further on the case I am on.

You don't know who is and who isn't in it. Inspector George's words repeating in my mind, I did not know who was a *brother* and who was not.

'Quite Miss, I am here with sad news.'

'Oh?' I asked.

'Can you tell me where you were last night?'

'I got in rather late last night, I was busying working.'

'Working, you say Miss? I do hope you were not working the streets Miss,' he replied, quite rudely.

'Certainly not my dear Inspector! I suggest you be a little more polite in your questioning before I show you the door!'

By Amanda Harvey Purse

'I am truly sorry to offend you, you are quite correct. In my line of work you get used to women working the streets at night, but of course the world is changing isn't it? Well, did you hear anything odd in the night?'

'It is funny you should ask me that, I thought I heard a scream.'

'A scream Miss?'

'Yes, but it was so fast and then there was silence that I had thought I had just imagined it.'

'Of course,' he said as he was writing something down in his notepad.

'I thought it was coming from next door so I went over to check.'

'Oh you did, did you?'

'Yes you see, Miss Violet was not in when I called earlier to give her cat back,' I said pointing to the ginger cat who was sitting on my window sill looking out. 'I thought the sound was from her.'

'You thought it was Miss Smith's scream?'

The Strange Case of Caroline Maxwell

'Yes, I mean. Well I just thought she might be back.'

'Ah, and so she seemed to be Miss,' was his reply.

'Well if she was, she certainly didn't answer the door to me.'

'No that she would not have done.'

'I am sorry Inspector, I do not understand.'

'Miss Smith could not have possibly opened the door unless she had passed on to the other world and her spirit was capable of opening doors,' he said as he glanced up at me. I was taken back, my head felt light and my eye sight changed suddenly and everything went blurrily. 'Oh Miss, I should have more tact, you are going to faint aren't you?'

'No, I will be quite alright thank you Inspector. It was a shock I can tell you.'

'You may want to sit down.'

'No, Inspector I am fine.'

'Miss Violet Smith was murdered in her rooms last night.'

By Amanda Harvey Purse

'Murdered?'

'That is what I said Miss, she was drunk yes but her throat was cut and *other things* were done to her.'

'Other things you say?' I asked.

'Yes Miss, it was quite a shock to see her like that Miss. Why I haven't seen anything like it since...'

'Since what, Inspector?' I asked.

'Well since him Miss,' he said as he looked away from me and to my open bag. 'You do know who I mean Miss, I mean I don't want to frightened you but Miss Smith's murder was very similar to one of the *Jack the Ripper's murders of 1888.*'

'Inspector surely you are jesting with me!'

'No miss, I'm afraid not miss. The room was a mess too; the murderer was looking for something, I only managed to see your note to her pushed to one side by the door because I have a keen eye.'

'I see.'

'Well thank you for answering my questions, if I have any more I will knock again.'

The Strange Case of Caroline Maxwell

'Very well Inspector,' I said. The Inspector took that chance to stand up and walk to my door, 'Do you think he is back?' I asked myself out loud. The Inspector thought I was talking to him as he answered me.

'There is a high possibly that Jack the Ripper is back, if I was you I would be very careful, very careful indeed.'

...

I don't really want to mention to you dear reader the thoughts I was having when the Inspector had left and I was alone once more, but they were so vital to this story I feel I must urge myself to explain. I was seeing my room, my belongings and my possessions but they were different than normal, they were lighter coloured and less detailed. They were like the scenery on a theatre stage; they were just a faded background for the images I saw in front of them.

The images of the death photographs of the Jack the Ripper victims were floating across my eyes, they were horrid and atrocious. I tried shutting my eyes as if that would stop my thoughts, but it just made the moment worse, I started seeing the photographs not in black and white but full flown colour, I saw the dark horrifying red blood dripping from their bodies.

They all arrived in front of my eyes in the correct order and if they were all politely waiting their turn to show their deaths to me, but there was one more to the list.

There was poor, poor Miss Violet...

There was a part of me that wanted to know what actually had happened to her, I wanted to actually see her to say sorry and wish her my best in her new spiritual life whenever it takes her. Why would this mad man want to kill you Miss Violet? What had you done to make Jack the Ripper notice you and come out of retirement? You wasn't a woman of the night, you didn't earn your money on the streets. You were a polite young woman who was working hard with teaching children the wonderful music I had often heard you play. You didn't have any bad habits, you didn't drink.

Wait one second, Miss Violet you don't drink did you? Something wrong and quite possibly erroneous is going on here.

She was drunk yes but her throat was cut and other things were done to her.

The Strange Case of Caroline Maxwell

That is what Inspector Lestrade said, but that cannot be. Miss Violet wasn't a drinker; she was dead...*sorry Violet I didn't mean to say that.* She was not in favour of drinking, she thought it was vile almost sinful to drink and allow that liquid to control your bodies and change your attitude.

Why would she have been drunk?

I need to find out more information; I need to get in to Miss Violet's rooms without the police knowing, as I may not be able to explain the reason I was in there acceptably. I walked over to the window and peered out into the street. Inspector Lestrade was ordering his men about as two policemen carried an body shaped sheeting between them, down the main steps, passed the Inspector and around the corner.

Poor Miss Violet, I will get him Miss Violet. I will get the person that killed you, if it is the last thing I do...

My eyes gave a fleeting look back towards the Inspector, he was still talking to a policeman, the policeman gave a nod and the Inspector walked away from him. The policeman had been sent to guard the door; I would never be able to get into Miss Violet's rooms, well not through the front door anyway.

I paced my way through my room to the window on the other side facing the back of the building; Mischief was still sitting at this window so I started stoking her as I looked out towards the back door of Violet's rooms. I was faced with a shocking sight.

A pair of eyes was looking up at me...

When my senses came back to me I looked out again to see a policeman's face attached to the pair of eyes that had disturbed me, I quickly thought ahead and made the action of drinking tea with an invisible cup as if to ask him whether he wanted a drink, he shook his head and mouthed the words 'No, thank you,' and turned his head back to face the back yard.

'A little more planning is involved here,' I said out aloud.

'Meow,' replied Mischief.

I looked down at the cat; she was sitting there looking up at me intelligently. 'Yes, well I'm glad you

The Strange Case of Caroline Maxwell

agree,' I said as I lovingly tapped her nose. 'I suppose I must go out and get some meat for you, sweetie.'

'Meow.'

'What is the world coming to? Not only am I talking to a cat, but she is talking back to me.'

'Meow,' replied Mischief; I could only laugh as I placed more milk in her dish and a few crumbs of cheese beside it.

'Will that do for now?' I asked the cat. She jumped down from the window sill and ran over to the dish, smelled it and then smelled the cheese.

She looked up to me, made her now famous noise and started eating, 'I will take that as a yes then,' I said as I grabbed my bag and walked out of my door. I hope the market still has some nice pieces of meat at this time in the day and I feel a visit to the *chemist* is in order.

By Amanda Harvey Purse

Chapter Twenty Seven

As I walked outside the door I made a quick nod towards the policeman standing in front of Violet's door and he smiled back at me.

This policeman is far more approachable...

When I got to the market I noticed it was moderately assiduous at this late hour of the morning and I could see the cat meat stall was not there, some imagination is necessary for little Mischief to have some lunch.

'Get your last goose of the day!' a rather large woman shouted into the crowd of passersby. 'Get your goose fresh from me today,' I followed the voice and walked over to the stall.

The Strange Case of Caroline Maxwell

'Why if it isn't Mrs Oakshott! I have not seen you for many a year, how are you?' I asked.

'Agatha? Look at you all grown up,' she replied, my mother had known her from the good old days when they had spent time selling matches. When I was little Mrs Oakshott always had some sticky sweets for me, she was constantly kind and caring but for some reason she always called me Agatha...

'I am a little more grown yes,' I said looking down at my feet and then I glance back at the kind hearted old lady, 'what are you doing selling geese?' I asked.

'Got to change with the times love, more dosh in food these days, I raised these myself. Good old town bred geese and fresh from Brixton Road.'

'Is that so?' I asked looking at the last geese's to buy.

'But for you they are going cheap.' She said as she poked her finger friendly at my hip.

'Oh thank you but I was looking for something fishier. I might say.'

'Oh?' She said with a questionable look, as I had realised what I had said to her.

'I have a cat, newly required.'

'Oh of course, well is it a pretty little thing?'

'Yes, she is.'

'And does she give my little Agatha some comfort in these dark days?'

'I would guess she is beginning to.'

'Well then, she should have the best from Billingsgate.' she said as she handed me a dark, oily newspaper parcel.

'Oh Mrs Oakshott, I cannot take that!'

'Well you're a little too old for sticky sweets now, aren't you?' she asked as she poked with her bony jointed finger at my hip again.

'Thank you, I am sure she will make a meal out of this,' I said as I took the parcel in the other hand to that what was holding the chemist paper bag.

'Do you mind me asking whether she is indoors?'

The Strange Case of Caroline Maxwell

'Yes, why do you ask?'

'Has she been indoors for a while?' After a short pause, I had instantly begun to feel as if Mrs Oakshott was trying to hint towards something.

'Is there something I should know?' I asked as I turned towards her.

'Well I think you should pop over there to the fire bucket.'

'Fire bucket?'

'I won't tell anyone but I think you may need the sand from the bucket as someone may need to go wee wees.'

'Oh I see, thank you,' I said as I crept my way over to the bucket and took a few hand falls of sand and placed it inside the chemist bag, knowing that the original content of the bag was in a sealed bottle. I mouthed another 'thank you' towards Mrs Oakshott to which she nodded and I headed on my way home.

At home, I walked in and saw Mischief pacing the floor; she looked up at me with pleading eyes and meowed.

By Amanda Harvey Purse

'Ah I believe Mrs Oakshott was right,' I said as I placed an empty box on the floor and filled it up with sand. Mischief trotted over to have a look at what I was doing and plopped herself in the box but did nothing, she was just looking at me.

Finally I got the message...

'Oh okay I won't look at you,' I said as I moved over to the kettle.

I prepared a cup of sweet tea that was made even sweeter with the added ingredient of Latachosem I had purchased from the chemist. Mischief was now eating her fish as I turned to her and said 'That will do the trick,' she stopped eating at my statement, meowed and carried on eating. 'Glad you agree,' I answered back at her.

I carried the tea outside the front door and walked carefully down the steps, trying to not allow the dead leaves of the trees that lined my street to fly into it. The day was still as cold as the morning dawn, a sign that winter was on its way and it was an additional benefit to what I was planning to do.

Forgive me whoever is watching me, it is the only way and there will be no real harm.

The Strange Case of Caroline Maxwell

'Hello young policeman, what a horrid day it is becoming, don't you think?'

'Yes Miss, this is my first time guarding a murder scene and well, I don't mind saying I am cold to my bones!' He said as he was moving around on the spot.

'Well we can't have that; here have this lovely sweet tea, which will warm you up no end,' He went to grab the cup but stopped.

'Sorry Miss, but I don't think I am allowed to.'

'Oh I won't tell if you don't,' I said with a smile, he smiled back and took the cup.

'What's the worst that can happen?' He said as he gulped down all the contents of the cup.

'Precisely.' I whispered as I took the cup, said my goodbyes and walked back home.

Twenty minutes should be enough time...

One thing our neighbourhood tried to change was the community toilet that was placed at the end of the road; it was now looked upon as an outdated eye saw and now that many of us had outside toilets in our backyards it was seen as not essential to have it. But the problem was that a percentage of home owners did not have the money to install an outside loo and so needed the toilet at the end of the road. One of these home owners was Miss Violet, I often seen her in the early hours of the morning going off to the toilet that was placed just out of sight from our homes.

This fact believe it or not, was an advantage to me today.

Back inside my home with the smell of the fish lingering around the room I watched the young policeman who was new to guarding a murder scene from my window...

...

Twenty two minutes went by and the young policeman was moving uncomfortably within himself. I couldn't believe what I was watching, what had I done? I was feeling anxious and fretful, I felt like I was almost splitting in two, one half of me wanted to run outside and help to poor lad in his moment of need. But there was a part of me, a part that I feel ashamed to admit as it is rather too sinister for my own liking but I was watching this

The Strange Case of Caroline Maxwell

policeman with eagerness, it was almost thrilling and stimulating to watch this policeman appreciating that I was the only one who knew what was happening inside of him. The moment was coming and coming fast.

The moment happened three minutes later, the young policeman left his post of guarding his first murder scene for a more urgent matter of, *I'm guessing,* emptying his bowels in the only place he could do so, which just happened to be all the way to the end of the road and around the corner. *Isn't that just the way?*

I left my home and while whistling to myself managed to dig passed the first bush outside Violet's home looking for a piece of brass metal in the shape of a key, I came across what I was looking for and walked up the steps and entered her door as naturally as I could muster.

Once inside, my nature changed as I looked around at Miss Violet's belongings, the feeling I had looking at the waxworks of the Jack the Ripper victims was repeating. I felt I was prying into a life that I had no rights too.

Come on Amelia, think like Mr. Holmes, detached yourself if need be.

I looked for clues.

By Amanda Harvey Purse

There had been a mad struggle that I was sure of as the room was a mess, chairs were pulled to the corners of the room and the table that should have been standing vertical on top of the colourful rug was now laying on its side.

There was blood on the rug on the top left hand side, there was so much of it that I could see that it had leaked on to the other side and stained the wooden flooring underneath, but one thing was puzzling me...

Why has the rug moved? Surely the blood had marked the spot Violet died, she would have been lying right on top of the rug and yet the rug seems to have been moved.

I quickly whipped up the rug and investigated the wooden floor that was made up of small square panels, as my eyes passed across the floor they noticed in the left hand side a corner of a wooden panel was raised up slightly above the others. I bent down and wedged my fingers around the raised edge and lifted up, to my surprise the panel moved and there was a secret compartment underneath.

The Strange Case of Caroline Maxwell

It was empty, apart from some scraps of white and blue paper. As I lifted each piece out of its hiding place I could not believe what I saw.

There was one small piece of paper that seemed to have been burned at some point but what was left was a heading, a very important heading. It was of a shield with a red cross within it and black lions surrounding it, there in front of me was the heading of the City of London Police Force.

Why would Miss Violet have papers from the City of London Police Force? And who would be looking for them? Is this why she was killed? Did Miss Violet burn them and why was this action taken? Did someone want to make sure they were destroyed by fire? Did Miss Violet get in the way?

I quickly grabbed all the pieces of paper together and placed them in my pocket, I put the wooden panel back in its place and threw the rug on top, I left the house and deposited the key back in the bush where it came from. As I was about to re-enter my house I heard the footsteps of a man running, I glanced over to see the young policeman back at his post looking nervous but more comfortable.

By Amanda Harvey Purse

I had just made it in time.

It was curious, as I looked at the policeman and was sure he wasn't looking at me, I began to feel the hot burning sensation of a pair of eyes on me again. I glanced up and down the street and saw no one or at least that is what I first thought but then in the corner of my eye I caught a glimpse of a small grubby figure that was leaning on the lamppost.

My eyes stayed with this intriguing little cocky scamp, he must be a chimney sweep as his face was blackened. He was wearing a flat cap and small brown suit that had seen better times and was covered in dirt. His feet were bare and stained as the boots he owned are tied with their lace around his neck.

He met my gaze and topped his hat off to me as he ran off down the street, as I watched him leave I saw him manage to jump on the back of a coach that was also leaving the same street.

I walked into my home and shut the door. Although I smiled at the thought of the cheeky chappie, I couldn't help wondering how long he had been watching me...

The Strange Case of Caroline Maxwell

As night came I realised I had spent hours thinking about this one piece of Police documentation, *what was written on it? What made it so important it had to be burned and then killed for?*

At last I gave up and headed for a lay down, as I got myself comfortable in bed and closed my eyes, one thought startled me awake and made me sit upright.

Did the second stain on the flooring now match the first stain of the rug? Did I place the rug back in its right position? Would anyone notice the difference?

By Amanda Harvey Purse

Chapter Twenty Eight

I must have fallen asleep as I awoke to the sound of scratching; Mischief wanted to go out, I couldn't blame her; she was used to going out.

I got up and stared at the cat, 'I'll let you out if you promise to come back here, not next door. Here is your home and if you promise to come back you will have more fishy fish,' I said waving the leftovers of the fish Mischief had eaten last night. *What am I saying? She is no child, she is a cat.* 'Now do we have a deal?'

'Meow Meow.' she replied.

'Was that Meow Meow yes, or Meow Meow no?'

The Strange Case of Caroline Maxwell

'Meow Meow,' she paused and looked around the room, 'Meow,' she answered as she nodded.

'Glad to see you like your new home,' I said as I opened the window. As I watched her jump from the window sill to the wall to the floor and started chasing a spider into the undergrowth, I noticed the policeman who was guarding Violet's door yesterday was getting a stern talking too.

Oh no, I have been found out...

Inspector Lestrade grabbed the young policeman by his ear and dragged him inside Violet's house, after a few minutes I saw the Inspector and policeman leave the house once again with two extra guests.

Sherlock Holmes and Doctor Watson!

I opened the window wider to hear what was being said, 'Let this be a lesson to you, young lad. Nothing gets passed Inspector Lestrade, it took one look at the rug inside and I knew someone had been within that room!' the Inspector shouted.

Mr. Holmes coughed and said 'Well yes inspector, it is another feather in your cap!'

By Amanda Harvey Purse

The Inspector turned to face him but still talking to the young policeman when he said 'Well of course, Mr Holmes helped me pursue the idea, seeing the second stain on the wooden floor in the way you did of course.'

'Of course Lestrade,' Mr. Holmes replied and started to walk away, the Inspector carried on lecturing the policeman and didn't notice that Mr. Holmes had stopped, turned and was looking back into Violet's rooms. He then turned a little more glanced up and winked at me as if he had always known I had been watching him.

As I watched the celebrated detective and his good old sidekick walk back in the direction of Baker Street, I shut the window all the while knowing Mr. Holmes now knew it was *I who had entered next door.*

Well Mr. Holmes had decided not to tell the Inspector that I had entered next door, he knew it was connected with the case he had given me and didn't want Lestrade to know anything of it. I was not going to be the one to inform him either.

I had more important things to do, the meeting with Inspector Dew was due soon and I had to walk all the way to the East End. I made my way through the busy streets

The Strange Case of Caroline Maxwell

until I reached the dirtier streets and back alleyways of Bow Bells, Whitechapel. By now it was quite dark and gloomy, thoughts that I was now in the Ripper's killing ground was pushed to the back of my mind as I entered the library and the warmest of its new electric lighting hit my face.

The library itself had an eerie sense of loneliness; my shoes creaked on the shining marble flooring, the sound left my feet, echoed around the room and entered back inside my ears. As I stepped further inside the one room the smell of musky old books itched my nose, and delighted my senses. For you see being a writer of some sort, I take great pleasure in seeing many books all lined up in a row. All the while knowing; that if I was to take one book off the old wooden shelves I would be instantly transformed into another fictional world, trusting the writer to lead me to the end of the book.

I always thought that if I didn't make it as a journalist I would be a writer of fictional novels, to see my name on a number of books, all lined in a row would be such a delight to me.

'Miss?' asked a polite and high toned voice. I turned to see an elderly gentleman standing behind a

By Amanda Harvey Purse

wooden desk, looking at me. He was trying to stand up straight but with his age, his legs bowed and there was a slight arch to his back. He had the whitest of hair on his head and same colour moustache that I had ever seen, but I could not see the colour of his eyes as his arching forced his head to tilt to some extent down, and with the dim lighting in that corner to which he had placed himself, made it hard for me to pick out another features.

'Oh hello,' I said to him as I moved faintly nearer to him. 'I am meeting a policeman here; can you tell me whether a policeman has been in?'

'A policeman you say,' he said pausing to think.

'His name is Inspector Dew,' I said trying to help as I passed the old man my card, I had wanted to act more acceptable in front of this Inspector than I did the last ex-Inspector. So I had made a few cards with my name on it, nothing fancy for you see dear reader I couldn't afford fancy but it said my name and the word 'Writer' on it because somehow the word 'Journalist' did not seem quite right.

'What Walter you mean? No Walter hasn't not been in here, in truth Miss, Walter doesn't get the time to visit

The Strange Case of Caroline Maxwell

Whitechapel anymore, since he was taken off his beat,' the old man said as he looked at my card, raised one of his thick, bushy eyebrows and placed the card into his small pocket within his waistcoat.

'You seem to know of him.'

'I have worked here for many years Miss, I am as old as the books here Miss and Walter Dew was a young policeman here when I started. He was a nice fellow, always checking in here to see if there were any break-ins. He knew everyone and everyone trusted him. It was a little sad to see him promoted and leave this area but we are all very proud of him, as if he was one of our own. One of the family, I should say. I'm sure he will be famous for catching some criminal or another in future years.'

'He sounds like a man devoted to his job.'

'Oh yes Miss, he certainly is. But you see most policemen who were around sixteen years ago and were involved with the horrible scenes we were left with, are normally devoted to catching criminals.'

...

'You are talking about Jack the Ripper aren't you?'

By Amanda Harvey Purse

'Yes, this used to be such a quiet place. Now we are famous for a murderer and probably always will be, it is quite sad really, if you think about it in that way,' he said looking further down towards the desk, so he was now not looking at me at all.

'The Inspector was involved, I know with the last woman.'

'You are different I can see that,' he said still without looking at me.

'Excuse me?' I asked a little caught off guard.

'I was just thinking to myself, you are different.'

'I know that is what you said, but I was just wondering why you said it.'

'Oh I see, well I don't like to make presumptions, but I thought you were different the moment I saw you, then you hand me a card that clearly states you are a writer. I often think that a card defines someone don't you think?'

'Defines someone, you say?'

'Yes well, take your cards for example. They are clean cut paper, not the best quality but not the worst,

The Strange Case of Caroline Maxwell

which tells me you want to be professional, but there is a side to you that thought you don't want to waste money on high quality pieces of card that people normal throw away at the end of the week. So you are sensible, a sensible young lady that works for her bread and butter, very different indeed.'

'I believe you are right,' I managed to say before the old man carried on, it was funny really, the more I listened to this old librarian the more I felt as if I was in a lecture room being taught 'the meaning of people'.

'Then you say that,' he said in a heartily tone.

'What? I just said I believe you are right,' I replied.

'No, no, my dear that is not what I was on about.'

'Oh?'

'You said something before that,' he said as he turned to face me, his face still cast in a dim shadow.

'I did?'

'Yes, my dear. You said 'woman'. You said 'the last woman' can see how very different you are, even if you do not grasp at what you said?'

'Yes I said the Inspector was involved with the case of the last woman.'

'That you did, my dear. Most people would have said that sentence in another way, they would not have been able to help themselves but describe the last person as 'Victim'. Most people would have said 'the last victim, Jack's last victim' but you said 'woman'. You said it innocently enough I grant you, but that is what makes it all the more caring. You said 'woman' because you meant 'woman' that is how you see her.'

'I have never thought about it before.'

'Why should you? But to everyone else it shows you care without thinking. You have got to understand, my dear, those who knew her all thought of her as a person not some murdered pieces of flesh. She was somebody, not just Jack the Ripper's toy that he used and then destroyed when he got bored. It is nice to see that we locals are not the only ones to think in this way, but you do too and with you being a writer. Well, my dear it is all a little...'

'Different,' I answered.

'Indeed,' he old man simply responded. There was a long pause as I felt very touched by how much the

The Strange Case of Caroline Maxwell

women who were killed were thought of in their own part of the world. It is easy to imagine, the women as something rather than someone. Even just sixteen years on the women that just happened to be in the wrong place at the wrong time were starting to disappear into myths and be something of a fairy tale, a *Grim* Fairy Tale.

I could not help but notice the books that I had cherished when I first came in here and I wondered if in a few years there will be books on these very shelves about Jack the Ripper. Maybe there will be a whole section devoted to him and what he has done and these poor women, who will be mentioned in every one of these books, will fade into the background. They will have their part to play of course, because without those, people will not be in fear of the mighty Jack the Ripper but their part will get washed out behind the unknown mask of the famous serial killer.

These women will seem to be fiction for most generations, their lives, their families, their thoughts, their dreams all pushed onto a few pages within an entire book as if the writer wrote about them on a whim before he gets to the 'good part' of guessing who Jack the Ripper was. These women were more than that and being here in their own part of the East End, standing in front of a local man I was just beginning to understand the unique situation I have been placed in.

This was never about me riding on the coattails of a madman; this was never about me being another journalist to write about the famous Jack the Ripper. Other journalists after me will never get this chance to feel for these women in the proper way, to mourn after them as human beings before they turn into fictional characters of legend. I am given this chance to write about these poor women while they are just that, women. That is why I am different, that is what Mr. Holmes had seen and known from the very start...

Maybe, just maybe Mr. Sherlock Holmes has a heart and cannot detach himself away from every emotion. Maybe just maybe, Mr. Sherlock Holmes cannot let this case go, not because it is unanswered but because the story has not been told in the proper way. It has not been told in the view of the murdered women.

'Yes, it was quite heartbreaking for him really, Walter knew her, you see,' the old man carried as if there had never been this emotional moment between us.

The Strange Case of Caroline Maxwell

'He knew her?' I questioned as I moved nearer to which he moved further away, so I stopped which in turn made him stop. There was something strange about this old man, it almost seemed as if he didn't want me to see his face as anytime I moved closer, he moved further away like a childish game. I guess I was just imagining it, after all I knew being in Whitechapel at this time of night had already transformed me into a shaking wreck, no matter how hard I tried to act normal and professional.

'Yes,' he carried on, 'Walter always looked after the ladies of the night shall we say and she was one of the loveable ones, cheeky but polite. Walter would have done anything to save them, he blamed himself.'

'No doubt he did, I guess many policemen did at the time and still do.' I said glancing down at the marble flooring.

'My sentiments exactly.' the old man sadly said, 'Is there anything else I can do for you? As I am sorry to say but I am closing.'

'You are closing already?'

'We always close early today.'

By Amanda Harvey Purse

'I don't understand, I was told to meet Inspector Walter Dew in here at this time.'

'I can't help you there Miss, but it sounds as if you have been put on a wild goose chase.'

Something is telling me this old man was correct but why? Why would Inspector Godley have lied to me, to drag me here? To drag me to the streets of Whitechapel, the Ripper's killing ground...

As I left the library I heard to the old man lock the doors after me and once again I was on the damp, cold alleyways of the East End alone, or that was what I first thought when I started my walking pace for home.

The Strange Case of Caroline Maxwell

Chapter Twenty Nine

I had got no further than a few paces when I felt the returning burning sensation of someone watching me, at first I thought it was my imagination for I was allowing this case to control my every sense of being but I was being a fool.

Yes I am on a Jack the Ripper quest of sorts, which has brought me right on the same streets as his victims but it is silly to think that the bogie man is still upon us, and for him to be following me now is quite ridiculous and yet I can distinctly smell tobacco of the Canadian variety and cheap gin coming up close behind me...

By Amanda Harvey Purse

I stopped my walking pace to stillness and when my breathing returned to the same speed I took the courage to face my fears and turned around.

I was greeted with the sight of a horrid man, standing inches away from my own face; he wore a large floppy hat that curled down at the ends, from years of wear and tear no doubt. I could not see his eyes but I knew he had a pair of them for I felt them burning into my soul, I was so close to him that I could see his thick ginger beard was flickered with grey strands and what looked like stale bread crumbs within it. Suddenly as if he knew I was looking towards his mouth area, he opened it to smile at me, showing me his lack of teeth and his bad breath.

'Hello Missie,' he simply said.

'You have been following me,' I stated back at him without a tumble in my voice.

'And what exactly, of that miss?' he asked as he stood there bold as brass.

'I mean that I would like to know why you have been following me?'

'Oh you would, would you?'

The Strange Case of Caroline Maxwell

'Yes, I would as it comes.'

'Well Miss, you see it's like this. I was in my local *as it comes*; minding my own business as I normally do and this fella comes in and walks right up to me. He asks me if I'm busy, if I have any work on. Well you see the docks have been laying off people everywhere, and times are hard as they say, so say I haven't any work, this fella then smiles at me, quite snake like, me thinks. He buys me a drink and I drink it, he offers me a job.'

'This is all very touching, a day in the life of an East End bum and all that but, why are you following me?'

'Because my dear, you are the job.'

'I am what?'

'I was told that a smart young lady would be walking out of the Whitechapel Library at seven o'clock and there you were, I was told to follow you until we reached a dark alleyway, I was going to chose the alleyway further up but as you have stopped here, here will have to do.' He said as he shoved me against the cold, slimy brick wall. The sensation of pain running across my back was considerable and it made me drop my bag, the brute still had hold of me when I asked,

By Amanda Harvey Purse

'Why are you doing this?'

'Like I said miss, I was told to.'

'By whom?'

'Well in truth Miss, I have no idea, but I will be paid well and that is all that matters in the end,' he replied as he slapped me across the face with some significant force to which I knew I would have a bruised cheek in the morning, if I survive to see morning that is. 'I was told to tell you to leave the past in the past, for you are on a dangerous path and next time you might not live to tell any more stories, have you got the message Miss?'

'Yes, I understand,' I said with difficulty as my jaw was hurting and stiffing up.

'Then I have done my job and will get paid,' he said when suddenly another pair of footsteps came rushing into earshot.

'Put that young lady down!' shouted what I thought was a middle aged policeman as he stood by the side of me, 'Down I said! Come on now fella, you don't want me to take you to the station now do you?' he asked to which the brute dropped me.

The Strange Case of Caroline Maxwell

'Well this wasn't a part of the deal,' he said and ran off into the smoky atmosphere and disappeared. When the brute dropped me I slid down the wall until I hit the floor and I stayed there.

The policeman bent down and asked 'Are you alright Miss? That ruffian had you tight and strong back there.'

'He sure did,' I said rubbing my cheek.

'What did he want?'

'To pass on a message, I guess.'

'Oh Miss, you are not getting yourself into trouble are you Miss? There are loads of horrible thugs on the streets of Whitechapel. Bad things happen here.'

'Yes I can see that,' I said as I tried to stand up but in the end I needed help from the policeman and attached myself to him. 'When you mention 'bad things' you are talking about Jack the Ripper aren't you?'

'I can see why you would think that; he has made this area famous hasn't he? But no, I try my best not to talk about *him*; I was actually thinking of the Wainwrights.'

By Amanda Harvey Purse

'The Wainwrights you say?' I asked.

'Of course you seem too young to remember, I am sorry to have mentioned the case.'

'No, it is quite alright, please tell me.' I told him to which he gave me a questionable look. 'It might take my mind away from what has just happened,' I replied.

'What a strange lady you are, I have never known a lady other than my flower that is, to rejoiced in crimes.'

'It has always been in my blood, you see I have always wanted to be a crime writer.'

'Is that so? Well it would make a difference, reading of a crime from a woman's point of view I guess, you are sure you are alright Miss?' he asked.

'Yes, I am quite alright.'

'Then I will tell you about the Wainwrights, on the walk to your house, just to double check that you get home without more trouble.'

'If you must, might I ask what a kind old City Policeman is doing in the East End?' I asked as I glanced at his uniform and making a mental note of the crossed shield placed on his policemen's helmet.

'I live here miss, I was planning to move up west to be closer to me loved one, my flower but I guess I have to stay here now,' He said looking down at the cobbled stones.

'Oh? And why is that?'

'My flower has passed on, last night in fact.' He whispered. There was a silent moment between us and then with the shake of his head this policeman's head he changed the subject.

...

'The year was 1875 as I recall, being such a young boy at the time, years just roll into one and another these days.'

'Wait a minute, how old are you?' I asked as he laughed at my question.

'Yes well, you wouldn't have been the first to think I am younger than I actually am. My skin seems to relish this London smog. I'll carry on if you didn't mind.'

filled with chloride of lime and a hammer, a chopper and a spade nearby. But although the body couldn't be identified, local rumour spread that it was one Miss Harriet Lane who had been missing for a whole year.'

'Did this, Miss Harriet Lane know Mr Wainwright?'

'Yes, you could say that. Miss Harriet Lane was a milliner working on the same Whitechapel Road when she met Mr. Wainwright, she knew he was already married but soon a 'Mr and Mrs Percy King' were married.'

'Let me guess, Mr and Mrs King were Mr Wainwright and Miss Lane?'

'You are correct, Mr. Wainwright now had two families. One under his real name in which he had five children and one as Mr King who had two children, he was paying 'Mrs King' five pound a week for the care of his two children.'

'A sum worth a *King's* ransom indeed for Mrs King, I would say.'

'Quite so Miss,' the policeman said with a heartily laugh, 'You sure are quick with the witticism Miss.'

The Strange Case of Caroline Maxwell

'I have been told this many times, it has not always been a helpful tact of mine.'

'I can imagine that some men might take offence to a charming lady with an intelligent mind, some men Miss but not me. I have been around strong minded woman all my life.'

'You talk as if you could chain yourself to the gates of Downing Street with all the other women, it would get the press buzzing.'

'That it would certainly do,' he replied laughing. 'But I think my flower did enough protesting for the both of us,' he seemed to drift off into a world of his own, saying his lover's pet name again. He was in pain, emotional pain but in a time such as this a man must not show his pain, something I find uncontrollably wrong. I tried to pull him back to the crime story he was talking about, but this time it was more for him than me.

'Mr. Wainwright was paying his second wife a lot of money,' I mentioned.

'What? Oh yes that was what I was talking about, but then Mr. Wainwright lost his job and his double life fell apart. Mrs King got drunk and threatens to tell Mrs

Wainwright all about the relationship she has been having with her husband.'

'Ah I begin to see.'

'Quite Miss, Mrs King was never seen again.'

'So he was hanged?'

'Very much so Miss, you know, now I think back I even watched a play about him once, in some back street theatre. It was a delight to watch and it was going well so I thought, until it got to the hanging scene.'

'Oh, what happened?'

'Something went wrong and the actor playing Mr. Wainwright almost got hanged in real life as well!'

'That's terrible!'

'Quite Miss, but it heighted my thoughts that horrid men have the devil behind them, but that night the devil must have got confused.'

'I can see why you would feel like that. This is my home,' I said pointing to my door. 'Thank you for carrying me all this way; it must have taken you well out of your way so I appreciate you helping me in my time of need.'

The Strange Case of Caroline Maxwell

'You live here Miss?' he asked as he let me have my own weight back again and without seemingly taking any notice of anything I had just mentioned to him.

'Yes,' I answered a little surprised by the suddenness of his question. 'Why? Does that bother you?' I asked as by the look upon his face I could clearly see that something was wrong with him.

'In a way Miss, it does,' he said looking sadly towards my ex-neighbour's door. As I gazed at his expression I could see more than sadness, I could see utter despondency. There was sorrow in his eyes, there was grief. Suddenly with the word 'grief' rolling around inside my head, things began to click into place, *'My flower has passed on, last night in fact.'* Was what he had said to me before the Wainwright case had entered his head and before he had spoken a single word of it. This policeman is a proud man, his boots are cleanly polished and he had gone to the trouble of polishing his buttons and waxing his moustache. He knew he had let his guard down to an unknown lady, a lady who seemed to be interested in crimes.

This policeman thinks quickly, much more quickly than any of the policeman I saw in Scotland Yard. So to cover him he rapidly changes the conversation with flair, a conversation he knows would divert the opinion of this young lady's thoughts of him, for after all he is a policeman and can judge the character of some unknown being faster than most. He judged that this lady was a quick thinker, a lady with deliberation of someone's temperament; he did not want this lady to believe him to be a soft touch as if it would hurt his pride, so he gave a crime case to think about and I fell for it. But now, in that instant I knew why he was hiding his grief, his flower was my ex-neighbour.

'You can learn a lot of things from the flowers,' I mentioned almost as a whisper.

'What?' he asked at that last statement of mine, that had a certain Mr. Holmes ring to it and it had broken his heart-rending mood.

'Your loved one was Miss Violet Smith wasn't she?'

'My dear, dear flower,' he whimpered, holding back his tears and all the while knowing his cover of his pride was blown.

'Would you like some tea?' I asked.

The Strange Case of Caroline Maxwell

'Yes Miss that would be very kind of you.'

By Amanda Harvey Purse

Chapter Thirty

We both entered my rooms, I lit a few candles that I had left lying around on their stands and instantly felt the warmth across the top of my thumb knuckle running down to my thumbnail, I turned slowly around to see that the policeman had made himself at home and placed himself on the one remaining chair I had left. I smiled at him and he started laughing.

'What is the laughing matter?' I asked.

'I was just thinking that it is close to Hallows Eve.'

'Yes?'

'Well let's say, I'm ready for my ghost story.'

The Strange Case of Caroline Maxwell

'What?' I asked as I watched him point at me, up and down. I took a fleeting look at myself and noticed I was half in shadow and half lit in the flickering glow on the candle I was holding, I knew at once what I must have looked like from the policeman's point of view. 'Oh yes I see what you mean now,' I said as I held the candle at waist height instead of just below my chin. 'But please no talk of ghosts tonight, I feel as if this case, this strange case I am on is full of ghosts that have laid in conflict and turmoil for many a year.'

'I am guessing it is also leading you into trouble Miss, going by the state I found you in tonight.'

'Quite right,' I said as the thought of what that ruffian had done to me entered back in the foremost of my mind leading me to instantly start rubbing my jaw again as the pain had returned like a bad penny.

'Are you really fine Miss? Should I have taken you to a hospital?'

'No, I'm fine. A little battered and a little bruised but nothing to worry about... Now you wanted some tea didn't you? I'll just place the kettle on the fire,' I said as I moved about my room, knowing all the while that the policeman was staring at the wall between mine and Violet's room. 'So can I ask the name of my knight in shining armour?'

'Oh yes, sorry about that, the name is Collard, Edward Collard. But you can call me Teddy.'

'Well there you go, PC Teddy,' I said as I passed him a steamy hot mug of lemon tea.

We had sat in my cold room with only the light from three candles, two of which were placed half way up the slightly damp walled corners of my little space and one that was now placed on the small wooden table that stood in between us, as we drank our hot drinks, allowing the warm liquid to heat up our insides. We had not said another thing to each other for a long time as if we can only focus on one task at a time and somehow we had both decided that drinking our tea was more important than talking.

The silence was mysteriously not strange, it felt homely and comforting to have someone sitting here enjoying my company without even having to say so. Although I was quite fond of the situation I had found myself in, after what I had been shockingly put through this very night, it was me that broke the stillness, by just

The Strange Case of Caroline Maxwell

glancing up at my window to see a pair of shining cat's eyes staring back at me.

'Oh yes, I think you will know my new lodger,' I said as I walked over to the window and opened it allowing Mischief to wander, very slowly I might add, in. She ran straight to her dish, passing Teddy without even a glance his way. As I shut the window, I heard Teddy proclaim.

'By Jove! It's little Mischief! I had forgotten all about you,' he started stoking her, to be honest I don't think Mischief was paying any attention to Teddy's actions as her concentration was firmly on the fact that there was no food in her dish and the look upon her face was saying that 'she has not trained me well enough yet'. 'Well I can see you have made yourself at home here, thank you for doing that Miss.'

'I would not thank me for it; to be honest I don't think I had a choice in the matter. Although I think she is after her dinner,' I said as I walked passed Mischief and Teddy to get to my cupboard to find some cheese, that I crumbled into to pieces and placed on her dish, to which Mischief made a certain noise and tucked right in.

'Well at least I know she is being looked after.'

By Amanda Harvey Purse

'I don't quite know who is looking after whom; she has certainly given me company, one up side to this quite ghastly case I have found myself on.'

'If you don't mind me asking, you talk of a case that you are working on, this case is very dangerous I can see, I was wondering if you were maybe some sort of police...woman?'

'A policewoman, you say! I have never heard of such a thing!' I laughed.

'I know it sounded a little odd but I have always thought that one day there will be women in the force.'

'Really? Well I can't see that happening anytime soon.'

'It might happen sooner than we all think, if you are not working for the police, what do you do?' He asked as he placed his empty mug on the table and sat back in his chair, 'I mean I don't even know your name.'

'That is very true, my name is Miss Amelia Christie and I'm a writer of sorts.'

The Strange Case of Caroline Maxwell

'Writer hey? Well that is a surprise and you have found this case that has put you in danger? I must say you seem strong willed.'

'In truth I did not realise I was in any danger at all until tonight.'

'Well I hate to say this, but I wager all my experience in the force to say that I think you are and living next-door to what happened to my Miss Violet well I cannot help but think there is evil afoot here.'

'You think what happened to me tonight and what happened to Miss Violet is connected?' I asked as I placed my mug on the table as I did so I glanced down at my hand and noticed my hand was shaking for Teddy had just said the one thing that had been playing on my mind in the long silence we had shared.

'That was what I was thinking.'

'Why so?'

'The ruffian, I knew him or should I say I met him before.'

'Oh, where?'

By Amanda Harvey Purse

'Or more importantly when?' he plainly said.

'What?'

'I met him coming out of a police station with a policeman, sixteen years ago. He had been arrested then released you see.'

'Once a ruffian, always a ruffian.'

'Quite, but he was arrested for something a little more depraved than slapping someone around a bit, although I am sure what he did to you must of hurt of course.'

'It did a bit, what was he arrested for?'

'Well he was arrested for being Jack the Ripper.' He said as he sat forward, allowing the candle to light up just his face as if him mentioning Jack the Ripper wasn't enough to scare me, now Teddy's face looked foreboding.

...

'Jack the Ripper!' I proclaimed in a state of shock. I must have said it quite loudly as Mischief stopped eating to look at me, 'Sorry Mischief, I did not mean to say that so

The Strange Case of Caroline Maxwell

loud,' Mischeif carried on eating, while Teddy carried on with his story.

'Yes, he was one of the first few the Metropolitan Police arrested of being Jack.'

'And what happened to Miss Violet...'

'Has made the police think that Jack's back.'

'Inspector Lestrade has told me that.'

'It is all too much a coincidence, don't you think?'

'To be honest, I don't like what I am thinking.'

'And what with the missing papers...'

'Yes,' I said in a dreamily way. 'Wait, what did you just say?'

'Oh it's nothing, probably nothing anyway. You see, no one knew about them so why take them?'

'You said papers, papers from the City of London Police by any chance?'

'Well, yes in a way Miss, you see I was doing some researching on someone and well I wasn't meant to be doing it, but something seemed to me to not be quite right and well I like to do my own digging around sometimes, but if my bosses found out that I was doing it on the wage they would not be too happy. So I often took what I found out home with me, or more to the point to Miss Violet's and told her to keep them safe.'

'And she hid them in a secret compartment in the wooden panels in her room, under a rug.' I said as I moved over to my bag and started searching through.

'How did you know that Miss?'

'Because I have the remains of the burned papers here,' I said as I showed them to him.

'These are them! They *were* after them! Well I'd be! This means only one thing and a horrifying conclusion!'

'What is that?'

'That Jack the Ripper is back and knows I am after him!'

'It seems I am not the only one who is in danger.'

The Strange Case of Caroline Maxwell

'Quite, I must leave as you may have someone following you and if he sees me, well it will not be pretty,' he said as he took his turn to leave.

'Can't you at least tell me, who Jack the Ripper is?'

'Not if you life depended on it, in fact your life may well depend on *not* knowing who Jack the Ripper is!' Within a fleeting moment Teddy Collard had left me and Mischief, alone, feeling a little nervous and unable to sleep.

By Amanda Harvey Purse

Chapter Thirty One

So Jack the Ripper was back and it was he that killed Miss Violet Smith, Jack the Ripper was just next door to me two nights ago, killing my neighbour while I was asleep. All those years ago I felt as if I had missed out on something, something innovative and new because of my young age. Not once did I think of myself as lucky to not have seen or experienced the fear this murderer caused, to lie in bed and wonder where Jack the Ripper was or what Jack the Ripper was doing? Would he kill again? Would he kill me? Would he kill someone I knew?

Well now I am lying in bed wondering where Jack was and I am wondering what Jack the Ripper is doing now. Will he kill again? Will he kill someone else I know? Will he kill me?

The Strange Case of Caroline Maxwell

It is as if what I am doing, what I have done has somehow brought the famous serial killer back to life. As if Jack the Ripper has jumped out of my notebook and materialize back into human form to run around killing innocent women again.

As if I am Victor Frankenstein and I have recreated a monster.

Is this all my fault?

Before I knew it, it was morning and things seemed different and a little clearer in the natural light, all the ghastly nightmares and dreadful thoughts of my childish bogie man seemed ridiculous and quite impractical really, I laughed at how silly I had been. I had been in Whitechapel for one night and look what it had done to me, it turned a quite sensible young lady into a shivering wreck that jumped at every noise London had to offer her. Mischeif was fine and slept right through the night, making the occasional purring noise with every twitch of her whiskers or jerk of her legs. But of course she had, had her forty winks, what was a serial murderer on the loose mean to her? What does the name Jack the Ripper mean to a cat? Nothing, but what does it mean to me, to everybody else?

By Amanda Harvey Purse

Because it may well be the morning again but the truth of the matter is Miss Violet has still been murdered by someone wanting to leave me a message and just so I remembered the message I was followed and had the message literally slapped in my face.

Did Jack the Ripper know I was on a case that involved him? And if so why did it bother him? After all that had happened last night I had forgotten the real meaning of my case, the real reason I have found myself in this situation.

I must find Caroline Maxwell

I had found her words, now I must find her. There was only one place I can look for her and that was the one place she mentions in her eye-witness report, her father's lodging house, Crossingham's in Commercial Street, *Whitechapel...*

...

In truth it did not take me long to be in the East End of London once more, I could lie to myself and say it was because of the thrill of the chase, the not knowing where this lead will take me in my own adventure. But the reality was I just wanted to get there, find out what I need to know

The Strange Case of Caroline Maxwell

and get back again as quick as humanly possible to feel safe and secure within the confines of my home and to see a friendly face, all be it feline.

Although I was walking along the streets of Whitechapel in the bracing coldness that the winter mornings brings, nothing seemed that different to me here, than it did last night. There still seemed to be danger in every dark alleyway, the streets and houses that lined in row alongside it was still dirty, the foul stench of rotting animals and polluted river that was lying minutes away from me just behind a row of shops entered my nostrils at every step I took. But the most shocking thing was although I knew it was a bright, sunny day because it was when I left my house; somehow for some unknown reason to me, the streets of Whitechapel were still clouded in smog. The smog wrapped itself around me, as if it was squeezing the life out of me, making it hard for me to breathe or even see further than a few feet.

No wonder this was Jack the Ripper's playing ground.

I managed to find Crossingham's lodging house finally after a few wrong turns and a few wrongly knocked on doors. It amazed me to know that there were so many

By Amanda Harvey Purse

lodging houses in this small area, yet alone on this one street. I have heard about the poverty and homelessness in the East End, I had seen the maps Mr. Booth had made out of years of researching, but to actually see the amount of obviously illegal lodging houses that look more like dilapidated ramshackles than any type of home was even more disheartening.

I tapped on the door of Crossingham's to see a large amount of green paint, flake off and land on the top of my hand. As I shook the dry paint off my hand the door opened with a creak and there stood a middle aged woman, her hair was dark and tied up in a cloth that looked as if it had originally belonged to a set of curtains, with a few hair strands hanging loosely down around her ears. Her eyes were dark and hooded with slight bruising around each one, her skin was pale, but if you think it was palely white, you would be wrong because her skin was more a palely grey. She was not well I could tell as she smelt badly, she smelt of deathly decay. Her dress was old and ripping apart in areas and she had no shoes on her feet.

'Yeah, what you want?' she asked between coughing.

The Strange Case of Caroline Maxwell

'Sorry to bother you, I am looking for a Mr. Maxwell.'

'There hasn't been a *Mr.* Maxwell here for many a year.'

'Oh I thought Mr. Maxwell owned these premises.'

'You... a...Copper?'

'No.'

'Well come in then, so I can warm up a bit,' she said as she opened the door wider, I walked in and she shut the door sharply. The hallway was a dark and gloomy affair and I was glad when she opened one of the inside doors and allowed some light in. She left this door open and went to the worn, red armchair by the fireplace. I could tell the fireplace had not been used for a long while as there were cobwebs covered in thick dust where burning wooden logs should have been. 'You gonna sit down, or stand there like one o'clock half struck?' she coughed.

'I am sorry,' I said as I moved into the dust filled room that smelt badly of mould and sat on the only available seating, a small wooden, three legged stool that stood opposite her.

By Amanda Harvey Purse

'Sorry for what?'

'I am sorry I am bothering you, you are quite ill. Maybe I should leave you to your peace.'

'Talking to you or not talking to you, it is not going to change how I feel.'

'You should be in hospital.'

'Do you think they will give me a bed?'

'Why not?' I asked, to which she laughed so hard she coughed up a lump in her throat and spat it out in the fireplace.

'You have never been in a queue at the hospital then, but then I could tell that by just looking at you.'

'I am sorry I will not nag at you.'

'To be honest, it is rather nice to hear nagging. It has been a long time since I have heard nagging.'

'Do you own this place?'

'Now I do, Mr. Maxwell was my granddad.'

'You are Miss Caroline's daughter?' I asked shockingly.

The Strange Case of Caroline Maxwell

'You know my mother?'

'It was your mother I was trying to find.'

'Check the graveyard, although it is not wise to do so for your health, the pile is getting quite high and the smell...well if you think this place is bad, you ain't smelt nothing yet,' she coughed.

'Your mother is dead?'

'For a good sixteen years now, I was young I didn't understand. She went out one night and never came back, alive anyway. Now I know she was a street walker and very ill, she died in the cold, my granddad found her just around the corner. She was five minutes away from being home.'

'How very sad...' I said.

'It is very common, not for the likes of you of course, but the likes of us...the likes of me it is common, you live, you die. Sometimes you are living while dying,' she said as she coughed again, louder this time.

'Sixteen years ago you say? After she was in court you mean?'

By Amanda Harvey Purse

'In court you say? My mother was never in court, well not that I remember anyways.'

'Well maybe you were too young,' I whispered more to myself rather than this young woman.

'Maybe, sorry I wasn't much help, you seem a nice lady,' she said as her head rolled to the side and she looked towards the fireplace.

'It there anything I can do?' I said hopelessly.

'There is one thing.'

'Anything I can do.'

'Make sure my boy is alright, he would be at least seven by now. His name was Rupert, he was taken from me because I was young and couldn't cope with him and he went to the Madame's Home for lost boys in the West End. I tried seeing him but they don't allow it because I am...well look at me,' she said as she coughed again, 'I had heard he had ran away from that place and some gent was looking after him, I tried finding him but I am getting worse by the day. I cannot look anymore.'

'I will find him.'

The Strange Case of Caroline Maxwell

'Thank you, please close the door on the way out, I cannot get up.'

'You stay there,' I said as I got up, and moved towards the front door, while I heard her whisper,

'I can't go anywhere else.'

By Amanda Harvey Purse

Chapter Thirty Two

Walking back from the sad sight that I was greeted with at Crossingham's I was confused about how I was feeling. A feeling of complete sadness had taken over me, how could someone live their life like that? How can the same person have so much heart break? She is sitting in that cold, damp and unloved place, feeling cold, perhaps damp but feeling ill and unloved all the same. She is alone; her mother is dead and died in a horrid and depressing way, her son was taken away from her and she has tried to find him with no luck. It is all very sad and I had to leave her because there was nothing I could do, apart from one thing and that one thing will be very hard to do. How do you find a seven year old boy, who could be walking the streets in this large city of ours?

The Strange Case of Caroline Maxwell

Also and I will admit it that I was feeling let down in some idiosyncratic way, this was the end of my adventure. How could I find out what all this had meant if the person that caused it was now dead? How silly was I to not even think this could happen? I mean it's been sixteen years, that is enough time for evidence to disappear, never to be seen again and that's exactly what has happened. Caroline Maxwell held the key, held the answer to an unsolvable case, a case that the famous Mr. Holmes had put me on to, a case that has led to a dead end, literally.

I know it is juvenile of me to feel disappointment; to feel frustration even if it is anti-climax of an ending, after all I had seen from the different people I had met. The sadness I saw in Inspector Godley's eyes of having years of seeing horrid sights, the anger and the distress of not being listened to or understood from Mr. Fredrick Abberline and the feeling of complete aggravation of being a failure. The love and tenderness I saw from his wife, which is because she is in no doubt she will never see the true character of her husband again.

The misfortune and grief I saw in P.C Edward Collard's eyes, now that he has lost his true lover by the madman he has been chasing. The despondency and wretchedness I saw in Miss Caroline Maxwell's daughter, seeing life as something to give her pain, of feeling alone and unable to just end her life.

All this and I am feeling disappointed that I have no article to write about! I never realised how selfish I was being until that very moment, it made me stop in my tracks and tears just fall from my eyes like some uncontrollable force wishing me to break down.

'It can't be that bad, love,' said a voice from beside me. I turned to face the voice and realise I had stopped right in front of a newspaper seller. He was a tall man, taller than me by a few feet. He wore a brown bowler hat, slightly tilted forward so I was unable to see his eyes; his beard was dark, thick and very long. His clothing was well worn and almost falling apart in areas, his hands were grubby and he smelt of rotting fish. I would guess that selling papers was not his first line of work and that he was sent away from the docks this very morning.

'Oh sorry, I didn't realise I had stopped here in front of you.'

'Nothing to say sorry for, I mean it is not everyday a man such as I, meets a lady such as you on my travels.'

The Strange Case of Caroline Maxwell

'That is kind of you to say so, but I am not feeling such a lady today, I have been very selfish.'

'You selfish you say? I don't think so, if you don't mind me saying, you have a kind face and no doubt have a warm heart. Whatever has happened to make you think that, I am sure you did everything you were meant to...'

'Again, you are very kind. I must go home and stop blocking your path.' I said as I just wanted to get home and just see that cat of mine.

'Please, I know it's not much but take a paper, free of charge.'

'No it is quite alright.'

'I insist,' he said more strongly, there was something in the tone of this man's voice that reminded me of someone else, but again it must be my mind playing tricks on me.

'Well in that case, I insist I will pay,' I said as I took the paper in one hand and threw some coins into the seller's tin with the other hand and turned to walk off home. As I did so, I heard the seller shout out to me,

By Amanda Harvey Purse

'Things will be alright, you wait and see!' What a kind, old man I thought and his kind words stayed with me until I entered my home.

...

Inside my home, Mischief was meowing at me for some food, after feeding her I sat on the bed and laid out the newspaper in front of me, intending to read it but Mischief had other ideas and decided that I had brought the newspaper for her to lay on and after going around and around in three, small circles she finally determined that the paper was to her liking and laid down, going quite quickly to sleep, purring. I tutted to myself but began to stroke her as it was only the natural thing to do, as I did so Mischief stretched out, pushing back on my hand with every stroking of her body and the purring got louder. After a while the pushing stopped and I knew she had truly fallen asleep, I tried to read the paper around her, but I was only getting to read half the stories, so I gave up.

It was then that I noticed a small, white piece of paper between the pages of the newspaper, curious at what this was I slowly pulled at it so not to wake Mischief up. When I had completed this task successfully I noticed that

The Strange Case of Caroline Maxwell

there was writing on it, but more importantly the note was addressed to me...

> *Amelia,*
>
> *The path to true enlightenment never runs smoothly; do not give up the fight. The fight is the only way of feeling satisfied at the end of a good adventure, after all if everything was easy to complete, what would be the point of completing it? There are still answers to find; questions that are running around in your head will never be answered if you give up now. Unexplainable things have happened, you must not forget them, and you must push on.*
>
> *The task you seek may seem to have halted, but there is another route. You are in the closing stages of your adventure, but it does not end here.*
>
> *You must head south from here; to the south east you must go,* **where smoke falls on water.**

It was handwritten by a man, an intelligent man with good education. The paper is thick and of the highest quality, the ink is pure black without the slightest hint of purple so it is not a cheap value ink. Although I was feeling a little traumatized by reading a note that seemed to know

By Amanda Harvey Purse

all about me and what I have been doing, there was something at the back of my mind that was saying to me I had seen this style of writing before, but from where?

This letter was commanding me to push on in this strange case of mine, but how can I? Miss Caroline Maxwell is dead, anything she may have been able to tell me is lost and was lost sixteen years ago with her. This letter states that there are still unanswered things that have happened and in a sense it is very true in what it states, Miss Violet Smith has still been murdered, I was still threatened on the streets of Whitechapel and I still get the sense someone is watching me but how does the writer of this letter know that?

The writer seems to suggest that Miss Caroline Maxwell being dead is not the end and that there is another way to solve this case, the writer suggests the answer is somewhere else, out of London and to the South East. If that is right, then South East from London is in Kent but where? Where in Kent must I go? And who will look after Mischief? I needed to get in contact with P.C Teddy again and just hope he is safe.

The Strange Case of Caroline Maxwell

<u>Chapter Thirty three</u>

'You need me to do what?' Teddy asked looking quizzical at me. As he ushered me into what looked like an empty Inspector's office.

'To look after Mischief, I wouldn't normally ask, but I am going out of town for a few days.'

'Oh is that so? Do you think that is wise with you know who about?' he whispered.

'Do you think he will follow me?' I questioned foolishly, I was a fool to even want the answer to that question.

'I don't know and that I suppose is the point. Look I can see you are determined to go so can I ask where you are going?'

'I don't know.'

'What?' he asked as he quickly turned on heels to face me.

'What I mean to say is, I know it is in Kent but where in Kent I don't know. I've been given a lead on the story I was writing about but it is rather cryptic and I don't quite understand it yet.'

'A cryptic clue hey? That does sound very Sherlockian.'

'Indeed,' I laughed, then suddenly I went silent, my mind was racing and I was unable to concentrate on one single thought.

'What is wrong?' P.C Teddy asked me, I had heard his voice and something in the back of mind was telling me he was asking me a question and that he was waiting for an answer, but I did not answer him. 'What is wrong Amelia?' with all the Victorian etiquette pushed to one side between us. 'You have such a strange look upon your face.'

The Strange Case of Caroline Maxwell

'There was something there, something that had popped into my mind and popped straight out again. It was something in what you said.'

'What did I say?' P.C Teddy asked.

'Something and nothing don't worry about it; I'm sure I'll figure it out at some point.'

'Well maybe I can figure out the cryptic clue for you, put a policeman's mind on it so to say, what do you think?'

'We can gave it a go, it is somewhere in the east of Kent, and the line is: *where smoke falls on water*,' I said shrugging my shoulders.

'Where smoke falls on water you say? But smoke doesn't fall, it rises.'

'That is the point I guess, it wouldn't be a cryptic clue if it made sense from the first time you read it, would it?'

'So true, I am going to have to think about this one, do you mind if we sit down? I've had a hard day of walking to and fro and need to rest my bones,' he asked as he moved towards the wooden chair behind a wooden desk.

By Amanda Harvey Purse

'Of course,' I said as I moved towards the other chair that sat in front of the desk.

Now I was seeing P.C Teddy as someone else, I don't know whether it was the first time I saw him in his role as a policeman but there was something in sitting opposite him, with a rather large wooden table that had one glowing lamp on it and a selection of paperwork on it that gave me the chance to have a real look at him. He seemed more dynamic and strong, he seemed to be a man you could trust, no wonder Miss Violet had fallen for him. While he was deep in thought I watched him light up a cigar, allowing the smoke to rise as he said it would.

'Where the smoke falls on water,' he repeated to himself in a whisper.

I had no idea where this clue was leading, or where it would take me, but something else was bothering me. What had Teddy said to me that made my mind spin with all different manner of thoughts?

'I can't see a way through it.' Teddy said again to himself, 'I think someone is playing a trick on you,' he said while turning around in his chair to face me.

'What did you say?'

The Strange Case of Caroline Maxwell

'I think someone is playing a trick on you, I mean I just don't get it, smoke always rises, it always rises, I mean look,' he said pointing to his well smoked cigar. I looked over to his cigar; I watched how the dark smoke raised up towards the ceiling as more burning tobacco burned away, falling to ash.

'No you are right, smoke never falls, but ash does,' I said slowly.

'What did you say?'

'Ash falls.'

'In the east of Kent, you had said.' he said as he moved towards some books on a bookshelf, as he chose a book and started flicking through its page he asked me 'What was the rest of the clue?'

'On water, where smoke falls on water,' I repeated.

'That was it, I got it!' he proclaimed and tapped at the page sharply.

'You have it? Well then where do I need to go?'

'There,' he said as he handed me the railway book he had been holding, I looked down the page and there,

By Amanda Harvey Purse

sure enough was a name of a town in South East Kent where smoke falls on water.

'I need to go to Ashford.'

...

Leaving London again my heart was in my mouth, I had no idea why I was leaving, and I had no idea when I would be back. All I knew what that I had to finish this adventure and for some reason I believed the adventure will end in Ashford.

I was now sitting on the train watching the countless fields and farmyards go rushing pass me; I had placed my hat above me on the shelf and my bag to the side of me.

The day had turned out to be one of those shiny deceitful days that if you were looking out of a window, like I was doing right now, you would have thought it was the height of summer but if you were to step outside you would be faced with the bitterly cold temperature that an English winter brings.

I turned to my notebook that was now full of details, statements and odd little words that I had thought

The Strange Case of Caroline Maxwell

of throughout this case, I had no plan or inspiration to carry me through once I got off this quite empty train, where was I to go? What was I going to do? And more importantly why was I going to Ashford? It was then, while these thoughts were running around my head that I first met my travelling partner for the rest of my journey.

My travelling partner took the form of a quiet, elderly man wearing red suede and brown tweed, his white beard was pure in colour and freshly groomed as I could smell the lime juice he had used on it from where I was sitting. He chose to sit in the seating furthest away from me and the window of the train, so that I was unable to study him quietly, patiently and without being seen by using the reflection in the window glass. He sat down quietly as if he had almost missed the train; he crossed his legs and leaned back, hard in the chair, breathing fast and heavily.

'Are you alright Sir?' I asked him, turning away from the window to face him.

'Me Miss? Yes I am alright, not used to running for the train that is all, it is running a little early,' he replied in a Kentish tone.

'Is it? I didn't realise.'

By Amanda Harvey Purse

'Oh yes Miss, I know my train times, I always carry a 'Bradshaw' around with me, when out and about,' he said as he lifted a small, brown book out of his inside pocket and waved it about in the air, only to put the little book back into his pocket again as quickly as he brought it out.

'Where are you headed?' I asked.

'I go to Canterbury Miss, got to change at Ashford, where are you going? If you don't mind me asking that is.'

'Not at all Sir, I am travelling to Ashford.'

'Ashford you say? That is a nice quite railway town; I think it has a farmer's market there too. You are visiting I see as you seem to be a London lady.'

'Why yes I am visiting.'

'Any reason why?'

'To get out of the smoke I would say, see how others live and what not.'

'Oh,' he said disappointingly, why was he disappointed with my answer? Why would he care? 'Well I like little Ashford.'

'You seemed to know it quite well.'

The Strange Case of Caroline Maxwell

'Do I? Do I indeed?' he smiled, 'Well my daughter went to the British School there, I was much impressed with the school and its teachers, it is a delightful piece of building work, you should really take time to see it. It's on West Street, the Ashford's Congregational Church spend many a year raising funds for it and I must say and have said to the Reverend Alfred Turner that it was funds well spent!'

'I will make sure to do that; do you know where I could stay at all in Ashford?'

'There is a little inn in the high street, between the butchers and bakers called The Rosebud, they are normally quite good and their beers are top class!'

'Oh really, why thank you for being so informative Sir,' I said it was something in the way he smiled that made me think he had visited The Rosebud Inn a few times for their top class beers, but I didn't mention what I was thinking.

We said nothing more all the way to Ashford, which allowed me time to write a few more details in my notebook, I had just finished writing and began to tap my pencil on my notebook when I heard the call for Ashford

By Amanda Harvey Purse

Station where I must admit I was eager to stretch my legs so hastily put my notebook in my bag and quickly jumped off the train only to look back and see that there was now nobody in my travelling carriage. Where had the elderly gentleman gone? I hadn't seen him get off the train, he had just disappeared...

    I had walked a few steps along the platform and saw the train I was on, pull itself off with a cloud of energy, it was at that moment when I realised that my hair was blowing around annoyingly in the cold wind across my eyes and catching itself in my mouth, and that the only reason why that was happening was that I had left my hat on the train!

The Strange Case of Caroline Maxwell

Chapter Thirty Four

Ashford was indeed a quiet town; quiet of people anyway as there was certainly the sound of cattle being walked down the tiny roads to get to a rather large building with wooden fences in a line in front of it, probably the market house, was loud and so very bizarre to me. The sound of different pitches of mooing and the sound of their cowbells ringing hastily with every step their little hooves took them was very strange for me. I being a person used to hearing the odd horse trot pass my window pulling a cab along, or hearing some fight between two persons going on outside, being in a village where there are trees and countryside with every turn you take was extremely curious to me and got my journalistic senses running.

By Amanda Harvey Purse

I moved along a few streets heading to where I thought would be the high street, when I could not walk any further as I was faced with a huge building blocking my path. With three archways within the brickwork showing three doorways, I looked up towards the top of the building, pass the broken windows and cast iron drain pipes in the direction of the roof and I felt a little dizzy. I started tapping my pencil on the side of my leg, as I had forgot to put it back in my bag when I got off the train, with every tap, I made a clicking noise inside my mouth, it was another way of keeping me calm.

The building stood so tall and masterful that it took me by surprise; I must have been standing there, staring up at this monster of a building for quite some time when a rough voice from behind me entered my thoughts.

'Ere, you after I wash my lovely?'

'What...What did you say?' I asked as I turned around to face a horrid looking man, with a flap cap, dark bushy eyebrows, his face was greasy and covered in dirt, his mouth was cracked and incrusted with flakes of dry skin, he was wearing a dark coloured flannel shirt and brown overalls that were rolled up at the ends of his legs as if he was too small for them. He leaned, in a cavalier

The Strange Case of Caroline Maxwell

fashion on his well used spade and he allowed a stick of corn to droopily hang from one side of his mouth.

'Are you after a wash, me saids? Coz if you were like, it is now closed it is.'

'What is closed?'

'That building my love,' he said pointing over my shoulder towards the huge building I was just looking at. 'Opens at eight, shuts at one, aye so it does.'

'I am sorry I do not understand you.'

'Nah, me sees that alright,' he laughs. 'New ere isn't you? Well it's not often the likes of me sees the likes of you, nah so it is. Ave you not seen the baths before, like? I thought there were still some in London, so I did.'

'Oh that building is a public bath, now I understand. Wait! How did you know I am from London?'

'Saw you get off the train, didn't I? With your hair all flying around and looking a right muddle, I thought to meself, we ave a right one ere. I was worried like, that you didn't know your way. So I followed, not closely like, not in the way to make you scared or nothin. I saw you looking at this building for quite some time, and me thinks you are lost or are wanting washing, I don't know what ladies want after a long journey these days, so I wait before talking like.'

'That was kind of you; I'm assuming that was you being nice.'

'Me love? Me always kind love, so are you lost or wanting washing? Coz me misses, can run you a bath from the cast iron if you like, but it will take a while and there be a few kids running around like.'

'No, I am fine, thank you. I am in fact lost and was looking for the high street. I was looking for the establishment called The Rosebud Inn.'

'Ah, the old Rosie, well I show you the way. You were headed in the wrong direction Miss, this is the part of Ashford called Newtown.'

'Newtown?'

'Oh yes Miss and newly built I should say, built for the railway workers on the lines, hence the public bath.'

'Oh I see.' I said taking one last look at the enormous building before I followed this quite interesting stranger.

The Strange Case of Caroline Maxwell

...

The horrid looking man seemed to be not as horrid in personality as I first thought; he seemed to me as being quite a jolly fellow and proceeded to explain the history of Ashford, before the railway had came to this small town. He was a farmer by trade but did a little gardening for elderly gentleman and ladies of the town, whenever the season turned too cold for them to do it themselves. He seemed really sympathetic to other people's needs and I could quite imagine him helping an old lady across the street without even thinking about it. He was thoughtful enough to carry my bag, allowing me to warm my hands up by placing both of them in my pockets and caring enough to not ask why I was carrying a pencil outside of my bag but he carried it all the same. After walking a few more minutes I found myself standing outside The Rosebud Inn, with the delightful smell of home cooked meals being served.

'Looks like we are still in time for lunch, me takes it you are hungry. But me never knows I don't eat that much you see, drink loads though. But don't tell the wife like.'

By Amanda Harvey Purse

'No I won't, yes I am hungry although I didn't know it until I smelt that food.'

'Rosie does a mean roast, with dumplings and veg. A big slap of beef too with oodles of gravy to boot, you won't find any better, but again don't tell the wife,' he said as he chuckled to himself.

'No, I won't,' I said chucking myself. 'But that does sound very appetizing.'

'Well I leave you here, otherwise I'll ave a few wallops and my misses won't see me for days!' he proclaimed as he handed me back my bag.

'Best be on your way then, thank you for everything,' I said as I waved him off.

'Always a pleasure misses, always a pleasure so it is,' he said as he left me and started whistling a merry tune. It was a while afterwards and when I was tucking into a hearty roast dinner, that a thought had occurred to me, the kind old farmer must still have my pencil!

The Rosebud Inn, wasn't quite as quaint as it sounded but it had some old, history charm to it, apparently some of King Charles's men had stayed in this town and

The Strange Case of Caroline Maxwell

hid themselves in this very Inn on their way to France, something the Landlord had the delight of telling me. I told him and a few locals that were listening and shrewdly observing, that I had come to visit a sickly aunt as I felt broadcasting what I did for a living didn't get me far in the last Inn I stayed in, they seemed to buy my story. Whether it was because of the way I told it or that they were so merrily drunk and didn't truly care I don't know, but that was my story and I was sticking to it.

Once in my somewhat quaint room, alone, I allowed myself to start thinking of what to do next, yes I had a coded message stating I should come to Ashford to complete my adventure, so I came to Ashford but where do I go from here? Who do I see?

Right, think Amelia, think over everything. What was this adventure? What was this case? Start at the very beginning, Mr. Holmes believes that one of the five victims of Jack the Ripper was wrong on one account, he believed Inspector Abberline knew which one was wrong and he wasn't allowed to say at that time. Inspector Fredrick Abberline told me that Sherlock was right, but that I needed to find Miss Caroline Maxwell. Miss Caroline Maxwell was an eyewitness in the Miss Mary Kelly part of

By Amanda Harvey Purse

The Ripper case, she wrote and then said in court, that she had seen and spoken to Miss Mary Kelly hours after Miss Mary was dead!

I saw in her witness account that her father had a lodging house in Whitechapel. I go to Whitechapel I don't find Miss Caroline, but I find her daughter who tells me Miss Caroline died sixteen years ago, it must have been just after she wrote the eyewitness report for Inspector Abberline, but her daughter knows nothing of her mother being called to court. Yes her daughter would have been young, but would she have been too young to not know that? She seemed honest, she is ill and dying so she has no reason to lie to me. I next get a coded message in a newspaper saying that this was not the end of my adventure, how did the writer know I had come to a dead end?

Was there really someone following me in Hampshire? Are they still following me now? P.C Teddy had suggested so, when I told him I was coming here, I had been warned with a few slaps and a bruised back from my night in Whitechapel to stay away, someone knows I am on this adventure and someone does not want me to finish it. Could that same someone, have given me that coded

The Strange Case of Caroline Maxwell

message to lure me away from London and the people I know, to hurt me? Or did that someone lure me away from London to do something even worse to me?

'There is a high possibly that Jack the Ripper is back, if I was you I would be very careful, very careful indeed.' The words of Inspector Lestrade started to ring true in my ears...

By Amanda Harvey Purse

Chapter Thirty Five

My mind was filling up with quite ghastly and horrid thoughts; I was picturing Jack the Ripper walking slowly and confidently on some wet and sodden cobbled stones, his cane splashing in every puddle, he crosses the road without looking for cabs because his dark and menacing eyes were firmly set on where he had to go. He knew where he had to go, because he had planned it all out in his head, nothing he ever did was without logic or reasoning, that is how he had survived through the myth, he was a legend in horror because he was never caught, because he thought things through, he didn't act on a whim. His knife slips out of his long sleeve of his overcoat, he catches it at the handle, the gas lamp light now shining on his killing blade, he still moves forward. He can hear his victim laughing now, maybe she is singing, he looks down at her long skirt that has ripped in areas and was swaying across the stones as she was moving backwards and forwards, her hat is loosely tied around her neck and was bobbing around on its own accord, now Jack the Ripper focuses on her neck, he can see the skin, the living and breathing skin, he moves closer and strikes...

    Oh my! I felt a tight and knotted feeling inside my chest, I then noticed I was rubbing my own neck as if that would stop Jack the Ripper's knife from slicing it. I was unable to breathe and I felt the walls of my room closing in on me. I needed some fresh air and decided to have a nice, friendly country walk, where there were no murders, no madmen willing to slash at my neck and no talk of Jack the Ripper.

    At first I had no idea of where to go, I paced along the high street looking into windows of the shops, the beautiful bakers with their sweet smelling cakes and bread on the shelves and a benevolent looking woman within, elbows deep in flour smiling and humming a joyous tune to herself. It all allowed me to breathe again and to think that the world is not a dangerous place at all. I turned towards a fountain that was placed in the centre, its fresh water

By Amanda Harvey Purse

splashing out and birds, tweeting while washing themselves in that liquid. No, I thought the world is not a horrid place; there are not murderers at every corner, there was not a stench of death and rotting flesh here. Here is beautiful, here you could start again, you could wash the smog and diseases from your skin and breathe again, it is so different from London, it is so new. I could have quiet easily imagine staying here and never returning to London, never completing my adventure.

As that thought passed through my mind, I turned once more towards the shops, to see a butcher in his window, hanging up a dead pigs head, it's neck still covered in clotted blood. That was all I needed to bring me back down to the situation at hand, you cannot get away from it because murder is everywhere, I cannot run away from it, Jack the Ripper will always be there, somewhere haunting me. I keep forgetting my adventure is not about him, but his victims, the lives he took with one sweep of his knife.

I felt helpless and lost, I did not know where to turn and by chance I found myself looking at a street name and wondering where I had heard it before. West Street?

The Strange Case of Caroline Maxwell

'It's on West Street, the Ashford's Congregational Church spend many a year raising funds for it and I must say and have said to the Reverend Alfred Turner that it was funds well spent!' Of course! The elderly gentleman that was my travelling partner had mentioned there was a school on West Street.

'It is a delightful piece of building work; you should really take time to see it.'

And so I shall...

...

West Street turned out to be a quite long and peaceful road, with many twists and turns along the way, by the time I had reached the top of the hill to be able to see the school on the other side it must have been the end of school time as I watched a gust of school children leaving the premises as fast as their little legs would carry them.

As I walked passed every single one of them I noticed, every child was smiling, laughing and joking with their friends. The colour in their cheeks was such a charming and delightful sight to see, as sadly I have not seen many children that were happy in mind and in spirit in my lifetime. Then as I approached the school itself, I saw a little girl with ginger hair tied up in two small white bows, sitting on the bench outside looking around and into the school doors which were still open.

'Hello,' I said. 'Are you waiting for someone?'

'Yes Miss, my brother, said a squeaky voice, without turning to face me.

'Oh, has he not come out yet?'

'No, he hasn't,' she said in a huff as she turned around and slumped further down on the bench. By the way she had folded her arms and scrunched up her face I could tell she was unhappy about being kept waiting.

'Would you like me to keep you company?' I asked.

'It's alright Miss, I am used to waiting for him. He always gets himself in trouble and Miss Maxwell always has to keep him behind.'

'Oh I see, does your brother always get told off?'

The Strange Case of Caroline Maxwell

'Not really, not in the way my daddy tells him off, she is quite kind to him but I always have to wait here, I just want to go home!'

'Do you like your teacher then?'

'Sure I do Miss!' She said as she seemed to cheer herself up. 'She makes me laugh sometimes Miss, because of the way she talks!'

'The way she talks?' I asked.

'Yes, not like me and not even like you, but differently. It is pretty the way she talks; she said once that she comes from Ireland.'

'Oh I see, she has an Irish accent.'

'That's it Miss,' she said pointing at me with her little pink coloured fingers. 'That's it, you got it. We call her 'The lovely Irish Lady', because she is just that, lovely.'

'That's nice to hear, I think that is your brother coming now,' I said pointing to inside the doorway and down the hall at a little young boy who was running to get out. The little girl turns to look and then nods her head. The little boy reaches us, looks quizzical at me and then grabs

By Amanda Harvey Purse

his sister's arm and they walk off together down the road with what sounds of arguing with each other. I turned to look at the school again, the gentleman on the train was right; this British School was very picturesque to look at. Wait!

I started running back along the road trying to catch up with the children I had just met, 'Excuse me! Excuse me,' I shouted.

'Why? What have *you* done?' asked the boy towards me.

'Nothing, I just wanted to know what your sister had said to me.'

'You forgetful or something?' the boy answered.

'Come on Jim, there is no need to be horrible, she is a nice lady,' said the girl. 'What did you want to know?'

'What did you say about your teacher?'

'She is Irish,'

'No, it was not that.'

'She is lovely?'

The Strange Case of Caroline Maxwell

'No, that wasn't it either.'

'I don't know much else about Miss Maxwell,' she said shrugging her shoulders.

'That is it! Her name is Miss Maxwell! I don't suppose you would know her first name, by any chance?'

'No, sorry Miss that I don't,' She said sadly as if she felt my disappointment.

'I do,' said the boy suddenly. Both the girl and I turned to face him. 'Yes I saw it once on a book or something, her name is Caroline. Miss Caroline Maxwell.'

'I always thought she would have a pretty name,' said the girl. 'Does that help you Miss?'

'Yes that helps me very much indeed! More than you know!' I said as I turned from the children in a mad dash back to the school, probably leaving the children in a confused state.

By Amanda Harvey Purse

Chapter Thirty Six

My speed slowed as I entered the school, it seemed like a normal school hallway, with children's paintings and writings, one whole wall even had the alphabet written all over it. Just a normal school hallway, you would think dear reader but at the end of this hallway was a door, a normal looking door you would assume. I get nearer and nearer to this normal looking door, to see that it is slightly open and the light from the windows inside the room lighting my way for inside this normal looking room holds the key, the reason, my answer to this case, this *strange case of Caroline Maxwell.*

I stand outside the door for a few minutes breathing quietly, collecting my thoughts. I knock on the door, quietly at first, too quietly perhaps as I got no answer from

The Strange Case of Caroline Maxwell

within. I tapped a little harder and pushed the door fully open and the sight I saw was disappointedly *normal*. I wanted an exploding, shining light or trumpets playing, or birds singing or something, but all I got was a normal looking woman sitting behind a normal looking table, writing perhaps a normal report. Everything seemed utterly normal, too normal.

Her red flowing hair was not ginger but pure red, *blood* red I would say if I had the confidence to do so, she looks up at me. Her beautiful face is clean and freshly coloured with rosy pink cheeks, she was older I know in years than she looked, someone could quite easily believe this woman was in her thirties rather than her forties. I move closer without saying a word and oddly enough she isn't saying anything either, she is just watching me move closer towards her. Time seemed to have slowed down, I seemed to not be moving at all but I was getting nearer to her all the same.

My eyes were focused on mainly one part of her, the part of the body that had always interested me, the part of the body that I had used for my career to understand people I am talking to and oddly the same part of the body in which a Jack the Ripper victim was identified alone by.

By Amanda Harvey Purse

It was in her eyes, her bright emerald Irish coloured eyes, eyes that were full of wonder and delight, eyes that could melt your very soul. It was in those eyes, that the answer to my adventure was finally shown to me.

...

'Miss Caroline Maxwell? Or should I call you by your real name?' I said as I stood a few feet away from her. She stands up and faces me.

'Who sent you?'

'Mr. Sherlock Holmes.' There was silence, as if she was thinking over my answer, until she finally asked.

'How did he find out?'

'The same way he always does,' again there was silence.

'What are you planning to do?'

'I haven't made up my mind.'

'What can I do to make up your mind?'

'Tell me your story.'

The Strange Case of Caroline Maxwell

She sits back down and offers me a seat opposite her, I sit where she points and she glances out of the window, 'Where would you like me to start?'

'Start and finish where you like,' I said repeating what Mr. Sherlock Holmes had said to me at the very start of this adventure.

'How much do you know?'

'Enough.'

'How long have you known it?'

'I could say I didn't know any of it, until I walked in this door and looked into your eyes, but the truth of the matter I guess I have known for quite some time, ever since I met Ex- Inspector Fredrick Abberline.'

'He told you?'

'In his own unique way I guess he did, but I wasn't listening fully.'

'He is a great man.' She said still looking out of the window.

'He saved you. Like he saved many people he believed were under his protection.'

By Amanda Harvey Purse

'Yes,' she said as she looked down at her hands, 'Yes, not only did he save me but he gave me life.'

'A new life I would say.'

'Yes, a life I had never known existed,' she said as she stared at me forcefully but with tears in her eyes. I smiled kindly at her.

'Tell me about it.'

The Strange Case of Caroline Maxwell

<u>Chapter Thirty Seven</u>

'I was born some years ago, on the Irish plains. My family had been travellers for many generations, so I didn't see anything wrong with my life at first, we were moving from one beautiful sight to another, our family were very close because of the way we lived. Then I grew older and my thoughts were changing, I wanted more than I was getting out of life, I was noticing how different we truly were compared to the rest of the children my age.'

'I was six almost seven and I didn't know how to read or write. I couldn't even write my name or tell anyone my name, we had our own language that only we understood but if I bumped into another child from outside the camp, they used to laugh and make fun of me. They called me names, told me I was a dunce.'

By Amanda Harvey Purse

'I thought my luck would change when we moved to Wales and father got a job working as a foreman in some ironworks. With the money coming in, my mother Ellen decided I was the one out of all the children that had the most promise and sent me to school. I enjoyed every minute of it and quickly picked up things, within a month I could write my name and was understanding what was being said to me. But that caused problems at home, my other brother and sisters starting taunting me, saying I wasn't a real gypsy no more, that I thought I was better than them, they said. I learned quickly how to pretend I wasn't that bright and that I needed other people's help when I could quite easily do things myself, something I used later on in my life.'

'In truth I began to forget how bright I was, I met Mr. Harry Davis and fell in love, or what I thought was love because I was only sixteen. He seemed to be a knight in shining armour; he had his own place and had a fixed job, working down the mines. I tried to leave the family camp many times to be with him, but every time my father caught me and dragged me back. At the time I hated him, he didn't seem to understand that Mr. Harry and I belong together. The only way I managed to leave the camp was by telling my parents I had married Mr. Harry in secret and that there was now nothing they could do to stop us being together, we didn't truly marry but my parents were fooled enough, they seemed to just give up on me in the end.'

'Life with Mr. Harry was delightful, I was quite happy pretending to be his wife and doing all the roles a wife does, but then Harry died in an explosion at work and I lost everything, not just the man I loved but his home and the money coming in. I tried going back to my parents but they didn't want to know. I was on my own until I heard of a distant cousin living in Cardiff, apparently making a life for herself, so I left for Cardiff. I found out very quickly how my cousin was making a living and that is how I went to the streets for the first time, my cousin taught me a routine of pretending to be young and dim-witted to fool clients. I picked it up straight away and made my cousin a lot of money.'

'But then I made a mistake, a mistake of the womanly kind. I didn't know what was happening to me but when I started to show, my cousin was very angry and took me off to an infirmary of some sort to have my baby. All throughout those months, I was cold, often starving and alone, I had to pay my way by doing sewing, or washing floors in the place and when I was too big to do anything I

By Amanda Harvey Purse

was sent into a dark and gloomy cell, I was to stay inside that cell not seeing anyone but a hand that passed my gruel through a opening in the door until I had my baby. When my baby was born, I knew it wasn't quite right but it was healthy, I didn't find out whether it was a boy or girl as my baby was taken away from me and I was never to see my baby again. The next day I was thrown out into the street with no money, I found my cousin and was told she had no business for a used up girl but as I was her cousin she would give me money to leave Wales, never to dirty up her doorstep again.'

'I took the money and moved to London as I had seen the posters saying that England was the land of new hope, all I had ever known was to work the streets so I went to the brothels of the West End. I pretended once again that I was young and foolish; I never told anyone that I had, had a baby. It was all going well; I met some posh gentlemen who paid well for my services. I never knew quite what these gentlemen did for a living, but they seemed to all know each other and greet each other in a strange way.'

'One of them then offered to take me to Paris in France, he promised me the high life and I fell of it all

The Strange Case of Caroline Maxwell

because I thought I deserved some miracle to happen to me after all I had been through. But it turned out to be not how I had hoped, so I left him to come back to London, by this time I was told I was too old to be working in the West End and that I should travel eastwards.'

'I moved to Ratcliffe Highway and didn't really know the danger I was in until I met The Nichols Gang, the gang was mainly made up of four people but in truth there was always the threat that there was more hiding in the shadows. They claimed to be a protection gang and if I was to pay them money every month, they would protect me against bad clients, or other gang members. I was still a young girl on my own, so I paid up until I couldn't pay up any more. I got beaten, there was not an inch of my skin left that didn't have a bruise or a cut on it, and I was left for dead.'

'That is when I met Mr. Morgan Stone, he was a young doctor who helped me back to health, he seemed kind and caring at first but then he changed. Apparently being with a previous street walker was not helping him climb the medical social ladder, he started to drink more and use me. I felt as if I was street walker again but this time I was not getting paid.'

By Amanda Harvey Purse

'Somehow, while drinking in a pub I met Mr. Joseph Flemming, he was just a normal person like me, he worked hard being a plasterer and seemed to like me very much, I thought I could trust him so I told him everything that had happened to me, he seemed to love me even more. Then he disappeared, I later found out that Mr. Morgan had beaten Mr. Joseph and told him to stay away from me. I wanted to leave Mr. Morgan so I told him, I had a disease and that he would be likely to have it too, I don't know why I said it, I wanted to hurt him and that certainly hurt him, he threw me out and I began to walk the streets of Whitechapel.'

...

'I met Mr. Joseph Barrnet, he showed me care, not love but care. From the start it seemed odd the way he cared for me, we were lovers and yet we didn't seemed to be lovers. It was only later; I found out that I reminded Mr. Joseph of his Irish mother and things started to fall into place. I had taken the place of his mother in some odd fashion. He was very strong willed but nothing like what I had dealt with before, I was able to manage him and we moved into together, we moved around a bit and I was feeling like I was in my family camp again so I told Joe, I

The Strange Case of Caroline Maxwell

wanted a place, one single place no more moving. He found 13 Miller's Court.'

'Things were alright, until I started helping my fellow street walkers. I had been through so much I just wanted to help anyone that was having problems, I helped Miss Maria Harvey a few times but I always knew she would be alright, but it was Miss Belle that I really worried for, she was young, younger than I was when I started, she seemed so alone. So I allowed Miss Belle to stay with me and Mr. Joseph. Mr. Joseph was not happy, he claimed I was keeping with bad company but I found out later he had tried to get his way with her and she didn't play ball. Joe and I had a row about it and Joe got violent and managed to break the window. I never did get that window fixed.'

'He left, but the look in his eyes was horrid, he seemed mad. I thought he was mad, I did not feel safe and I began planning a move somewhere else, after all I was a traveller by birth, I thought I could move and start again quite easily so I held back on the rent. I knew Mr. McCarty wouldn't mind too much as he had a soft spot for me and my services.'

'Then came the night of the 8th November, I stayed out longer than I normally do, Miss Belle was keeping

Miller's Court warm for me, just case I was back sooner than I hoped. I had told Miss Belle my plan to leave and offered to take her with me as long as she didn't tell Mr. Joseph.'

'I came back in the early hours of the next morning, I tapped on the door, and Miss Belle didn't answer. You know when you get that feeling; you can't explain it but you just know something is terribly wrong? Well I was feeling that way instantly. I slowly walked around to the broken window and pulled the coat I had been using as a curtain to one side, I looked through the window; the sight before my eyes was of poor Miss Belle. But it wasn't Miss Belle; it wasn't Miss Belle at all! I remember whispering 'Murder' or perhaps I said it louder than that, in truth I don't remember. To this day I don't know why I said it, it was so plainly murder, Belle had been murdered, of course I thought of Jack the Ripper for he was going around killing women like me, but there was something different in the sight I was seeing and I thought of Joe, could he be so mad that he could have done that?'

'I stayed around, watching all the policemen going in and out of Miller's Court, watching all the crowds. People were saying it was me in there; it was me that Jack

The Strange Case of Caroline Maxwell

the Ripper had caught with his knife. I was very ill, I had thrown up many times but I stayed watching, I don't know why.'

'I saw a man come out of the alleyway, he leaned on the brick wall, he was as sick as I. Then all of a sudden, he seemed to sense me looking him, there was a moment we were just looking at each other, somehow I knew that he knew who I was. I ran but he caught me, he took me into a quiet pub around the corner. He knew it would be quiet in there as most people were out on the streets wanting to get a glimpse of the next Ripper killing. He asked me my life story and I told him everything from the moment I was born, he allowed a single tear to fall from his eyes. He told me that this was my chance to run, I tried to tell him about Joe but he seemed to already know who had killed Belle. Then he looked out of the public house's window and saw who he said was his Sergeant, I didn't like the look of him at all, he seemed quite evil, I would have believed him to be the devil and reminded me of one of the posh gentlemen I had met in the West End brothel.'

'The Inspector then rushed a story upon me, saying that he would get me away if I was to claim to be a witness, I was to tell an unbelievable story, a story no one

By Amanda Harvey Purse

would believe or question me further. He said that this death was the second he had visited within a few days and that the other woman was called Miss Caroline Maxwell; she had sadly died from the cold while walking the streets and no one had claimed her yet. For all known purposes I was to be this Miss Caroline Maxwell for the rest of my life. And I guess I have been.'

The Strange Case of Caroline Maxwell

<u>Chapter Thirty Eight</u>

It was at this time, I remembered I had lost my handkerchief inside the Unsolved Crimes Room of Scotland Yard for I needed it now as my tears were falling uncontrollably. Mary turned to face me as she had told her whole story while looking out of the classroom window and said 'I have a tissue here,' she leaned back in her chair, pulled at a drawer in the desk and handed me a white tissue. 'Always have a tissue handy when dealing with children I say.'

'How can you be so strong after all you had been through?'

'After all I had been through? What about Miss Belle? What had she been through? Did she truly deserve to die in that horrid fashion? Did any of those women deserve to die by the hands of Jack the Ripper? For the rest of my life I have got to listen to people saying my name when they talk of The Ripper, for I was his last victim, I was Miss Mary Kelly while Miss Belle disappears into uncaring and unknowing myth.'

'You now think Jack the Ripper killed your friend?'

'What do you mean?'

'You had thought it was your lover Joe once.'

'After all this time, you don't want to think of it, to know that you had spent the last eighteen months with a murderer, or even worse a serial murderer.'

'You think Mr. Joseph Barrnet and Jack the Ripper was one of the same person?'

'It makes sense, doesn't it? Why would Inspector Abberline have helped me so much if I hadn't known who Jack the Ripper was?'

'I don't know, Mr. Abberline is a genuinely caring man, he always helped the people of Whitechapel that he thought was under his protection. But there was something in what you said. You believed Mr. Abberline already

The Strange Case of Caroline Maxwell

knew who Jack the Ripper was, a morning after the last murder, so he wasn't thinking of Mr. George Chapman then. What was he thinking? What did he know?'

...

Just then there was a gust of wind and the door to the classroom that I had shut burst open, the bright sunny day outside turned a dark and cloudy affair, the look upon Mary's face was of terror and frozen shock, she managed to mutter the words 'The devil, it is the devil!' I turned to see the stance of a man that I had once known, but he was different. His eyes seemed darker and menacing, the moving creatures I had only seen once before in a fleeting glance were running around madly inside his skin, I noticed them for the first time moving in his hands as he stood there with his right fist was clenched and his left hand was holding his cane. His long overcoat was hanging off him as if it wasn't his own coat; he had a smart appearance to him that I had never seen before, as if he was wearing some kind of uniform, but not of a uniform I had seen him in before. His head was partly covered in a black hood that was attached to black over coat.

By Amanda Harvey Purse

As he stood there, not saying one word I thought crossed my mind, 'here stood a man in a hood, and here stood a *brotherhood.*'

'You don't know who is and who isn't in it,' was the words that this man had said to me once, *and yet this is the very man standing before me in a brotherhood.*

And yet that was not the most deadly aspect of the sight before my eyes, as the man standing a few feet away from me also resembled to ghastly vision I had once of Jack the Ripper before he killed.

'Hello Miss Amelia Jane Reporter,' he announced.

'You, it was you,' I managed to say.

'Yes it was I, are things starting to make sense in that little brain of yours? I wonder,' he boomed as he moved forward.

'You killed Miss Violet!'

'Well I must admit it was quite delightful to find that you lived next door to her, P.C Edward Collard was getting on my nerves a bit, not allowing Jack the Ripper to disappear in the smog filled nightmares people were having of him. He had seen me release the man known as The

The Strange Case of Caroline Maxwell

Leather Apron and he was always looked at me like he knew and ever since then he has been on my case. So I thought to myself I could kill two birds with one stone, literally. I killed P.C Collard's sweetheart as a warning, but then I thought if I could kill her in the same way as Jack the Ripper to catch your attention Miss Amelia Jane Reporter, two warnings for two people with one body.'

'She was a real person, not just a body!'

'You say person, I say body, it's all really the same thing,' he said as he shrugged his shoulders. 'Then I thought you might need a bigger push to stay away, so I hire Leather Apron again to slap you about a bit and who do I see helping you? P.C Edward Collard! Well I knew I was at risk of you finding out about the brotherhood now as you seemed to so easily find out things, I had never thought of the oddness of Miss Caroline Maxwell until you had brought her back into my mind. Then I start thinking of how strange Mr. Abberline was with me from that day in the pub when he was talking to a 'witness', I thought then that he knew about me, but as the days went on he never said anything. So I forgot it until you told me Mr. Abberline never thought Jack the Ripper was Mr. George Chapman and it gets me thinking, who really was this Miss

By Amanda Harvey Purse

Caroline Maxwell? I started to following you, Miss Amelia Jane Reporter. I started finding out the things you had found out. And here we are.' he said as he pushed me to one side.

I had forgotten how strong he was when he shoved me into the Unsolved Crimes Room. I hit my head on the flooring and felt dizzy I looked up slightly in-between the school table legs and that is when I heard Miss Mary scream, a haunting scream that echoed in my ears as the sight I saw was of Inspector Godley holding Miss Mary Kelly roughly with a knife to her neck!

The Strange Case of Caroline Maxwell

Chapter Thirty Nine

'You should never have escaped Miller's Court my dear, look at all the hassle you have put me through!' Inspector Godley shouted in Miss Mary's ear.

'One thing I don't understand,' I said as I unsteadily got up from the floor. I don't know what I was planning; I don't even know why I was speaking for I knew as soon as he slit Miss Mary Kelly's throat, I would be his next victim. But that feeling itself gave me a sense of power, a sense of strength, I could do anything now I knew I was going to die, in any minute.

'Oh have I not made myself clear at all? Oh silly me!' he said in a jovial manner. 'Please go ahead, what do you not understand Miss Amelia Jane Reporter?' he said as he waved the knife at me but still holding tightly onto Miss Mary.

'Why kill all those women?'

'Why? You ask me why? Well I guess you would have to be a part of my father's brotherhood, to understand why.'

'Your father's brotherhood?' I asked.

'Yes my father's brotherhood, a gang so to speak. My father was the greatest criminal mind the world has ever known, but he would not have been able to do the things he had done without protecting his followers, his brothers. They were the highest in the land and my father protected them if they had little problems, shall we say and Miss Mary here bless her little heart, she was a little problem from her days in the West End.'

'I don't truly remember my days in the West End!' Miss Mary shouted.

'You think I will believe that?' Inspector Godley shouted back as he brought the knife back to Miss Mary's neck. 'You're a little liar! You lied in court, you're lying now!'

The Strange Case of Caroline Maxwell

'Why are you doing your father's work?' I asked trying to defuse the situation.

'Why you ask? Because my father is dead! My father was murdered!' He shouted as I saw the knife push deeper into Mary's neck, causing a small droplet of blood to appear.

'Murdered?'

'Yes, of course it was accepted by the police as an accident, but my father did not fall over the edge, he was pushed!' Inspector Godley said with so much hatred as he drove the knife in deeper into Miss Mary's flesh, that I wondered what had happened to this man? Was it simply the death of his father that drove him to kill? What had made a man named GODley turn into the devil?

As I watched more and more of Miss Mary Kelly's blood being spilling from the sharp point in which knife dug into her skin, I knew I had to do something to stop this, but I could not think of a single thing. I felt frozen to the spot in which I was standing unable to help, unable to scream I felt so utterly useless. Thoughts of my childhood entered my head, for that was the last time I had felt this useless, thoughts instantly running back of that cold night, of feeling those freezing damp cobbled stones under my bare feet. Thoughts of that gas lamp shining its light on a horrid, horrid scene. I felt worthless then and I had fooled myself all these years that I did not do anything because how could I? I was a little girl of six, I could not possibly understand what I was seeing, I was a fool to think that, dear reader for I felt the same totally inept feeling now. I had not changed at all.

Suddenly to bring me back to the moment that I was facing I heard a loud shot from behind me, the noise seemed to bounce of the classroom's wall, it felt as if my ears drums burst for everything seemed muffled and the sight I was watching slowed in speed as Inspector George Godley released his grasp of Miss Mary and falls backwards onto the floor, I did not have to look down at him to know that Inspector Godley, the mad man, the devil was now no more...

...

Miss Mary screams, her screams are still muffled to me at first and then in a flash my ears begin so work again and her screams were higher pitched. I look over to her and notice she is still holding her neck, as if there was still a threat to the part of her and steps to one side, looks down at

The Strange Case of Caroline Maxwell

the man who was willing to wait years to kill her. I was in shock at everything that had happened but somehow managed to force myself to turn from this scene to behind me and see two people I did not imagined I would have seen here and now.

I saw Mr. Sherlock Holmes and Dr Watson, who was holding a smoking gun!

Miss Mary was screaming madly, she was unable to control her actions; she was shaking hysterically as she watched the warm blood flow out of Inspector Godley's head and mouth. It was then I heard the voice of authority from Mr. Holmes as he quietly said,

'Watson, take her away from the sight,' Dr Watson instantly moved towards Miss Mary and leads her away as she began to sob on his shoulder, with Miss Mary out of the room Mr. Holmes turned his attention towards the dead body of Inspector Godley, he stood beside me while looking down at the bloodied mess that laid on the floor.

'Why did Inspector Godley do those horrid, horrid things?' I asked Mr. Holmes.

'Because quite simple, he didn't,' Mr. Holmes whispered back at me.

'What?' I said as I looked up sharply toward Mr. Sherlock Holmes.

'The person you see before you may well have taken on the role as Inspector George Godley, he may have trained hard to become an Inspector in the police force and he may well have believed he was Mr. George Godley for the amount of time he had played him. But I will tell you now that this dead man was not born with the name Mr. George Godley.'

'Who was he?'

'Mr. Albert.'

'Mr. Albert?'

'You are correct in what you say but then...'

'I have just repeated you, I am always going to be correct if I do that,' I interrupted him, all the while being reminded of how this adventure started.

'Indeed,' Sherlock Homes said with a smile before he carried on. 'I had deuced for some time now that there was the existence of an Mr. Albert, but I could never be sure, evil runs deep and evil protects evil, so they say.'

The Strange Case of Caroline Maxwell

'Who was this Mr. Albert?' I asked a little confused at what I was hearing.

'Fundamentally a nobody, he wanted to make a name for himself and stop living under his father's shadow, he had his father's mind, he had his father's patience but he was still naive to think I would allow him to complete his father's mission,' Mr. Holmes said shaking his head slowly from side to side.

'Who was his father?'

'Ah, now there was man! A man with the mind and intellect to entertain me, which has been sadly lacking been over these long years! He was the...'

'Napoleon of crime?' I interrupted again as suddenly a thought had entered my head,

'Yes, of course it was accepted by the police as an accident, but my father did not fall over the edge, he was pushed!' is what this dead man had said to me, knowing as I do now that Sherlock Holmes knew this man's father it made the word 'fall' in the sentence even more important and I began to realise who I was looking down at.

By Amanda Harvey Purse

'Quite,' Mr. Holmes said as he turned to me and smiled. 'Here lays the body of Mr. Albert *Moriarty*.'

The Strange Case of Caroline Maxwell

Chapter Forty

Back at 221B Baker Street I was feeling more myself and after having a delightful dinner, that Dr Watson and I tucked heartily into for as always Mr. Sherlock Holmes preferred his pipe to eating, I began to think over the adventure I had been on and how it seemed to last longer than the few weeks it actually did.

'Is there anything you would like to know?' Mr. Holmes asked through the smoke of his tobacco. Dr Watson rolled his eyes at the question. 'I see that Dr Watson would prefer if I left the case, this rather *Strange Case of Caroline Maxwell* where we left the dead body of Moriarty's son, back in Ashford.'

By Amanda Harvey Purse

'I just don't see how further talking about this case will help anyone, you had put a person at risk on a hunch Holmes!' Dr Watson said as he put down his fork.

'Oh, is that how you see it Watson?' Mr. Holmes said without looking at either one of us.

'Should I see it in another way then?'

'Well I will place all the facts in front of you and you will decide then and only then,' Mr. Holmes said as he turned towards the burning flames that were in his fireplace. 'First of all I will tackle the first part of your statement. You think I put a person at risk, who would that person be?'

'Well quite obviously Miss Amelia Christie here,' Dr Watson said pointing to me, and to be honest I was thinking the same. Mr. Sherlock Holmes had put me on a dangerous case that he had always known about, he must have known the dangers he was putting me into.

'You think I put her at risk?'

'Well yes Holmes! This case brought her face to face with none other than Jack the Ripper!'

The Strange Case of Caroline Maxwell

'Is that what you think Watson? Well putting that to one side, I would never have put Miss Christie is any real danger, or to put it another way I would not have put her in any danger that I thought she couldn't get out of.'

'But that is quite clearly what you have done Holmes!'

'You should know me better than that my dear Watson! I was with Amelia all the way through this adventure.'

'You were?' I questioned, while placing my fork and knife on the china plate and turned slightly in my chair to face the marvellous man that sat there looking into his flaming fireplace.

'Yes I was, let me remind you Miss Christie, you first met me as a cleaner within Scotland Yard who kindly helped you on your way.'

'That was you?'

'Yes,' Mr. Holmes said as he laid a photograph upon the side table, I moved away from the dining table and towards the photograph to see the death picture of Miss Mary Nichols, the first accepted Jack the

By Amanda Harvey Purse

Ripper victim. I had thought that there were five photographs in The Ripper file to start with and I was a little confused when I saw only four photographs when I placed them back inside the file.

The old man who was dressed in worn out garments that smelt heavily of gin, the old man who had a billycock hat which had casted a shadow over the man's eyes, while his whitening whiskers were long and grubby. I had thought of his crooked back that was causing him great anguish, now I knew it was only an act and that it was Mr. Holmes and he had indeed taken the photograph. I sat down on the chair opposite Mr. Holmes with only his fireplace between us as I felt I was going to need to sit down for this story.

'The next time I met you was on a lovely little train going to Hampshire, with my ugly looking face, full of boils and warts and long hooked nose, small round eyes and thin light ginger hair surrounding it.' He said with a smile, as he handed me back my piece of paper with my hand written note saying Mr. Fredrick Abberline's name. I wondered where that went. I smiled at the note.

'Something is humorous, Miss Christie?' Mr. Holmes asked me.

The Strange Case of Caroline Maxwell

'I was just thinking that you are known for your great mind Mr. Holmes, but how many people realise what a great pickpocket you are?' I said still staring at the piece of paper.

'A man of many talents, wouldn't you say Holmes?' said Dr Watson.

'I know how to do the things I need to do; next I think was my best disguise, a vicar but in truth that disguise was not new to me.'

'You were the kind old vicar?'

'Yes, of course I had to get hold of a bible first to fully complete my role,' he said waving a copy of the holy bible, a version I remember seeing in the lovely public house I stayed in, Mr. Holmes smiled at my recognition of this book.

Mr. Holmes had been the previous lodger of The Silver Horse public house who had upset the landlord's wife by stealing a bible. 'Oh I was keeping hold of this, I can now please Mrs Hudson by throwing it away,' Mr. Holmes replied as he held up a brown, rotting apple. In all other counts that act of Mr. Holmes would have confused many, but not me, for I knew it wasn't just any rotting apple, it was *my* apple the vicar had taken away from me.

'What sinful fodder!' I proclaimed.

'Quite right, quite right my dear,' Mr. Holmes chortled.

'Mr. Abberline had told me that he never met the vicar, I should have thought more into it.'

'That is quite correct of him, well not in my form anyway.'

...

With the apple being disposed of by Mrs Hudson and some freshly brewed tea placed in my cup, Mr. Holmes picked up his interesting story again. 'I decided to find out if you were able to see Mr Abberline like I thought you would and I was right, but of course I would be right.'

'You were the train conductor coming back to London.'

'Indeed I was,' Mr. Holmes said as he handed me back my train ticket. 'Now the next time you saw me, was more of a fortification for your safety than me finding out

The Strange Case of Caroline Maxwell

what you were doing, I am afraid. You were alone with a madman who can cover his tracks; I had to step in there.'

'I was alone with a madman?'

'Yes, you had managed to be alone with Mr Albert Moriarty but you thought he was then Inspector Godley, a curious name for him to take on I had thought but either way you were in so much danger that you could not have possibly known,'

'You were the policeman that called George...I mean Albert away from me back in the Unsolved Crime Room at Scotland Yard.' I said as thoughts ran back to the moment the Inspector looked so heartbroken over thinking that Ex-Inspector Abberline may have been involved in a secret society of the brotherhood. It was all a red herring, it was all an act to make me feel sorry for him while he had known it was him that was involved in the brotherhood.

'Yes I am sorry to say, that I took this,' Mr. Holmes continued as he handed my handkerchief with care I might add, over to me. All the thoughts of my bag lying on the floor and how the 'policeman' was ever so helpful picking it up for me came rushing to the foremost of my mind.

'I was upset it was gone, but I have it again so all is well again,' I said and Mr. Holmes nodded a silent 'thank you' at my statement.

'The next time I saw you, it was in my own person,' Sherlock Holmes said as he came a quick glance toward me and then back at the fire.

'You did seem to be out of breath, when I saw you at the window,' I said pointing to the window in question behind me.

'You saw that did you? That is interesting...' Mr. Holmes stated almost in a whisper to himself. As he said those words I was suddenly reminded of the moment I shared with Mrs Hudson in Regent's Park.

'He goes away for a few days at a time, on some kind of case I would imagine as he never tells me anything. I take the quiet time to clean his rooms, he then comes back in a mad rush and now it is just as big of a mess as it was before I did anything! All my hard work is down the drain!' Mrs Hudson had said to me, Mrs Hudson had basically told me in her own little way that Sherlock Holmes was on a case and had recently came back to his rooms in Baker

The Strange Case of Caroline Maxwell

Street. I should have thought Sherlock Holmes was still on the same case I was on.

'But I sensed danger for you so I had one of the Baker Street Irregulars, Rupert to watch you for a while. I can see you can look after yourself,' he said with his eyebrows raised and my mind went quickly back to the poor policeman I had tricked with my tea and I looked down, bashful. The little cheeky lad had indeed seen me enter my ex-neighbour's property.

'I had heard Mr. Albert Moriarty mention to you about meeting Inspector Dew the Whitechapel Library and I thought that was mighty strange and I did not like the thought of you going but of course I could not tell you to go home. So I decided,' he said with a flick of his hand 'To become a librarian of that said library and tell you that we were closing early, hoping you would go home before anything that Mr. Moriarty had planned for you actually happened,' He said as he passed me back my card I had printed and had given the kind old librarian. 'Sadly I was indeed wrong. Something that happens more times than you would think if you just know me by the stories my good friend writes of me. I am sorry I was not there for you.'

By Amanda Harvey Purse

I felt my jaw, the bruising had healed somewhat but it was still aching a little. 'I cannot be helped Mr. Holmes. You can be expected to be everywhere,' I said as I looked towards the great man himself, somehow I knew what I had just said did not comfort him so I carried on saying 'And what if you being there, would have put me in more danger? Mr. Moriarty had said he was watching me in Whitechapel, what if he had seen you helping me?'

'That would have indeed put you in more danger,' he replied sternly but he gave me a quick smile as another form of silent 'thank you' towards me. 'Then I had to pass you my note,' he said changing the subject.

'My cryptic clue you mean? P.C Collard had said it was very *Sherlockian*.'

'Sherlockian you say, interesting word I must admit.'

'It has your name in it Holmes, you are bound to like it,' laughed Dr Watson.

'Yes well,' Mr. Holmes said as he brushed off Dr Watson's comment. 'I followed you to Ashford as your travelling partner and dropped certain hints about a school.'

The Strange Case of Caroline Maxwell

'Yes, you were quite informative for someone I had just met,' I laughed to myself as I thought of silly I had been. Sherlock Holmes had led me through this adventure while I thought I was on my own.

'Thank you, I do try my best to be...informative, oh by the way; here is your hat,' he said as he reached behind the chair in which he was sitting on and passed me my hat. 'And while I am at it here is your pencil too, for I was also the man who showed you the way to The Rosebud Inn.'

'You are full of surprises Mr. Holmes!' I proclaimed.

'Isn't he just,' said Dr Watson as he rolled his eyes.

'I called for Dr Watson and his gun when I had noticed Mr. Albert Moriarty following you for quite some time; he is not as great at disguises as he thinks. He used chemicals and medicines to change his appearance.'

'Are they those creatures I saw moving in his skin?'

'They are the side effects of...being quite unwise. Mr. Robert Stevenson had once contacted me stated he had a visited from a very disturbed little man asking where 'Dr

Jekyll' had got his medicine to turn him into 'Mr. Hyde'...' Mr. Holmes stated has he gave me a questionable look.

'Mr. Moriarty thought Mr. Stevenson's book was true?'

'It is amazing how literature can seem so real to some people...' Sherlock Holmes smirked, but who he was smirking towards I have no idea, dear reader. 'I think you know the rest. I had always believed the lady I found to be working in Ashford as a school teacher was Miss Mary Kelly but I had to be sure and if I had found her I knew Mr. Albert also would.'

'It seems as if I was well looked after all the way through my adventure in that case,' I said remembering all the times I had felt eyes watching me, in those sad, depressing moments I had thought those eyes belonged to Jack the Ripper, I never once guessed the eyes belonged to Mr Holmes... 'I never saw anyone following me, Mr Holmes.'

'That is exactly what you should see, when I am following you,' was his simple reply, 'And it was more than just a hunch; wouldn't you say so now Watson?'

The Strange Case of Caroline Maxwell

'Yes, well... you always have an answer to everything!' Dr Watson replied as he shrugged his shoulders and carried on eating from his plate. Sherlock Holmes and I shared a smile as we watched Dr. Watson tuck into his food without a care in the world.

By Amanda Harvey Purse

Chapter Forty One

'Your adventure is at an end Miss Christie; I presume you will want to start writing your piece for the paper explaining all about it?' Mr. Holmes had asked me. I said nothing back to him; I had started to gaze into the warm, flickering flames of Mr. Holmes's fireplace. I was thinking over everything I had been through with this case and I finally realised I hadn't been through a lot at all, not compared to the people I have met along the way.

Yes I was sitting here in the famous residence of 221B Baker Street knowing the truth behind one of the greatest mysteries that had happened within the greatest murder case the world would ever know but I wasn't feeling contented or even the slightest bit jovial. The suffering and torment so many people had been through, all

The Strange Case of Caroline Maxwell

because of one man that killed five women sixteen years ago.

Ex- Inspector Fredrick Abberline can never truly allow himself to move on, knowing he had protected his Sergeant, his colleague, his friend. Whether Mr. Abberline knew how much he was protecting I can only guess at, but for someone that protected everyone he ever met, to have to protect a killer must damage your inner soul. He tried to constitute what he had done, by saving Miss Mary Kelly in the only way he knew how, by making her disappear into someone new, it just wasn't enough for him and Jack the Ripper haunts him still.

Miss Mary Kelly has had a life of the most unluckiest, unloved and harrowing. How she had survived a life so wicked at already such a young age, only to be faced with the depraved and horrific murder panorama I can only slightly envisage by having to look at the black and white photograph of 'Belle'. Miss Mary had suffered the worst kind of existence and yet, somehow she had managed to turn it all around, those children completely adored her and she did them.

Did I have any right at all to tell the story of Miss Caroline Maxwell? Was it my entitlement after what I had been through and risked for my career? Does what happened to me justify me telling the world the unknown life of Miss Mary Kelly?

'No, Mr. Holmes. I feel it would be an iniquitous of me to print a single word of this case,' I said still looking into the fire but picturing the soulless faces I have met.

'What will you tell your editor?' Mr. Holmes asked.

'There is a case that had developed within this case, a wrong that needs to be put right. This is what I will tell the editor, whether he will accept it or not is his problem for I will have filled my end of the bargain. This case has shown me something though.'

'Oh and what is that?' Mr. Holmes.

'Something I think you saw in me, am I wrong Mr. Holmes?'

'I saw something erroneous when I first met you, yes.'

'But you wanted me to figure it out myself...'

'Indeed.'

The Strange Case of Caroline Maxwell

'I am sorry but I seemed to be missing something, what is so wrong with Miss Christie here?' asked Dr Watson as he moved nearer to where Mr. Holmes and I were sitting. 'I for one can see she is the most delightful of all ladies.'

'Thank you Dr Watson for your kind comments but Mr. Holmes and I were discussing my *erroneous* career.'

'Oh?'

'It was not something new to me Dr Watson, in truth I probably have always known I am in the wrong career. But this case kept pushing me to admit it; I cannot tell you how many times in this adventure I questioned my journalist workings. I could not for an example, print the word 'journalist' on my card, for you see I have written something else,' I said as I showed Dr Watson my card.

'Ah, the word 'writer' seemed to be on your card Miss,' replied the doctor after he glanced at the card.

'Indeed.' Sherlock Holmes and I both said at the same time, to which we both smiled and Dr Watson laughed.

By Amanda Harvey Purse

'What will you do now Miss Christie?' asked Mr. Holmes.

'I need to finish something that has been hanging over me since I met Miss Caroline's daughter.'

'Ah I was wondering if we were going to come to that.'

'Yes, Mr. Holmes. I think we should come to it,' I answered. 'It is only fair.'

'Fair indeed, Miss Christie, fair indeed.'

'Can you two please explain what you are both talking about, I feel as if I am lost!' Dr Watson proclaimed.

I smiled back at Sherlock Holmes to which he gave me a quick smirk as agreement to joining in the teasing fun Mr. Holmes had shared with Dr Watson for many a year.

'We can't have the good doctor feeling lost can we Mr. Holmes?'

'Shall I bring him in then?' Asked Sherlock Holmes as he stood up from his seat and moved towards the door.

'Yes, please Mr Holmes.'

The Strange Case of Caroline Maxwell

...

'Bring who in?' asked Dr Watson as he still must have felt at a loss of what Mr. Holmes and I were talking about.

'The reason,' we both answered him together and then we both smiled.

'What?'

'I'll let you answer him Miss Christie, it would be a nice change to hear an explanation from someone else's mouth,' said Mr. Holmes as he pointed to me.

'The real Miss Caroline Maxwell's daughter had a son that was taken from her, she has been alone for many a year and she is now ill but still she looks for her son. Her son was in a home but he ran away and it was heard that a kind gentleman had taken care of him in such a way, I had promised to find this boy for her.'

'How very thoughtful of you Miss Christie,' said Dr Watson, but I carried on talking.

'It turns out I did not have to look too far to find the said kind gentleman who had taken care of this boy.'

By Amanda Harvey Purse

'When did you find out this gentleman's name?' asked Dr Watson.

'Just a moment ago.'

'What?'

'The next time I saw you, it was in my own person but I sensed danger for you so I had one of the Baker Street Irregulars, Rupert to watch you for a while,' I said repeated what Mr. Sherlock Holmes had said to me.

'That is how I knew about the real Miss Caroline Maxwell Watson; I knew she could not have written that eye witness account in The Ripper inquiry because she was already dead,' Mr. Holmes said picking up the story. 'I have always said my Baker Street Irregulars were of a different class, Rupert had found out about his mother and his grandmother and told me.' With that the door opened and a teenage boy stood in the doorway. 'Would you Mr. Rupert, like Miss Christie to take you home, to your real home?'

'Yes, please Mr. Sherlock Holmes!' he said in a boyish glee.

The Strange Case of Caroline Maxwell

With that, I smiled at Mr. Holmes, something so inconsequential to him had directed him to find the truth behind Miss Mary Kelly, all it took was listening to a small boy. As I took my turn to leave, I stood up and the conversation between Dr Watson and Mr. Sherlock Holmes ran through my mind.

'You think I put her at risk?'

'Well yes Holmes! This case brought her face to face with none other than Jack the Ripper!'

'Is that what you think Watson? Well putting that to one side, I would never have put Miss Christie is any real danger, or to put it another way I would not have put her in any danger that I thought she couldn't get out of.'

It stopped me in my tracks and forced me to ask one more question to Mr. Holmes, 'Mr Holmes? Will we ever know who was Jack the Ripper?' Mr. Holmes smiled deeply back into the fire as he sat back down.

'Hang on! Wasn't Jack the Ripper, Mr. Albert Mortarty?' asked Dr Watson to me.

By Amanda Harvey Purse

'I don't think so, do you Mr. Holmes?' I asked glancing down at the most famous detective in the world, a man whose mission it is to know everything.

'Maybe one day...' was his simple reply, somehow in those three unpretentious words I understood that Mr. Sherlock Holmes had always known who Jack the Ripper was and that one day I might be lucky enough to find out myself, but that was not the point of *this* adventure, maybe, just maybe it will be the point of my next adventure...

I said 'Goodbye,' to Mr. Holmes but as always it fell on deaf ears as he did nothing to change his look into the fire.

'Goodbye Dr Watson,' I said as I shook his hand.

'Goodbye Miss Christie, oh, by the way what is the accurate career for you if being a journalist is so erroneous?'

'My right career you ask Dr Watson? I will someday write crime novels, it is something I have always wanted to do; maybe I will imagine my own detective, which solves my little crimes by using his little grey cells. I will change my name I think.'

The Strange Case of Caroline Maxwell

'Oh? And what will your author name be?'

'Mrs Oakshott had always called me by a name I quite liked, Agatha. *Agatha Christie* has a certain ring to it, don't you think Dr Watson?'

'Very much Miss Christie, good luck to you!' I heard Dr Watson say as I left the living quarters of Mr. Sherlock Holmes, hand in hand with a Baker Street Irregular on our way to Whitechapel, to make a dying woman's wish come true...

By Amanda Harvey Purse

Saturday 9th November 1901 in The City of London...

The Strange Case of Caroline Maxwell

Chapter Forty Two

'I cannot believe my eyes! Is it really you? Is it really the person who I had hired so many years ago?' My sarcastic little editor said to me when I had entered his office. The office was cold and bitter as the wintry weather was setting in, it did not surprise me as this office always seemed cold even on the brightest of summer mornings. I had wondered how my editor coped with these constant icy surroundings in which he worked but I suppose he was heavily fed and maybe it suited his personality.

'Yes, I agree that I have not being in your office for a while Sir,' I asked.

'For well over a month my dear! I think you will find,' my editor's comment was spiteful and a little tactless but I will have to admit that no matter how insensitive his comments were, they are actually very accurate. I had not been in this office for about six weeks. I could lie to you dear reader and say that is was because I had started to write my crime stories but in truth I had only wrote a few lines and a handful of notes on this matter. I had been playing around with the idea of using poisons in my stories as thoughts of George Chapman the poisoner had never truly left me after I heard of his tale but no idea was solid in my mind. The reason I had not been in this office was because I wanted to send Mr. Fredrick Abberline just one version of my article, I wanted him to know I cared about the stories within his life that I only had to send him one complete account. With this in mind I mumbled to myself more than towards my editor,

'I had to make sure...'

'that your hair was right? You had the right dress to wear? I don't want to hear your womanly excuses my dear, I want results!' He bellowed me; I was a little taken aback by this statement but as I looked towards this little man sitting at his desk, I saw the notes he had written all in a mess lying at his desk. I saw the pale skin of his face, from days of worrying and I saw the dark rings around his eyes

The Strange Case of Caroline Maxwell

from the lack of sleep. All of this made me understand the stress feeling within that last statement towards me.

1...2...3...

'I had to make sure the contract was fulfilled,' I answered forcefully without replying to the statement my frustrating little editor had just said.

'Ah yes, this contract you had signed when you should not have done! I hope the article in your hands is worth the long wait I have given you!' My editor said as he got up from his desk and turned from me to look out of his window. I also took at moment to look out of his window, this time I could not see much as the frost of the November weather had surrounded every pale of glass, leaving only the centre as the pin-hole viewpoint. But what I could see was that snow had fallen; the cold winds blew the white dust of its icy coverings around the chimney tops of this great city, all the normal signs pointing to one conclusion that Christmas was on its way.

'I believe it is worth the wait Sir,' I said as I looked down at the folder I had written my article in. On top of the folder I had left a single white piece of paper out and placed it on top, it was to remind me of everything I have

By Amanda Harvey Purse

been through and what it all meant in the end. For on this single white piece of paper had the words...

My nightmares have ended, you are free to publish.

Mr Fredrick Abberline

'Oh it is, is it?' My editor asked, still looking out of the window.

'I believe so Sir,' I said as I place the single white piece of paper inside the pocket of my dress and placed the folder on his desk.

'By the way, what have you titled this article?'

'You've never asked me that before, I did not think you cared.'

'I always care what title you choose...'

'A Protective Policeman.'

It was then my editor turned from the window to face me, 'That will do, Miss Christie that will do,' he said with an agreeable nod of his head as he sat down at his desk. He picked up the folder and started reading it,

The Strange Case of Caroline Maxwell

stopped then put his little gold rimmed spectacles on as if he had forgotten I was still in the room and started reading again. *I knew it! I had suspected he wore glasses!*

I had thought it best to leave him reading my article so I took step backwards and turned on the spot. I had almost reached the door when my editor asked, 'Do you happen to know what the date is today, Miss Christie?'

'It is the 9th November,' I said.

'And do you know what happened on this day?'

'I remember all too well,' I replied as thoughts of the photograph of who I now know was 'Belle' entered my head for it was on this day in 1888 that she was found in the bloodied mess Jack the Ripper had left her in and the very day we all started calling her Mary Kelly.

'I was going to do a remembrance piece on it, if your article wasn't up to scratch.'

'Was you?' I said a little surprised.

'Oh yes, our public always trusts us to give them the political view of counties in far off worlds.'

By Amanda Harvey Purse

'I am sorry, I don't understand what you mean,' I said a little confused.

'Don't you remember Miss Christie? It was this time last year that China got back the control of Manchuria but they had secret meetings with Russia.'

'Oh, that was what you were meaning,' I said.

'Why what else happened on this day?' My stupid editor asked me.

'Nothing Sir, nothing at all happened,' I lied as I shut my editor's office door. How we forget so easily, do you not think dear reader...

The Strange Case of Caroline Maxwell

Epilogue

By Amanda Harvey Purse

Looking back over this whole adventure I now realise there is one significant missing part to my story, I had briefly mentioned how I met the greatest police consulting detective for the first time, but briefly it should not be anymore. So here is the only interview Mr. Sherlock Holmes has ever given to a young female reporter, Miss Amelia Christie of The Times Newspaper, London.

The Times

Christmas

Edition

It was with excitement I walked along the now famous Baker Street after, I must confess, getting a little lost with the odd numbering of that street. But finally I found the legendary 221B in gold plate above the celebrated black door.

To be honest reader, I couldn't believe I was there, standing outside this door. While it looked like any other upmarket door in this street and the area surrounding it, as the well-known Harley Street is only a few rows behind it.

The Strange Case of Caroline Maxwell

It was what was laying behind this door that interested me and of course you, the reader.

For here was the home of the most recognized man in Victorian England today, here was the home of Mr. Sherlock Holmes and I was granted an interview!

I tapped nervously, on the golden lion's face knocker and waited a few seconds. The door opened, and I was faced with a kind, warm hearted looking woman. Her light brown hair was turning slightly grey. Her face was the normal pale colour, of people who have spent their whole life in the London smog. The only colour that survived was the red mark on the bridge of her nose, which was obviously the cause of wearing spectacles.

Her smart, black maid's uniform was certainly well worn, a sign she had been a maid for a long time and the two white marks just above her knees showing she had been doing her spring cleaning today.

"Hello, can I help you?" she asked politely.

By Amanda Harvey Purse

"Yes please, I am Miss Amelia Christie of *The Times*."

"Ah, Mr. Holmes has been expecting a reporter from The Times, please come in."

So there I was inside number 221B Baker Street, being led up the carpeted stairs, to a dark brown, oak door. As I got nearer I heard from the other side of the wooden door, a man's voice say...

"If I'm not mistaken Holmes, here is the reporter from The Times now.

I can tell he is of medium build, I would say six feet tall, walks with a slight limp and he is young..." With that the door opens and I walked in.

"Miss Amelia Christie, from The Times," Mrs Hudson stated.

There was a round of laughter from within the room...

"Close Watson, close but no cigar!" The other man in the room laughed.

"Please take a seat Miss Christie," the now bashful man holding the door open said as he waved me in.

The Strange Case of Caroline Maxwell

"I am Dr Watson and this is Mr. Sherlock Holmes," he said while closing the door and pointing to his friend.

I sat down on the sofa, next to the fire as this cold winter was starting to affect me. I knew I was being studied as I moved across the room...

"Hello, it is nice to finally meet you two, after reading...."

"Yes, yes after reading 'A Study in Scarlet'," Mr Holmes said with a huff, to finish my sentence. Then he turned his back towards me.

"I'm sorry for my friend here, he doesn't much like my idea of writing about his cases and he doesn't like the fame I am giving him. It was my idea for this interview, you see Miss Christie," said Dr Watson.

"Oh I see and that does explains a lot. You see I was quite shocked that you two agreed to this interview in the first place..."

There was another huff from Mr. Holmes at that statement of mine.

"But what I was going to say Mr Holmes was after reading your 'Book of Life'.

By Amanda Harvey Purse

I just knew I had to meet the man who wrote it."

There was a quick turn in his seat as he faced me, he asked. "You have read my book?"

"Yes sir, very much so sir. But I must confess it was after my editor had read 'A Study in Scarlet' that he finally agreed to let me interview you Sir," I said.

"Yes well, some people don't have the aptitude to learn, they just want gossip, gossip and more gossip," Mr. Holmes replied.

"Quite so, Mr Holmes, but I must say gossip does sell papers.

Without gossip I would be out of a job, all reporters would be out of a job. In turn, there will no newspapers, so in turn there would be nothing to help you build a case on or nothing to put in your files over there," I said pointing to wooden shelving in the corner of the room.

There was silence...

Then laughter...

"Well, Miss Christie I must say you are very interesting indeed."

The Strange Case of Caroline Maxwell

"I am guessing that is what has given me this interview, but then I should never guess."

I could see in the corner of my eye, Dr Watson was giving me an assuring nod of his head.

I had answered correctly; I had passed the test...

Now down to business...

"Now Mr Holmes, our readers would like to know a few details about you," I said.

"Oh if I must, if I must," he replied, waving his hand at me.

"First of all, when and where were you born?"

There was a huff and a shake of his head.

"The questions were designed by my editor for the British readers," I said.

"I had thought so; ah the good old British reader ...The British Family...Big Ben...Stiff upper a lip and all that..." He said with a dreamy sarcastic laugh.

"Well I suppose my heart has been in the south of the country, Sussex with the countryside, the fresh air and of course the bees."

"The bees?" I questioned.

By Amanda Harvey Purse

"Ah yes, the bees, the wonderful bees." Mr Holmes replied as he seemed to drift off into a dream and did not really answer me. Maybe there will always be parts of Mr. Holmes that will seem to be a mystery to us and *maybe, just maybe it should always be that way.*

"Right then, when is your birthday?"

"The 6th of January," was the simply reply.

"So you will be celebrating soon, then?"

"I only celebrate a case well done..."

"You don't celebrate Christmas then?"

"Christmas! I quote from Dickens when I say...Bah Humbug!" I couldn't help but smile at his answer.

There was a tap at the door and Mrs Hudson walked in.

"A letter for you Mr. Holmes," she said.

Mr. Holmes snatched the letter from the silver tray Mrs Hudson was holding and waved her away; as she left the room she rolled her eyes.

The Strange Case of Caroline Maxwell

I turned my head back to Mr. Holmes to see him scanning the letter with the swift action we, readers have become accustom too.

"Watson! We must go! Off to Scotland Yard!" He said instantly.

With that, they both left the room sharply and with a quick nod from Dr Watson, the room was empty and I knew I had witnessed the start of a new case I will soon read...

Before I left the room, I couldn't help but look out of Mr. Holmes's window.

I looked down at the cab that was waiting, to catch the last glimpse of this fascinating man.

As I looked down I saw Dr Watson entered the cab, Mr Holmes was about to when he stopped and looked up at his window and nodded at me...

I knew then, I would be back here, at 221B Baker Street again, somehow with some reason but what that reason will be only Mr. Sherlock Holmes will know...

Reported by *Miss Amelia Christie*

By Amanda Harvey Purse

Author's Notes

As I came to the end of writing this novel I began to understand the history secretly weaved into this story and how maybe I should write a little bit about the Victorian and Edwardian history here...

Nellie Bly

Nellie Bly is mentioned by Amelia almost as if she was someone who she could look up to and this is why she could have thought of her that way. Nellie Bly was the pseudonym used by the American journalist, Elizabeth Jane Cochrane. She was born on the 5th May 1864 and died 27th January 1922; her journalist career was pushed into the limelight with her being the reporter who recorded a record-breaking trip around the world in seventy two days in the year of The Ripper.

Something that was so popular for its time that the writer Jules Verne, who she met on her travels, used it for his fictional character, Phileas Fogg in his novel *Around the World in Eighty Days*.

The Strange Case of Caroline Maxwell

As well as being an pioneer for female journalism, her forcefulness of getting a story at no matter what cost made her led the way in a new style of investigative newspaper writing. Her expose of a mental institution, where she faked her own insanity to become a patient is a great example of this.

She had to go through similar hard ships as Amelia Christie with her editor, having to use a fake name. The name taken was from the popular song by Steven Foster and it stuck. Writing articles about women's work in the factories and gardens got her name known enough to pluck up the courage to move to Mexico and write as a foreign correspondent which put her in danger and threats made on her life.

This did not stop her and next she turned her mind to the asylums and wrote her article, 'Ten days in a Mad House' where she was examined by a psychiatrist and she was able to fake her way into The Women's Lunatic Asylum on Blackwell's Island after practising a 'mad look' with the help of a mirror and oddly stating over and over again that she was NOT mad. The doctors then claimed she was 'positively demented'; once inside the asylum she was able to write about the horrid conditions, treatment and food the patients were given. Because of this, a jury launched an investigation where, Nellie Bly was invited and the outcome was better conditions and thorough examinations.

She followed the women's rights closely, covering the Woman Suffrage Parade of 1913 and even predicted that it would not be until the 1920's before women would get the right to vote. She died in New York City in 1922 of pneumonia at the age of fifty seven.

Irene Alder (Character within The Sherlock Holmes Adventures)

Within my story, I have Sherlock Holmes briefly comparing Amelia to Irene Alder. Irene Adler is a fictional character who is within one Sherlock Holmes's adventures written by Sir Arthur Conan Doyle, that story was called 'A Scandal in Bohemia'. This story had a slight importance to this story because it was first published in July 1891 but it was meant to be set in March 1888 (the year of The Ripper).

She is really the only female character that Sherlock Holmes was impressed by and the only one who got the better of him. Although she is possibly mentioned in

The Strange Case of Caroline Maxwell

another five stories, 'A Scandal in Bohemia' is the only one where the reader meets her and afterwards Sherlock Holmes only ever describes her as 'The Woman'. I thought that because my Amelia Christie was always going to be a strong willed woman, to make her seem different and that Sherlock Holmes was always quick to pick up on these things that Sherlock Holmes would have certainly have been reminded of Irene Alder as he spoke to Amelia.

Boar War

It is mentioned within my story, that Amelia's editor was involved in the Boar War. Which in fact should have been called The Boar Wars as there were two wars, the first was during 1880-1881 and the second 1899-1902. These wars were about The British Empire fighting against The Boer Republics called The Orange Free State and The Transvaal Republic.

The first Boer War was mainly a fight for the republics to keep hold of their lands from a British invasion, in which the British lost. The second Boer war was lengthier and involved a lot more troops from the British, which in turn meant a lot more deaths through combat and sickness.

By Amanda Harvey Purse

The reason I have Amelia's editor being involved in the Boer War was firstly because of the age the editor would have been within my story, but also because of a real life editor W.T. Stead (made famous at the height of The Ripper murders) wrote many articles on the Boar War as if he was there, seeing the harsh conditions and the starving people within the camps.

These wars could have been said to be the start of Germany thinking the British were weak and could have been one of the many causes behind World War One. Of course The Boar Wars greatly affected many people but the most famous was probably the novelist and poet, Thomas Hardy, who wrote the poem 'Drummer Hodge' about the wars.

Dates

The exact dates in which Amelia visits the editor in *The City of London* was another interesting part of my story, as each time the editor mentions to Amelia something that is news worthy which is also happening on that day. I use this for two reasons, the first as a form of the editor pushing Amelia to write a greater article because there is always news happening and secondly because what

The Strange Case of Caroline Maxwell

the editor tells Amelia is all true and it is another way to get true facts into my story.

The Cleveland Street Scandal

The Cleveland Street Scandal was a real case and happened in very much the same way as I have described in this story. It happened in 1889 and the male brothel was indeed found out by a telegraph messenger boy who had more money on him than what he should have done. Whether the press was paid to not mention it because of the 'higher up involved' is my fiction based on the fact that few famous people mentioned at the time as being involved with this case sued the papers for libel. The press never named Prince Albert Victor, the Queen Victoria's grandson, as being involved and there was never any evidence he had visited the brothel but there were rumours at the time. It was also these same rumours that help him to become a Jack the Ripper suspect.

Inspector Fredrick George Abberline

Inspector Abberline was probably the most famous policeman who hunted the famous serial killer called Jack the Ripper and he was indeed the policeman involved in

By Amanda Harvey Purse

The Cleveland Street Scandal. Frederick Abberline was the only child of Edward and Hannah Abberline.

Frederick was indeed a clockmaker before he went into the force, like I stated within my story but whether he never finished his clocks is purely my own fictional feeling of things that could have been. The cases Frederick dealt with as an up and coming policeman I have mentioned are true and wrote through my research of him. He indeed moved to Hampshire with his second wife and maid Mary Yates, although the story about Mary in fictional but he did have a lodger who sold a story about Abberline to the press.

It is said he did say, 'You've caught him at last!' meaning Jack the Ripper when his fellow policeman George Godley caught George Chapman.

Inspector George Godley

Inspector Godley was a real life policeman who worked with Inspector Abberline as I state in my story but the story of him being the secret son of James Mortarty is purely fiction on my part.

Born in East Grinstead in 1856, George Albert Godley first worked as a sawyer before joining the force in

The Strange Case of Caroline Maxwell

1877. At the time of The Ripper, Godly was a sergeant to J Division, he moved to H Division to help Inspector Abberline. He is often mentioned in The Times newspaper, which is mainly why I introduce him to Amelia. In 1902, George does arrest the famous poisoner George Chapman but by 1908 he retires from the force, he dies in July 1941 at the age of eighty four.

George Chapman

The poisoner George Chapman was real and his criminal ways was very much as I describe in my story. George being Jack the Ripper is a very old and well used theory as it was mentioned within a Jack the Ripper book only written fifty years after the actual murders and is of course helped by what Inspector Abberline is said to have stated when he got arrested.

Henry Wainwright

Henry Wainwright murdered Harriet Lane in September 1874 and buried in the shop/warehouse he owned until the smell got too bad. What happened the night Henry wanted to move her, was exactly how it happens in my story. Henry was sentenced to death and hanged on 21st December 1875.

By Amanda Harvey Purse

Inspector Lestrade (Character from the Sherlock Holmes Adventures)

Inspector Lestrade is a fictional character, who appears in numerous of Sherlock Holmes's adventures written by Sir Arthur Conan Doyle. It is said the name comes from a friend of Sir Arthur's from his days spent at the University of Edinburgh.

The Inspector appears in thirteen stories, one of which is similar to the scene set within my story, with the murder of Violet Smith. My favourite moment with the Inspector is set in one of the later Sherlock Holmes stories where, after years of what seems like fighting against the wit of Holmes, the Inspector finally states how proud of him Scotland Yard is.

London Zoo

Placing Amelia in Regent's Park was mainly to place her close to Baker Street, so she could have indeed met up with Mrs Hudson so the reader could find out an untold story of how Sherlock Holmes and Mrs Hudson met, as that has never truly been mentioned before. While in Regent's Park I have Amelia mentioning London's Zoo, which was there at the time I have my story set as it was

The Strange Case of Caroline Maxwell

opened on 27th April 1828, it was indeed used for scientific study but opened to the public in 1847 and the story of the American Bear is all true.

Inspector Walter Dew

Although this man is only mentioned in my story and does not actually appear, all that is said about him is true.

Walter Dew, was born in Northamptonshire in 1822 and left school at the age of thirteen, before going into the force he tries his luck being a junior clerk in Chancery Lane then going on the railways like his father. But in 1882 he joins the force in X Division and in 1886 Walter marries Kate Morris. A year later he moves to H Division and becomes involved with The Criminal Investigation Department when The Ripper strikes in 1888.

He later claims to have known Mary Jane Kelly by sight and believed that Emma Smith was the first Ripper victim. In 1898 Walter was promoted to Inspector and moves to Scotland Yard and in 1910 he becomes famous for catching Dr Crippen, who was said to have murdered his wife.

By Amanda Harvey Purse

You may think I have mentioned him here because of his connection with Jack the Ripper only, but sadly you would be only half right.

It is said that in his retirement he gave his comments and opinions on the 1926 mysterious disappearance of one real life crime writer called...Agatha Christie which is very important to the ending of my story and links him quite well in.

Inspector Collard

Inspector Collard is real but is mentioned within my story as P.C Collard and nothing about P.C Collard is the same as Inspector Collard but I wanted to mention him as his story is very sympathetic to how I believe policemen must have felt at the time of The Ripper.

He was actually living at Bishopsgate Police Station at the time of the only City of London Ripper victim, Catherine Eddowes was murdered. On hearing the news of her murder, it was Inspector Collard, who arranged house to house searches bringing the witness of Joseph Lawende, Joseph Levy and Harry Harris into The Ripper File. He also went to the scene of the crime, where he was handed various items from the victim.

The Strange Case of Caroline Maxwell

But what truly is caring, is that when he died just four years later he wanted to be buried in the same place as Catherine Eddowes so that he could protect her in death as he could not do in life.

Frankenstein

I mention few famous Victorian literatures at the time within my story, one of which is Frankenstein written by Mary Shelly. Apparently the story line came to her in a dream and while she, her husband Percy Shelly and Lord Byron had a competition to see who would write the best horror story, she wrote about her dream of a scientist who created life.

Ashford

Perhaps I mention Ashford within my story because of personal reasons, but in truth I wanted a town that would seem so different to Amelia than the smog filled streets of London. I wanted to suggest that murder could happen everywhere and it is quite often the case that when murder happens in a quiet town it seems more chilling, this was what I wanted the feel of the end of my book to be.

What I mention in Newtown actually existed at the time in which I set my story and Ashford being a railway and market town is all true. As well as the name of the school and how they got the funds to build it, is again all true.

I also wanted a town in which Sherlock Holmes would have known about, not necessity because of Mary Kelly, like I stated in my book as that is pure fiction on my count, but a town maybe that Sherlock had visited before, if only briefly. This is where Ashford fitted in quite nicely as Ashford is briefly mentioned in the Sherlock Holmes story of The Reichenbach Fall as a train station Sherlock Holmes and Dr Watson can use to get away from Moriarty.

Jack the Ripper

Finally we come to the main characters of this fictional story, Jack the Ripper was real but who Jack the Ripper was is still debateable. What the name does seem to stand for is highlighting all that was bad with the East End at the time of 1888. The poverty, overcrowding, lack of hygiene and lack of jobs, all become aware of to the government because of this serial killer. The victim's lives were so dreadful that it may even be said that Jack the Ripper ended the misery for them.

The Strange Case of Caroline Maxwell

The number of victims has always been questionable; some have said there were four and the number has risen to pass the twenties but mainly people have accepted that there were five victims and five victims only which all get mentioned with my story and the accounts of their lives within the narrative are all true to what we know of them.

Sherlock Holmes

This is the first time I have written this famous character within one of my stories; I will admit here this was a taunting task for many reasons. Firstly, I cannot express fully how much I feel affection for Sherlock Holmes. I thought it was when I was eleven that the Holmes bug hit me from reading the stories, but when I thought about it more I realised I was certainly younger, with my love for Basil the Great Mouse Detective film. But then I found Jeremy Brett's version of Sherlock Holmes and I was overcome all over again, sadly I found it a year after the great man had died but I own the complete collection on DVD, so I can bring him back on television whenever I like. So with Sherlock Holmes meaning so much to me it certainly worried me to write him in my story as I knew I had to do him justice.

By Amanda Harvey Purse

Secondly, it worried me placing Sherlock Holmes in a Jack the Ripper novel. Sir Arthur Conan Doyle never felt the need to do it and so many other people have wrote Sherlock chasing Jack. I did not want to the same, luckily enough this was not a 'who Jack the Ripper was' novel. My Sherlock, if I can call him mine, never chases Jack. He doesn't have to. Although I do use that fact that Sherlock Holmes was very good at disguises to help my story along.

Sherlock Holmes is a fictional character written by Sir Arthur Conan Doyle who first appeared in 1887, a year before The Ripper. Sir Arthur wrote four novels and fifty six short stories in a period of between 1887 and 1914. It is said the inspiration for Sherlock Holmes came from Sir Arthur's teacher from The Royal Infirmary of Edinburgh, Dr. Joseph Bell.

Sir Arthur's Sherlock lives at 221B Baker Street with Mrs Hudson and Dr Watson and has a brother called Mycroft. He killed Sherlock in a story set in 1891, but the public outcry brought him back with a story set before *the fall* and that story is probably the most famous story of Sherlock Holmes's being the Hound of the Baskervilles, which is why I mention it within my own story and also because it is said to be set in 1888 (the year of The Ripper)

The Strange Case of Caroline Maxwell

although that is still debatable. Instead of killing him for the second time, Sir Arthur retires Sherlock with his beloved bees as I have mentioned his likes, within my own story.

Sherlock and his method on more than one occasion have helped in real life crimes, hence to the main reason I wanted to join him in a novel where there is many true crimes within it.

Throughout my story, I either mention a story of Sherlock Holmes's or I secretly suggest a story. I do this mainly for other fans of the great detective, a sort of 'can you spot all the clues within my story?' I will not mention them here as it will be cheating, but it is up to you dear reader if you chose to read my story over again to spot them all.

Dame Agatha Christie

Although I have suggested Amelia can become similar to Dame Agatha Christie, with Amelia hinting at a future detective similar to Poirot, the detective Dame Agatha Christie has become famous for writing and the wanting Amelia has to write crime novels. My Amelia is otherwise very different to Dame Agatha Christie as I do

By Amanda Harvey Purse

realise Agatha Christie is her married name and she worked at a nurse before she put pen to paper, not a journalist but this is my fictional tale with my own fictional character. I suggest my Amelia could become similar to Dame Agatha Christie only ever out of respect for *The Queen of Crime*.

Dame Agatha Mary Clarissa Christie was born on 15th September 1890, two years after The Jack the Ripper Murders; in Devon she wrote sixty six detective novels, fourteen short stories and six romances which are under the name of Mary Westmacott. Her most famous characters are Hercule Poirot, Miss Jane Marple and Tommy and Tuppence. One reason she started writing crime novels was because she was a huge fan of Sir Arthur Conan Doyle's Sherlock Holmes, which seemed to tie nicely in with my story.

In 1926, she has her own little mystery when she disappears after her first husband asked for a divorce. This is disappearance was even wrote about on the front page of The New York Times, she was not found for ten days, where she was finally found in an hotel in Yorkshire under the name of her husband's lover. She never explained her disappearance and doctor's have guessed she had suffered

The Strange Case of Caroline Maxwell

from a nervous breakdown although like Sherlock Holmes always teaches us...*we should never guess*.

Finally to Mrs Caroline Maxwell...

Caroline Maxwell I suppose is the main character within this story, even though she does not actually appear in it, but it is because of her this story was able to exist so in that respect I feel she should be honoured here. I have changed the wording of the witness statement, I made her husband out to be her father, she may not have died in the way I have wrote but try as I could, I could not find her existence anywhere after or before her witness statement. I have hopes to find her some day, but until then all I can say is that there was a Caroline Maxwell in 1888, she wrote a statement and appeared in court, she was interviewed by Inspector Abberline and above all else...SHE DID CLAIM TO SEE MARY KELLY, HOURS AFTER SHE WAS MEANT TO HAVE DIED...

The rest I leave up to you dear reader...

Acknowledgement

There is so many people I would like to thank that have helped in their own little way, some probably don't even realised they have helped so I will try my best to mention them here.

Firstly my husband, he as I have stated in other books has taken an active interest in my hobby of Victorian crime, I can now have a conversation about Jack the Ripper and I do not have to explain who I mean or what they did because he either knows or mentions it, which makes me smile every time. He reads every one of my stories, often telling me when my brain has moved to fast for my typing fingers! He gives his honest opinion, claiming he likes everyone but there are certain ones which are more to his liking, normally the darker toned ones. Above all else, I thank my husband for always having faith in my writing and whenever I have a down moment he always tells me that this is what I was meant to do, that I have a natural skill for it.

Next my father, I do not think he quite understands my love for Sherlock Holmes as he is fictional and my father like the facts. But it is because of the knowledge he has given me, not just in crime but in the history of London

The Strange Case of Caroline Maxwell

that I feel confident to write in the period in which I do. Something that will never change and I always have got to thank him it for. Also it was him that gave me to idea of a young Amelia Christie through the Dame Agatha Christie route; it wasn't exactly what my father had suggested but very close.

To my mother, who is certainly quirky, I feel I must mention because she takes an interest in history especially Jack the Ripper as she has a personal reason for taking an curiosity in that crime, which I will not mention here because and I quote my version of Ex-Inspector Abberline here when I say, 'It is not my story to tell'. I thank her for being another person I can talk to about Jack the Ripper without giving me a funny look.

Next my thanks goes out to Jon Lellenberg and The Conan Doyle Estate, they were very patient with me and explained everything I needed to change within my book to make Sherlock Holmes sound right. I must say, although it will make me sound a little geeky but, I was very much like a excitable school girl when I got the okay and seal from them to publish my book. The reason for this was because I knew I could never get the okay from Sir Arthur Conan Doyle himself but from The Conan Doyle Estate I believe I have got the next best thing and knowing that they were not insulted by the Sherlock Holmes that appears in my story, gave me a confidence to push forward. So I thank you for the bottom of my heart.

My important thanks goes to two great men, Sir Arthur Conan Doyle and Sherlock Holmes, which might seem a little odd as one is not alive and one was only alive in pages but I feel I must thank them because without both of them, I may not have liked crime so much, I may not have enjoyed the Victorian era so I may not have written this book and more importantly I may not have become the person I am today, whether some believe I am geeky or not. I thank you always.

Now I have a very special thank you to say, there is a little blonde haired eight year old girl called Madison I feel I need to thank and I will explain why. This little girl did my husband and me the great favour in being our flower girl at our wedding, not only did she drop the petals down the aisle but afterwards, on her own accord she then picked them all up on her way out. You can't teach that, can you?

Well every time I have seen her, knowing what I write about, she has always explained to me her theory on who she thinks was Jack the Ripper. She would say quite

The Strange Case of Caroline Maxwell

forcefully that Jack the Ripper was Guy Faulkes, this makes me smile. Now, she will need some scientific reason what involves a time machine but the thought is there and in the mind of an eight year old and when I consider I was at the same age when I first read a Jack the Ripper book I cannot help but be touched.

Also I have to thank Madison because since she knew I was writing this book, every time I have seen her she has asked two questions, the first one being if I can write her a Harry Potter book? Which I could imagine has a few copyright problems and the second being, 'Is your book done yet? Is your book done yet? Is your book done yet?'

She asks this in the very fast and excitable way in which Madison asks most things and when I say 'No, it is not done yet', I always get the cutest screwed up face and the folding of her arms action as if that was the wrong answer and pushed me to finish it before I see her next.

So to you Madison sweetie, I can now say my book in finally done...

By Amanda Harvey Purse

If you like this...

Coming soon

The Adventures of Amelia Christie

Come join the Amelia you have come to know in *The Strange Case of Caroline Maxwell*, in her own adventures set in the Victorian and Edwardian era. Will she be able to solve all the crimes that come her way?

Stories will include:

The Gypsy's Diamonds, Murdered by a Ghost, The Escape Artist and many more...

The Strange Case of Caroline Maxwell

Author information

Amanda Harvey Purse is a 29 year old author and Sherlock Holmes enthusiast, who has spent the last twenty years researching Victorian Crime primarily studying the famous serial killer, Jack the Ripper.

When not writing, she is a volunteer of the City of London Police Museum where she has gives tours on the history of policing and crimes while giving lectures on Jack the Ripper to schools, businesses and local organizations, also she has helped with the researching of artefacts and documents held within the museum.

She is a very happy member of the Whitechapel Society to whom she has written the articles, A Protective Policeman, The Two Mary Kelly's and Did he almost catch The Ripper? Which she enjoys writing and always loves to learn new things about Jack through the society.

Amanda Harvey Purse lives in Kent with her loving husband Benjamin and her purrfect cat Binky.

Lightning Source UK Ltd.
Milton Keynes UK
UKOW04f0440171015

260718UK00001B/59/P